W9-CRP-550

Mici stepped inside her apartment. But for some reason, she stopped to listen. The room was silent. But she could not shake her sense of unease. She began to search her apartment. Nothing. Finally, she went to bed.

She hadn't been in bed long before she sensed that her bedroom door was opening. She stiffened under the covers. She heard a step. Definitely. No imagination. Before she could decide whether to make a run for it or pretend to be asleep, he was on top of her. In a single move he had one hand over her mouth, the other in her hair holding her head back against the pillow.

"Don't fight." The mask muffled his voice. "Make it easy on yourself."

Easy! *Mici thought*. No way I'm going to make this easy for you, mister!

Falling Star

Lillian O'Donnell

FAWCETT CREST • NEW YORK

A Fawcett Crest Book
Published by Ballantine Books
Copyright © 1979 by Lillian O'Donnell

ISBN 0-449-21395-1

This edition published by arrangement with G.P. Putnam's Sons, a division of The Putnam Publishing Group, Inc.

Manufactured in the United States of America

First Fawcett Crest Edition: November 1980
First Ballantine Books Edition: November 1987

He would not be back tonight, she was sure of it, yet she couldn't sleep. Julia Schuyler lay in her sweat-soaked bed listening while she waited for the booze and the tranquilizers to take effect.

She had learned through countless such hours to identify the sounds of night. They were many and varied for this was not a quiet part of the city. "The Tenderloin," it had been called in the bad old days at the turn of century, dubbed so by the venal police captain who, newly assigned to the sector, said, "I've had the chuck; now I'm going to get me some of the tenderloin." It had been squalid and dangerous then, and it hadn't changed. Its denizens came out after dark, their pale skins taking on the bluish tinge of the vapor lamps, the greenish or reddish glow of neon signs over porno houses, bars, massage parlors the way their more fortunate brethren absorbed the rays of the Miami sun. At dawn they crept back to dingy tenement rooms to fall into sodden sleep. Julia Schuyler catalogued their comings and goings the way some people counted sheep. These hot July nights with the windows wide open—nobody around there had air conditioning—it was easier than usual.

Tonight, however, Julia Schuyler wasn't interested in what was going on down in the street. Huddled in the dark, her flimsy nightgown soggy and plastered to her bruised body, she listened only for familiar foot-steps. Sweat soaked her black hair and trickled down to mix with the blood from the cut on her left cheek. The tiny, airless room was rank with sweat—the aftermath of what had happened and the fear of what still might come. She closed her eyes, which were just

5

about swollen shut anyway, so she could concentrate harder.

From the way the boards creaked she could tell whether it was Petersen in 4A staggering home, a bum looking for a flop, or an addict prowling for an easy "break and enter." She could interpret the moans of lovers on the landing, of the prostie steering a john upstairs, or of one of Petersen's brats getting smacked by his Ma. She recognized and ignored their cries just as she supposed they recognized and ignored hers. Like the rest of the tenants, Julia Schuyler didn't give a damn for what went on outside her own flimsy door.

He would not be back tonight.

Of course, she could call the police. She knew where that would get her. Nowhere. They were on the man's side every time. She'd seen the cops bound into the building on that kind of complaint. She remembered that poor wisp of a woman with the four slobbering brats calling in after Petersen had broken her arm for her. A piece of the bone was sticking out, but the husband claimed she'd slipped and fallen. Oh, they'd called the ambulance all right, and while she was being strapped into the stretcher, Julia had heard one of the cops whisper to the other:

"Maybe if I beat up on my old lady she'd act right."

They had laughed together.

Of course, she wasn't Helga Petersen, your ordinary household drudge; she was Julia Schuyler, star of stage, screen, and TV since the age of fourteen. If she went to the precinct and swore out a warrant, they couldn't ignore her. But that didn't mean they'd believe her. She could take her clothes off and show her bruises, and he'd say somebody else beat her up, or maybe he'd just give them the wink, the sad shake of the head and whisper: "She's always falling down." They'd take his word in the same way they took the word of that lout upstairs, all the more so in her case because even cops read the scandal sheets and they'd know her reputation.

So she drank. Nothing wrong with liquor. Drugs now, that was something else. Certainly, you couldn't mix the two; her psychiatrist had warned her so she was always careful with the tranquilizers. But alcohol —some doctors recommended it for relaxation of tension. The bible mentioned it as one of the benefits of man. Her father had been a heavy drinker and he had also been the most magnificent actor of his time. John Malcolm Schuyler had no equal, then or now. The tragedy of John Malcolm was that he had lost control, had let the booze destroy first his professional judgment, then his liver. He'd appeared in a series of execrable vehicles with his current mistress as co-star. He'd made himself a laughingstock. But that was at the end, the very end. Julia was forewarned. It wouldn't happen to her.

Suddenly the bed started to rock; her gorge rose; she couldn't control it. She turned over and heaved.

She didn't give a damn whether the police went for her story or not, Julia thought when the retching finally subsided, leaving her spent, gasping, and filthy. She was Julia Schuyler; her name had been up in lights, in headlines, her picture on front pages and magazine covers, and the story would be picked up. Reporters would jump on it. It would hit every paper in New York and L.A. The tabloids, God! The tabloids would have a field day with it. She could see the black scare headlines, the garish pictures of herself—at her worst naturally; they'd find a bleary shot taken at some bash where she'd had a few too many. She wasn't going to subject herself to that! Julia Schuyler, a has-been at thirty-one, could handle contempt, but she couldn't bear pity.

Footsteps on the stairs. She tensed. The tread was even, not favoring the right, without that slight halt as the weight shifted. Not him. She was sure. Almost sure. She hadn't really been paying attention. Oh God! she thought, not again, not tonight. She couldn't take any more. She pulled herself up against the headboard as she heard the key inserted into the lock, turned, and the door opened. Slipping out of bed, she stumbled to the bureau and grabbed the heavy, cast-iron frying pan she'd put there.

The lights went on in the living room. She screamed.

"Julia, it's only me. It's all right, Julia. It's all right."

Her knees wobbled. She managed a smile. "Did you bring anything to drink?"

He held out a brown paper bag. The shape left no doubt there was a bottle inside.

"You're a sweetheart." Julia Schuyler smiled and let the frying pan fall to the floor.

The two cops were parked halfway down Forty-fifth Street between Eighth and Ninth Avenues. All four windows of the patrol car were rolled down in the hope of sucking in a breeze. There was none. Raymond Emmenecher, the senior of the team, held the steaming container of coffee in his hands and wondered why in hell he'd sent Pace around for it. The stuff was too hot to drink and by the time it cooled it wouldn't be fit to drink. A glance at his partner, alternately blowing and sipping, blowing and sipping, made Emmenecher clench his teeth on a new wave of irritation. He had sent Pace for the coffee to get rid of him, to enjoy a few moments of blessed peace. The guy was driving him nuts.

Attilio Pace was blissfully unaware of the effect he had on Em. He was twenty-three, a victim of the first wave of firings due to budget cuts and had only just been rehired. Recently married, with a new house and a new baby, Pace couldn't afford another period of unemployment; all he wanted to do was please. He was always on the lookout for ways to entrench his position. He had it figured that if he could make that new grade, patrolman first class, his chance of surviving the new cutbacks, whenever they came, would be enhanced. The rank was similar to detective but without the gold shield. It was a merit promotion, and in theory you didn't need either a rabbi to push for you or a sensational bust to make it; still, you had to attract attention somehow. He figured the Times Square area should offer opportunity and when he heard that scream coming from a building across the street he thought he had it. He jumped, sloshing the scalding coffee on his own hand and over Ray Emmenecher's right knee.

"Christ! Watch what you're doing!" Emmenecher snarled as the stain spread. "I just had these pants cleaned. Hell!"

On one squad or another—Narco, Vice, Pickpocket, Pimp—Ray Emmenecher had worked the area in plain clothes for seven years. Suddenly, on the whim of the latest P.C., who wanted to emphasize "visible presence," he, along with a lot of others, was back "in the bag" as the cops called having to put on the uniform again. He hated it. Driving around in the damn car was like being shut off from the real world of the street. He was removed from the contacts, both civilian and criminal, he had so laboriously built up. Worse, if anything could be worse, he was being saddled with greenhorn partners, one after the other. As soon as he got one broken in to his reasonable satisfaction, they moved the guy on.

Pace stared in dismay at the damage he'd done to his partner's uniform. "Jeez, I'm real sorry, Em. That scream . . ."

"Relax, relax. That scream wasn't nothing more than a family argument or somebody on a bad trip. You'll hear a lot worse before you're through. This ain't a quiet neighborhood."

"Sure." Pace was ashamed of having overreacted. Still, he hadn't wanted to miss out on anything big.

"Will you please grab those paper towels and wipe up this mess?" Emmenecher indicated the brown puddle on the seat between them.

Pace complied with alacrity. He had the kind of watery eyes that seemed constantly on the verge of tears, never more so than now. "She sounded like she was getting raped."

"In this neighborhood?" Emmenecher snorted. "Forget it. We're supposed to be looking for kid prosties, remember? We're supposed to be making friends with them and gaining their confidence, saving them from the clutches of their pimps so they can be rehabilitated and sent back home to their mommies and daddies." He stared morosely at the damp patch on his knee. "Baby-sitters, that's what we've become. Goddamned baby-sitters."

*   *   *

Julia Schuyler didn't get out of the sack and on her feet till two-thirty the next afternoon. She made it to the kitchen and found one last can of beer in the refrigerator. It helped. At least it got her as far as the bathroom where one look in the mirror at her bloated face almost sobered her. But she'd seen that face in the mirror too often lately to be really disturbed. She hardly remembered what she used to look like, say . . . three months ago, six months ago. If she happened to run across a photograph of herself taken just that short while back before she'd broken up with Alfred, she was surprised at how pretty she'd been. Not beautiful. Julia Schuyler had never been beautiful—her face was square rather than the classic oval and her nose a trifle long like her father's—but her brown eyes were fine and her skin, in the pictures at least, clear and unlined, though that was partly due to the retoucher's skill. Yet no retoucher could put the brightness in her eyes nor impart the spirit implicit in the way she held her head. She had looked, Julia thought, not innocent—when had she ever been innocent—but unscathed. Even so recently. If she happened to catch herself on the late show, that took her even farther back and it was like watching a stranger. She cried then with self-pity. Where had it all gone? It was her birthright to be a star. What had gone wrong?

Slowly, Julia applied makeup. It didn't help much; her hand wasn't steady enough to do a good job. What she needed was another beer. She'd throw something on and go over to the deli for it; Tony was a good guy, he'd put it on the tab. After that she'd really fix herself up and go and see. . . .

She stopped and stared at herself. What was she, crazy? Julia Schuyler didn't gussy herself up like a raw kid for her first audition. Julia Schuyler didn't go begging. She called people; she told them what she wanted and they went and did it for her.

"Sue me for nonsupport?" Alfred Cassel repeated, stunned. "Is this some kind of new trick?"

10

William Zipprodt shook his head.

Cassel stared at Julia Schuyler's emissary in disbelief; then he threw his dark, handsome head back and laughed. It was a bitter laugh and forced, but Cassel was, after all, an actor and an exceptionally good one. After a while the laughter came more easily till the rolling gusts were almost genuine, till his narrow face, romantically pale with thin, sculptured features, high brow balanced by sensuously full lips, became red and rubbery with merriment, till his slim, elegant figure was wracked with laughter and he started to choke.

William Zipprodt, Billy Zip for short, was not overly impressed, or at least he was impressed only by the technique. He remembered that Cassel and Julia had once played a laughing scene in a show—what was the name? He couldn't remember; it hadn't lasted, but the laughter in the scene had built in just this way and ended in choking tears, too.

"She means it," Billy Zip said.

Cassel let the tears subside. He groaned. "I am supporting her to the best of my ability. I'm turning over every spare cent I have. Don't let this fool you." A sweeping gesture encompassed the living room of the relatively modest suite which was prestigious only for being in the Algonquin Hotel. "I'm living on credit. And I'm not indulging myself, either. You tell Julia. I need this setup for business. I've got my producer coming up here, my director. They bring prospective backers. What are backers going to think of the man being sold to them as a big star, a big box-office attraction, if they find him holed up in a furnished room?"

"I understand."

"Of course you do, Billy; any sensible person would, which naturally eliminates Julia. Still, she's been the route herself; she ought to remember."

Billy Zip flushed in embarrassment. Though he had a certain elegance and considered himself cosmopolitan, Billy at forty-six still nurtured the illusions of his youth regarding the great or near great of the theater. He was devoted to both Julia Schuyler and Alfred

11

Cassel, had served them in one guise or another for over ten years. Their talent and flamboyance fed a need in him which he had been forced to stifle when he faced the reality that he wasn't going to make it as a stage designer. He found a niche for himself as a stage manager, the executive officer, so to speak, of a theatrical production, the one who implemented what others conceived, the liaison between crew and cast. As such Billy Zip was competent, even skilled; he dealt with inferiors and equals energetically and efficiently. It was only in the presence of the stars that he became humble. When Julia Schuyler and Alfred Cassel separated, he had been deeply torn, but finally loyalty to Julia won out. She was the weaker; she needed him. To have Julia Schuyler, daughter of the great John Malcolm Schuyler, dependent on him fed his ego. Still, it was hard to take her side against Cassel. Billy's jowls quivered. His eyes were anxious behind their tinted glasses.

Cassel put a hand on his shoulder. "Don't take it so hard, Billy. This is just a ploy. What Julia wants is for me to drop the divorce. She's trying to make me nervous. You tell her that if she sues she won't get anything, and she'll ruin any prospect of ever getting anything. What good is it going to do her to ruin my reputation? Nonsupport, that's a lousy label to pin on a man. It could cost me the show, and then where would either one of us be?"

"I've already told her that."

"Tell her again."

"I will."

"And don't worry. Julia has no more intention of dunning me before the play opens than any of my other creditors and for the same reason: the well is dry now, but it may be overflowing later."

The two men were silent for a moment, sharing concern for the woman each loved in his own way.

"How is Julia?" Cassel asked quietly. "What's she doing with herself these days?"

"Waiting for the phone to ring."

Cassel sighed. "Drinking?"

Zipprodt nodded.

"I wish she'd get off the sauce."

"Maybe if you went to see her, talked to her . . ." Zipprodt suggested.

"I lived with the woman for six years and I couldn't straighten her out," Cassel muttered.

"I mean about this nonsupport business. I think all Julia really wants is to know that you haven't forgotten her, that you still care. I honestly think that if you go over there . . ."

"Maybe." Cassel nodded as though to himself. "Maybe I will go over there and try to talk some sense into her. It's worth a try." He slapped a hand on the stage manager's shoulder and steered him to the door.

As soon as Zipprodt was gone, Alfred Cassel sprang to his telephone. When it was picked up at the other end, his tone became elaborately casual, as it had been with his visitor.

"Oscar? How are you? How are you feeling? Good, that's good. I was wondering, have you heard from Julia lately?"

"Yes, I have," Oscar Brumleve replied. "In fact, I've been meaning to call you." He paused. "She wants to sue you."

Cassel groaned. "Then it's true. Billy just told me. You talked her out of it, of course."

"I'm sorry, Alfred," the lawyer replied. "I tried. I told her that a suit like that would be seriously damaging to your career. I also pointed out that it would be defeating her own interests. But you know Julia. At the moment what she wants is to hurt you, even if it means your losing the show. Later on she'll be sorry, naturally."

"Naturally." Cassel echoed bitterly, a vise tightening across his chest. "What are you going to do?"

"What can I do? If I don't go ahead, she'll get somebody else, some shyster who won't give a damn about either one of you. But don't worry. It's just a question of going through the motions. She'll drop it before it gets to court."

"Meantime she'll ruin me!" Cassel cried. "You can't

13

do this to me, Oscar. You can't file this charge. For one thing, it's false and you know it. I'm giving her every cent I can spare."

"Do you have canceled checks?"

"I've been giving her cash."

"That wasn't very smart."

"Hell! I didn't expect to have to prove it!" Cassel groaned. "Oscar, you can't do this to me. I'm your client, too. You can't represent us both."

"I'm aware of that."

"You're dumping me?"

"You must have realized that if Julia agreed to bring action for divorce I'd be representing her."

"That's different."

"She was my client first," Brumleve pointed out. "And her father before her."

"It doesn't matter who's right?"

"John Malcolm Schuyler was my client before Julia was born."

Cassel did not like being reminded of his wife's father. Once he had admired Schuyler—the actor, not the man—had even emulated his style, for Alfred Cassel was basically a classical actor. He had dreamed of playing the great Shakespearean roles and what finer model could he have had than Schuyler? In many ways, Cassel was much like him. He had the elegance, the flair, the voice. He supposed—hell, he knew—that was what had attracted Julia to him. And he to her, he admitted. To have John Malcolm Schuyler's daughter rate him in the same category as her father was the supreme compliment. He had married Julia thinking they could help each other, only to discover that where it had taken John Malcolm sixty-two years of licentious living to destroy his talent along with himself, Julia was likely to do it in half the time. Cassel was not going to let her drag him down with her.

Though he was talking on the telephone with no one in the room to observe, Alfred Cassel drew himself erect and placed his right foot at an angle to his left, slanting his body as though posing for the photograph-

14

ers. "You need publicity, Oscar? Business slow? Looking for new clients?"

"I didn't expect that from you, Alfred," Brumleve sighed.

The lawyer was retired, had been for several years. He was also a very sick man. Everyone knew it. "I'm sorry, Oscar. It was a cheap shot," Cassel apologized.

"I'm sorry, too. I wouldn't do this for anyone but Julia."

"Sure. Do me one favor, Oscar? Hold off for a few days? Give me a chance to talk to her, to try to reason with her. Do that much for me?"

"Of course. You know what I think? I think she just wants you to give up on the divorce. Maybe if you move back in with her? Maybe that's what she's after."

Now it was Cassel who sighed. "We both know what she's after and we both know I can't give it to her. I wouldn't if I could."

2

It was a decent middle-class neighborhood, a pocket of the old ways and the old morality. Situated just across the Queensboro Bridge from Manhattan, it was bordered on one side by the Pennsylvania Railroad yards and on the other by acres and acres of graves. The house had been the end house in a row of neat, red-brick, one-family dwellings identical as paper cutouts that stretched block after tree-lined block. It had had a lovingly tended garden with the standard patch of front lawn individualized by a family of gaily painted plastic ducks perpetually waddling across it. The house was now a gutted, blackened shell, a rotted tooth in the otherwise gleaming row. The garden, flooded by water

15

and smothered in chemicals, had become first a swamp, now, after being trampled and baked by the ninety-degree heat, resembled a lumpy pie-crust. The plastic ducks, melted down, were somewhere inside.

Bare-legged, bare-armed, red-gold hair twisted into a knot and pinned on top of her head, wearing a faded denim sundress, Mici Anhalt picked her way through the debris. Tall, slim, and agile, Mici with her arms outstretched as she carefully placed one foot in front of the other looked like a child balancing on an imaginary line on the sidewalk. A gust of hot wind threatened to blow her off. It came from across the polluted waters of the East River and bore no relief, but rather noxious fumes from the city and more heat. This was no day to be examining an arson site, Mici Anhalt thought, her blue eyes tearing. This was a day to be home in Greenwich, sitting on the shady back porch looking across the field to the apple orchard, listening to the soothing midday hum of the cicadas. Maybe she'd go up this weekend. It wasn't so much the oppressive heat that Mici wanted to escape but the nagging, niggling stresses that had been building up in her work for . . . longer than she cared to admit.

Even in a job one loved—and Mici loved her job—there were bound to be difficulties from time to time, she thought as she sat down to rest on what had once been the front stoop of the burned dwelling but was now a fragment of broken steps leading nowhere. There had been misunderstandings, disagreements with colleagues before, but they'd never lasted. What troubled Mici Anhalt now was a change in the atmosphere, a barrier between herself and the other investigators. It wasn't because she was the only woman on the staff. She didn't know what it was. She had countered by being friendlier and it hadn't worked. Mici was puzzled.

Maria Ilona Anhalt was not used to being rebuffed. She liked most people and expected to be liked in return. Even her nickname, Mici, the Hungarian spelling for Mitzi, was an endearment meaning "honey" or "darling." She was extraordinarily pretty, in fact strik-

16

ing, with that tall, fine figure and that mass of red-gold hair. Her skin was clear and unfreckled, exceptional for a redhead, and her light-blue eyes had a way of turning pale under stress until they became almost colorless—translucent. Mici Anhalt was thirty-three, but she seemed younger because of her energy. In fact, it was her spirit that pulled it all together: her enthusiasm for whatever she happened to be doing and her complete absorption in whomever she happened to be dealing with. When Mici Anhalt talked to you, you were the focus of her attention completely and without outside distractions. It was devilishly flattering, and completely sincere.

Mici came from a closely knit family. Her grandfather, Laszlo, had escaped from the Communist revolution in Hungary after World War I and on arriving in his new country immediately bought the house in Greenwich where her father, Paul, grew up and married and where she had been born. She was used to loving and being loved, which wasn't to say that she wasn't tough. She wouldn't have survived in the world of professional ballet otherwise. But after two years with the Joffrey, Mici Anhalt found herself oddly restless, and when the company went to Seattle that second summer she joined the ranks of volunteers for Kennedy during his presidential campaign. There had been plenty of competition there, too, but she'd taken her knocks and given as good as she got. As a member of the Attorney General's staff during John Kennedy's term, she'd learned about the wheeling and dealing, the *quid pro quo* of politics. After Robert Kennedy was assassinated, she returned to New York but not to the ballet—she'd progressed beyond that limited sphere. Mici had become dedicated to criminal justice. She got a job with the Vera Institute and was assigned to the Victim/Witness Assistance Program. It opened her eyes to the victim's plight.

With all the current concern for the rights of the criminal, Mici soon realized that the rights of the victim were all but forgotten. Time after time, the criminal was back out on the street while the victim

17

still lay in the hospital; often the criminal was out repeating his crimes while his first victim still struggled to pay the medical bills. Ostensibly, the awesome forces of law and order were arrayed behind the victim. In essence, he was alone. Once the criminal was caught, nobody paid any attention to the victim. He was abandoned to his pain and his sorrow and the ugly memories that would be part of his life forever.

Mici moved over to the New York State Crime Victims Compensation Board where some attempt was being made to help the victim of crime financially and medically. First, of course, those needs had to be assessed. Mici's job, often referred to as social worker, was actually similar to that of an insurance investigator. Usually it was enough to confirm the identity of the victim-claimant through a birth certificate, a marriage license, and the like; to check his financial status, his insurance coverage, extent of injury, and extent of his medical policies. But if there was any uncertainty regarding the claim, Mici Anhalt didn't quit till her client got every benefit available to him under the law. That was why she was out here now in the midday heat examining the burned remains of Karl Spychalski's house. The unemployed ironworker was one of the borderline cases. If there was any evidence in his favor that had been overlooked by the police and the regular insurance investigator, Mici intended to find it.

Wiping the film of sweat from her face with a tissue from the straw satchel she carried, Mici got up and resumed her examination of the area.

As many slum landlords knew, and others were rapidly learning, it wasn't easy to determine the cause of a fire. A bomb might leave evidence, but matches thrown on a trash heap or an old sofa doused with kerosene went up in flames along with everything else. What could Mici expect to find that the Arson-Explosion Squad or the Fire Marshal had not found before her? Or the agent for the company that carried the insurance on Karl Spychalski's house? None of them had been able to make a determination as to the origin of the fire, yet Mici Anhalt went on looking.

18

"You there! You! What do you think you're doing?"

Startled, Mici looked around. She couldn't see anybody.

"You. I'm talking to you. That's private property. You're trespassing."

A slight, frail figure appeared from behind the vacant house next door. She was old, at least eighty, Mici thought. Her hair was snow-white, a halo of sparse curls through which the sun shone, unmercifully revealing portions of pink scalp. Her skin was crazed like fine china, and she was dressed like a girl in pale-blue cotton sprinkled with rosebuds, white stockings, and white shoes. She had a cane but didn't use it to pick her way across the uneven terrain; in fact, her step was so light she seemed to float over the ruts and fissures. A ghost at midday, Mici thought and smiled.

"You've got a tongue in your head, haven't you?" The voice was high and feisty.

"You must be Mrs. Feirick."

"Never mind who I am. Who are you?"

"I'm Mici Anhalt, Mrs. Feirick. I'm an investigator for the Crime Victims Compensation Board. I rang your doorbell just a while ago." She had rung all the doorbells on both sides of the street. Only one or two people had answered, though she was certain nearly everyone had been at home.

"I heard you." Marge Feirick tilted her head sideways as though sizing up the interrogator. "I was having my nap."

"I'm sorry I disturbed you."

"I didn't get up, did I?"

"No, ma'am."

"So then you didn't disturb me." This bit of testy logic seemed to give the old lady satisfaction. "Well, what did you want?"

"I wanted to ask you about the fire. I wondered whether you saw anyone around the house before it started."

"Did you talk to any of the other people on the block? What did they say?"

"I talked to one or two. Neither of them saw anything or anyone."

19

"Me neither."

Mici hadn't really expected any other answer, yet she was disappointed. "How about the Geramita boys? Had they been hanging around?"

The old lady jerked her white head toward the silent houses with their shades drawn against the heat. "What did they say?"

"They didn't see the boys."

"Me neither."

"If you don't know anything and you didn't see anything, why did you bother to come out and talk to me?"

"I wanted to see what kind of young woman you were. Now I see that you're no different than the rest of them—no patience and no respect for your elders."

"It's not a matter of respect, Mrs. Feirick. A crime has been . . ." She stopped. She had been about to say that a crime had been committed, but she didn't know that it had. That was what she was trying to determine, whether in fact there had been a crime, whether the fire had been of natural origin or deliberately set. Karl Spychalski had accused a pair of teenage boys, Robert and Damian Geramita, of starting the fire. If the suspects had not been juveniles they would surely have been arrested on probable cause, Mici thought, but probable cause didn't mean a thing where juveniles were concerned. The tragedy was that the children knew they could get away with just about everything, including murder, at least till the age of sixteen.

The Geramita brothers were the local bad boys, hardly in the league with delinquents in other parts of the city—they didn't carry knives, use or deal in drugs—but they showed disturbing tendencies. Many a day when he should have been in school, Robert could be seen weaving down the street obviously drunk; at thirteen, he had already learned that you could get a good high on alcohol and you wouldn't get busted because alcohol was legal. At fifteen, Damian was deflowering girls of eleven and twelve, though he did go outside the neighborhood for them—so far. Combining these hobbies, the boys held liquor and sex parties

20

in the summer in the backyard of the empty house next to the Spychalskis. The parties went on most of the night and into the morning. The sounds not only disturbed Karl Spychalski's sleep, but they embarrassed his wife and frightened his two girls. They were not the kind of sounds he wanted the women of his family to be forced to hear. Against Rose Spychalski's earnest pleading, he called the police and complained, naming names. Two days later every window on the first floor of his house was broken.

Spychalski took matters into his own hands. Though fifty-two, the ironworker was accustomed to handling heavy weights and clambering over steel girders at great heights, and he was still both strong and quick. Dark-haired, with a heavy, black growth of beard which he could never shave really close and bulging biceps in arms and thighs, he was physically intimidating. The boys were gangling youths who had not yet reached their full growth. It was no match. He got them both on the same day, one at a time; he could do that because they went to different schools—one to junior high and the other to high school. All Karl Spychalski had to do was wait for each boy to get off the school bus and then grab him. Each was momentarily stunned, without the wit to run. By the time the boy recovered, the ironworker had pulled him behind some shrubbery, thrown him across one knee, pants shamefully pulled down, and administered a blistering, old-fashioned spanking.

Each boy yelled, of course, and, as soon as he was released, ran. But neither one ever told, not his parents, not his friends. Karl Spychalski had counted on that. He had counted on the boys not confessing the humiliation to anyone but each other.

It would have been better for him if they'd told everybody.

A week later to the day, a neighbor—Mrs. Feirick as it turned out—had spotted the boys lurking around the Spychalski garage. Evidently she hadn't learned yet to fear the young for she came out of her house to scream and shake her cane at them and thus alerted Rose

21

Spychalski who was in her kitchen. Mrs. Spychalski smelled the smoke and saw the flames and was able to call the fire department in time to limit the damage. Again Spychalski refused to listen to his wife's advice. A woman who took her marriage vow of obedience seriously, Rose seldom argued with him and now that he had high blood pressure she almost never disputed with him. Not that she could have stopped Karl; he was determined to bring the Geramita boys to court.

At the hearing the boys' lawyer denied everything, beginning with the backyard parties and responsibility for the broken windows. When Spychalski charged that the fire was retaliation for the spanking he'd administered, the lawyer denied the spanking. He admitted his client's culpability in the fire—could hardly do otherwise since they'd been caught in the act—but dubbed it a childish prank that got out of hand. The judge found in the boys' favor. He reprimanded them and sent them home, and he warned Spychalski to stay away from them.

Indignation sent the ironworker's blood pressure soaring. He had a seizure on the courthouse steps. Medical bills wiped out the last of the Spychalskis' financial reserves. Unemployment benefits were suspended because, being sick, Spychalski was not available for work should work be offered—though for the past seven long months it had not been.

Two weeks after the debilitated and frustrated man was back from the hospital and down at the hiring hall, there was another fire. Rose Spychalski, on her way home from the weekly trip to the supermarket, turned the corner in time to see her house a torch. She also saw her two girls leaning out of the window of their second-story bedroom, screaming. She dropped her groceries and ran.

Once again Spychalski brought charges against Robert and Damian Geramita, but there was nothing to support them, not even the testimony of a Mrs. Feirick. The neighbors weren't talking. Pressed, they admitted to knowing about the backyard parties that took place next door to the Spychalskis but professed to have no idea as to who attended. Regarding this, the most recent and most devastating of the two fires, no one had seen anything, heard anything, knew anything. Who could blame them? They didn't want their houses burned down.

Meanwhile, Rose Spychalski lay at the Jacobi Hospital Burn Care Unit with second- and third-degree burns that would permanently disfigure her face and arms. The two girls, Natalia and Sophia, were dead.

"What I'm trying to do is substantiate Mrs. Spychalski's story," Mici explained.

"Are you calling Karl a liar?" Mrs. Feirick demanded. Her frail figure stiffened, her rheumy old eyes challenged. "Karl is a good, decent, hardworking man." Raising her cane, the old lady shook it at the girl as though about to call down a curse on her.

"I believe him, Mrs. Feirick," Mici assured the irate woman. "That's why I'm here, because I believe him. Others don't. What's needed is proof that the fire wasn't just an accident."

"I see."

"The way it stands now it's Mr. Spychalski's word against that of the boys and their parents."

"How about the first fire in the garage? I was a witness to their setting that. I testified."

"Yes, ma'am, I know. I wish your neighbors were as civic-minded and showed as much courage. Unfortunately, proof that Robert and Damian took part in those backyard parties . . ." Mici paused to choose her words. "As long as no one can definitely place Robert and Damian at those parties, the broken windows afterwards can't be blamed on them. If no broken windows, then no spankings, and the garage fire becomes not a retaliation but an isolated prank to which Mr. Spychalski overreacted. It all hangs on those backyard parties."

"Why didn't you say so? You're not very good at your job, are you, girl?" Mrs. Feirick scolded. "I can tell you about the parties. Orgies for depraved children. Terrible. This is the curse that God has put upon our generation—that our children are monsters. Do you have children?"

"No."

"Then you are blessed."

Mici got her back on the track. "How about the Geramita brothers? Did you actually see them at the parties?"

"I saw and heard them. Many times."

Now we're getting somewhere, Mici thought.

"I could look right into that backyard." By a series of sidesteps in place, she turned her body about forty-five degrees and raised her cane to point in the direction of her own house. It was one block behind the Spychalskis' and raised slightly above theirs on a ground elevation. "I could look right down into that backyard and see everything."

"Uh . . . it would have been nighttime, of course," Mici reminded her. "I suppose they must have had some kind of light—lanterns or a bonfire?"

"I have cat's eyes. I can see in the dark."

Mici let it go; she could check the street lighting, also the almanac for the phase of the moon on the night or nights in question. "It would help Mr. Spychalski if you would make a list of the dates when you saw the boys at those parties and if you would be willing to make a formal statement."

Mrs. Feirick smiled sweetly. "Of course."

Mici was delighted. "That's very good of you."

"It's my duty."

"I wish your neighbors felt that way. Most of them won't even admit they were home the afternoon of the fire."

"I was home," Mrs. Feirick said. "I was upstairs taking my nap when something, I don't know what, woke me. A noise . . . like a dry wind. We don't get that kind of wind here much—rustling, sinister. When I was a girl back in Iowa during the drought, we had winds like that; they burned the crops; they took the topsoil right off the fields, blew it away in clouds. . . ." For a moment she was lost in her recollections; then she shook them off and returned to the present. "As I was saying, I heard this sound, like a sigh, and it woke me. I got out of bed and went to the window. There

24

was a flickering light over at the Spychalskis'. The day was cloudy so I knew it couldn't be a reflection of the sun on a window. It could have been candles, but why would they be burning candles in the middle of the afternoon? Then I saw two figures run out the back door. . . ."

"You actually saw them?" Mici couldn't believe her luck. "Were you able to recognize them?" *Of course not,* Mici silently answered her own question, *if Mrs. Feirick had been able to identify them, she would already have told the police.*

"It spread so fast, so fast. . . ." A wild light flickered in the old woman's eyes much like the flames she had just described. "Are you a Catholic?"

Mici blinked. "Yes."

"According to the faith, a child is supposed to know the difference between good and evil, between right and wrong, at the age of seven. These children won't ever know it; they weren't taught. And that's our fault." She pointed a bony finger. "Yours and mine."

Mici winced. Though she assumed that Mrs. Feirick was generalizing, she was becoming distinctly uneasy. "Were you actually able to recognize the running figures?"

"I knew who they were—demons spawned in hell."

Mici's heart wasn't in it, but she tried anyway. "I mean, were you able to see their faces well enough so that you could identify them in a court of law?"

"Yes, yes!" The fragile figure shook with almost religious fervor. "Yes," she repeated earnestly.

Mici was somewhat reassured. She took another look at Mrs. Feirick's house up on its rise. From the second story, where she assumed the bedroom to be, Mrs. Feirick would certainly have a clear view into the entire row of backyards, including that of the Spychalskis. If the boys had made their getaway through the kitchen door, they would not have been likely to head for the street but back through one of the side yards and in her direction.

"I saw them, I tell you. I saw them as clearly as I see you."

25

"Would you be willing to sign a statement to that effect?"

"I've said so, haven't I? Why do you think I'm telling you all this?"

As far as Mici Anhalt was concerned, the return to testiness meant a return to normalcy. She was relieved. Then she was elated. "I wish your neighbors had your courage, Mrs. Feirick."

The old lady smiled sunnily. "I'm not afraid. I'm alone now. If anything happens to me . . . well, I've had a good life and there's no one to mourn me." —

The simple statement touched Mici because it was neither maudlin nor an appeal for pity. She did wonder, of course, that none of the various investigators who had covered the neighborhood before her had discovered Marge Feirick and gotten her testimony. Well, maybe she hadn't been home on the particular day, or they hadn't asked the right questions. So she'd struck it lucky; nothing wrong with a little luck once in a while. Only one small point remained to be cleared up.

"About the backyard parties, Mrs. Feirick. Why didn't you call the police and complain the way Mr. Spychalski did?"

For a moment the old lady hesitated; then she smiled a sweet, sad smile. "To protect the girls, to spare them. I was sorry for the little girls. So young. Debauched. I didn't want their shame to be made public."

"Their names wouldn't have been mentioned," Mici explained. "The names of juvenile offenders are never . . ."

"But I was wrong. Wrong!" Marge Feirick cried out as though seized by a spirit, as though testifying at a revival meeting. "And I have been punished. I had no right to make a judgment. *Judgment is mine, sayeth the Lord.* I have been punished. I bear the scars of the fire on my body the same as Rose Spychalski does on hers. I am crippled and bent by the sins I have permitted to flourish around me. Crippled and bent . . ."

She seemed to shrivel; bending down and leaning on her stick, she turned from a sprightly old lady into an old crone. "My bones are broken, my body consumed by the murders, the rapes, the kidnappings. Every day, every day I am tortured. I suffer . . . the pain . . . the pain. . . ."

The nerves at the back of Mici's neck tightened; a cold chill passed over her.

"You call on me, girl, and I'll testify any time to whatever you want . . . whatever. . . ."

Mici backed off, one step and then another. "I will. Yes. I'll be in touch. Thank you, Mrs. Feirick. Thank you . . ."

Backing off and murmuring reassurances, Mici made it to the street where she turned and walked as quickly as she could back to the reality of traffic and elevated trains and the jackhammers of Con Edison repairing underground lines. Just as well that Marge Feirick hadn't been discovered by police or other insurance investigators, she thought. If they ever did interview her, even her testimony about the earlier fire in the garage would become suspect, and Karl Spychalski's hopes of proving arson and pinning it on the Geramita boys would suffer a severe setback.

3

"Nice of you to drop in."

"I'm sorry, Adam. The time just got away from me."

Adam Dowd's homely, pitted face showed his displeasure. "You could call in now and then. Just to let us know you're still on the job. I assume you are still working for us?"

Mici Anhalt flushed. She had hoped to get through the big main room and into her own private office without anyone's noticing. As luck would have it, Supervisor Dowd emerged just as she was scurrying by.

Or was it luck? Had Adam been watching for her? If so, he must be very annoyed indeed. Still, it wasn't like him to be sarcastic. Suddenly Mici was aware of the silence around her; nobody was typing or phoning. She sensed that nobody in the row of private offices was doing anything but listening, either. It wasn't like Adam Dowd to make a reprimand in public.

She apologized again. "I'm sorry, sir. I wasn't near a phone."

"Mind telling us where you were?"

Us? Mici stiffened. What was going on? Was she reporting to the whole damn office? "I went to the scene of the Spychalski fire. I interviewed some of the neighbors."

"And?"

She hesitated. She could feel the expectancy as they waited for her answer. Her blue eyes narrowed and turned pale. She tilted her head defiantly. "Nothing, sir. Nothing new." She'd be damned if she'd report her interview with crazy old Mrs. Feirick under these conditions. Besides, what she'd said was true; the interview had no credibility. Mici waited a beat; then, her eyes now faded to a cold translucence, she made a slow sweep of the room establishing contact for a moment with each and every person in it. It was like restarting a clock: all the parts went into motion at once; suddenly everyone had something to do and was very busy doing it. Now Mici turned back to her boss. "If that's all, sir?"

"No, it isn't. Step into my office, please."

Not one head was raised; not one pair of eyes so much as glanced in her direction, but everybody heard. Seething, Mici strode past the supervisor and into his office. She could hardly wait till he followed and closed the door.

"What's going on?" she demanded hotly. "What have I done?"

Despite his concern Adam Dowd could not repress a smile.

"It's got to be more than my being out of touch for a few hours to warrant that harangue out there."

Dowd frowned. "I'm afraid it is."

"What? Would you care to explain?"

With deliberation the supervisor crossed to his desk and sat down. "Clay Marin was in a couple of hours ago. He said he had an appointment with you."

"Damn." Her outrage was stopped in full spate. She flushed. "I forgot all about him. It went clean out of my head. I'm sorry, Adam. I really am."

"I know that Marin isn't one of your favorites." She started to protest, but he waved her to silence. "I don't like him much myself. He's a whiner and a complainer, but he has cause. And anyhow that's not the point. You can't work just with the people you like."

"I know that."

The supervisor clasped his hands over a small but developing paunch and considered the only woman on his investigative staff. He had liked Mici Anhalt from the first moment she had walked into his office for a job interview two years ago on a day in July almost as hot as this one. He remembered it particularly because the air conditioning had broken down and not one of the job applicants had dared refer to it by so much as wiping his brow—till Mici.

"If I'd known you were running a sauna I'd have worn my bathing suit," the good-looking redhead had said.

Dowd had thrown his head back and roared. "I wish you had," he'd retorted.

She came with a good background in criminal justice. She appeared enthusiastic about the concept of victim compensation, and after a check of her credentials he'd hired her. She had fulfilled his expectations. She was dedicated, no clock-watcher, and she had an intuitive feeling for the pattern of a case. He'd encouraged her to think and act independently. Maybe he'd encouraged her too much. To that extent Dowd felt responsible for her present predicament. Adam Dowd was nearing fifty. Big, balding, with that growing paunch and scarred complexion, he was certainly not attractive, but he was a kind man and a fair one and everybody liked him. Yet he was also lonely. His two

29

sons, though unmarried, no longer lived at home. His wife was a secret drinker—though by now she was the only one who considered it a secret. To Dowd, Mici was like a daughter and he'd treated her as such, unconsciously at the beginning. That was part of the problem, too.

The rest of it was Mici herself. Maybe she was too dedicated, too intense for the job. Her exuberance could be either endearing or overwhelming, depending on the point of view. He sighed and leaned forward; she was thirty-three years old and should be able to face reality.

"You can't slough off the dull cases and work only on the ones that appeal to you."

"I honestly forgot about Marin."

Dowd waved that aside. "Wally saw him. The point is that your missing the appointment brought the resentment to a head."

"Resentment?"

"The other investigators feel that you're getting special treatment. They feel you get all the good cases."

"But you assign the cases."

"That's right. I try to match case and investigator. I consider the investigator's special talents. It appears that I have an extra high regard for yours. Perhaps too high."

"That's a lousy charge."

His smile was tight. "I do regard you highly." Dowd sighed again. "Another complaint is that you spend too much time on these special cases and are therefore not carrying a full load. Which in turn means that the others are carrying more than their fair share."

Now she understood the scene he'd played outside. She came forward and took the chair beside his desk. "I'm sorry, Adam. I'll watch myself in the future."

"You step on a lot of toes, Mici. You have very little patience with anybody who thinks or reacts slowly. You don't mean any harm, I know that, but you just forge ahead and they're humiliated. You're too quick mentally. Excellence is more resented than admired."

She felt the warmth as her cheeks flamed again. "I

30

had no idea. I will try to attract less attention. I promise."

Dowd unclasped his hands and drew them across his face in a gesture of weariness and helplessness. "There's more. There's resentment because your claims are approved more often than anybody else's."

"Maybe that's because they're prepared better," Mici snapped indignantly. "Did they ever think of that?"

"The settlements your clients get are big, almost always maximum."

"Come on, Adam! That's really too much. The commissioner makes that decision, for heaven's sake. I have nothing to do with it." She tried a laugh, hoping to get Dowd to join in. When he didn't, she pleaded, "Adam, you can't be taking that part of it seriously?"

"It was Mr. Cornelius who remarked on it."

Mici gaped. The state board was appointed by the Governor and consisted of ten commissioners, two of whom were assigned to the New York City office. One of these was J. Hammond Cornelius. The other was Louis Weyerhauser. All cases handled by the office were divided between them and, based on the reports filed by the investigators in the field, one or the other made the decision as to whether or not the claim should be granted.

"Mr. Cornelius thinks your reports may be slanted in the claimant's favor, unconsciously, of course." Dowd's homely face was graver than ever.

Mici sucked in her breath. "Do you think they are?"

"You're working in a bureaucracy, and unilateral decisions are frowned on. Face it. You've got to go through channels. The ultimate action may be the very one you would have initiated on the spot and it may come hours, days, or weeks later, but it's been sanctioned. That's the game. Those are the rules. You are not in business for yourself. You are not handing out your own money."

"You can't slant figures," Mici retorted hotly. "That's what I report principally. As to circumstances, there are sometimes borderline situations, gray areas that can be interpreted either in the victim's favor or against

31

him. Maybe I do give him the benefit of the doubt, but I thought that was our policy."

It was almost an accusation, and Dowd knew it was as close as she would ever come to one. He acknowledged that he had encouraged her to bend in the vitim's favor. "I also told you that we are neither a charity organization nor a social agency. Compassion is a fine thing, but we are dispensing public funds. Now that the victim is being informed of his rights by the police at the time the crime is reported, the claims are pouring in and the money is pouring out. We've got to stick to the rules."

"There are still hardship cases."

"Sure, but it's not up to you to decide which ones."

She had made that judgment many times in the past. "I'm sorry if I've embarrassed you, Adam."

He could not let her take the full blame, for the truth was that she had not made those judgments without his knowledge and approval. "It's not up to me, either."

For a moment their eyes met and the bond between them was as strong as ever.

"I don't want you to be caught in the middle, Adam."

"I won't be, not as long as you watch your step. Okay?"

"Okay." She rose but she was still uneasy. She had the feeling that he hadn't told her everything. "Adam . . ." She hesitated. A flash of intuition sent a chill through her and brought out goose bumps. "Do you want me to resign?"

"Of course not. Don't be ridiculous. It won't come to that." He answered quickly, too quickly and too heartily.

Oh my God! she thought. It had come to that. It had been discussed. She left the supervisor's office reeling.

Fired? Mici had never considered the possibility. It wasn't fear of not finding another job but fear of having failed, of having been rated inadequate to the job she had. The talk with Adam Dowd had shaken Mici Anhalt on several levels. She didn't know which allegation surprised or hurt the most. Her honesty had never

32

before been questioned. Oh, Mr. Cornelius had admitted that if she was indeed slanting her reports it was done subconsciously—or had he? Could it in reality have been Adam who made that suggestion to the commissioner in order to protect her? And was she going overboard in favor of the claimants? In Mici's opinion, the poor unfortunate who walked through the door marked Crime Victims Compensation Board needed sympathy as much as monetary assistance. Of course, one had to maintain perspective; of course, one couldn't afford to become maudlin. She'd always thought that she had maintained proper balance. As for the attitude of her colleagues, Mici was more disappointed than angry, but she didn't feel like facing them right away. Glazed vision and a low ringing in her ears acted as a protective barrier as she passed along the row of doors to her own office. It was broken by Wally Lischner coming out of his office and colliding with her.

"Oh." She forced her usual bright smile. "Thanks for seeing Clay Marin this afternoon, Wally."

"For you? Any time, sweets."

As usual he leaned too close, almost pushing her into the wall and asphyxiating her with his cologne. Thin, slightly sallow, with medium-long, wavy hair brushed forward into bangs over his eyes, sideburns, and a rather elegant beard, Wally Lischner wasn't bad-looking. If you liked the type. Unfortunately, Mici did not. He went in for the macho bit, wearing everything skintight, shirt open to the waist revealing the gleam of a gold medal amid manly chest hair. In the office he sported a safari-type jacket that just happened to fall open whenever he leaned over one of the secretaries at her desk. They seemed to appreciate it.

When she'd first come to work there, Wally had made a play for Mici so strong and so insistent that she'd thought the only way to deal with it was to agree to go out with him and get it over with. It had been a bad mistake. He'd made a heavy pass, one she'd had more than the usual trouble parrying. The next day at the office had been embarrassing for both of them. They avoided each other, and for a while Mici thought

33

that was the way it was going to be for good. She didn't like that kind of situation, but what could she do? To her relief he got over it. The only thing that Mici could complain of in Wally's treatment of her afterwards was that he was overfriendly, suggesting an intimacy between them that hadn't taken place. There were plenty of times when she'd been on the verge of rebuffing his public advances in a way that would leave no doubt in anyone about her feelings. Somehow she never did.

Mici squirmed as he put his arm against the wall blocking her passage. She choked back the familiar urge to tell him off; of all the times to do it, this would be the worst. "What did Marin want?" she asked instead.

Lischner shrugged. "What does he ever want? To cry on somebody's shoulder."

"I'm sorry you got stuck. If I can ever return the favor . . ." Too late she realized the opening she'd given him.

"You can. Easy." He leered good-naturedly.

She laughed. "Come on, Wally, you know how I feel about office romances."

To her surprise he grinned and dropped his arm. "You can't blame a guy for trying."

For a moment she stared in disbelief, then flashed him a grateful smile. Just as well she hadn't been smart with Wally Lischner, Mici thought as she went on to her office. At the moment, he might be the only friend she had.

4

"My God! She's finally gone and lost her marbles!"

The words were at odds with the presence. Delissa Grace was a Junoseque figure in her flowing scarlet draperies with the white scarf binding her brow to hold back a mass of frizzed black hair. She had a broad, pale face with large, widely spaced, and brilliant eyes, a prominent, slightly hooked nose, and a high, noble brow—the whole forming an ample canvas upon which the passions could be portrayed and transmitted across the footlights.

"You're not going to let her get away with it!" It was a demand, not a question.

"Calm down, Dee, please. Take it easy." Eyes half closed, Alfred Cassel lay slouched against the cushions of a black-velvet sofa positioned in the center of Delissa Grace's living room so that people could move around it freely like actors on a stage.

She now stood behind the sofa looking down on Cassel. "You've got to do something. She could create a very nasty scandal; she's crazy enough. And you could lose the show. Do you realize that you could lose the show?"

At that he opened his eyes and looked up into hers. "I am not going to lose the show—and neither are you," he added pointedly. "She can't make the accusation stick. For one thing, because it's not true and she knows it."

"Fine. She knows it, you know it, I know it, but she can make you look pretty cheap while you're trying to clear yourself." Delissa swept around to the front of the sofa where she could deliver herself directly to his face. "She doesn't even have to take you to court; all she has to do is tell her story to a reporter."

Cassel sighed. How was it that he always got involved with temperamental, overbearing, domineering queen bees who tried to consume their mates? He was himself a mild man, introspective, and above all rational. "If that's what she intended she would have done it without sending a warning through Billy Zip and then Oscar. No. The whole thing is an elaborate form of blackmail."

"For what? What does she want?"

"Ah . . ." he shrugged.

"Does she want you back?" Delissa Grace was very still awaiting his answer.

"We wrote each other off romantically a long time ago. I think she'll take action for the divorce after she's made me squirm a while."

The actress flung herself down beside him, threw her arms around his neck, and kissed him, forcing his head back among the pillows. After a pleasant and relaxing tussle, they leaned against opposite ends of the sofa regarding each other with satisfaction.

"Darling," Delissa cooed, "it's a question of your image. Maybe it wouldn't matter if you were doing character work, but you're a leading man, a romantic leading man. The women in the audience are going to look up on the stage and see you making love to the leading lady and remember that you abandoned your wife and that she had to sue you to get her rent and grocery money."

"Ah, thanks, luv. You've certainly made me feel better."

"I'm trying to make you face reality. Julia can ruin you if she persists."

"All right, all right." He got up and paced. The way they were playing the scene it was his turn. "What do you suggest?"

"Don't ask me. She's your wife."

"She's sick, Dee. She's sick and she's desperate. What she needs to get well. . . . You know what it is as well as I do."

Not a muscle in Delissa Grace's expressive face twitched.

"She's fighting for her life, her professional life—it's one and the same."

"What does she want from you?" The actress asked the question despite herself; her voice quivered as she asked and the quiver was not acting.

"You know damn well what," Cassel replied. "She wants to be in the show. She wants me to ask to have her in it. She wants me to demand that she be in it."

"There's no part for her."

"Of course there is. Yours."

"Mine?" Delissa Grace's emotions followed one another so quickly none lasted long enough to be portrayed.

36

Finally, she began to laugh in broken spurts as though feeling her way in an insufficiently rehearsed scene, then gaining assurance. "Mine! She can't play Teresa. No way. It's ludicrous even to suggest . . ."

"Hold it. Stop right there," Cassel ordered. "Julia Schuyler can play any damn thing she sets her mind to, and don't you ever forget it. She's come a long way from the Hollywood brat she used to be—half Shirley Temple, half Bette Davis. They exploited her too soon, before she was ready. But she's got the talent. It's there."

"She got it from her father."

"Okay. It's got to come from somewhere. Where do you think you got yours? All talent is inherited."

"My people weren't actors. I had to claw and scratch for every damn job I got."

"Maybe Julia would have been better off if she'd had to do the same."

Delissa Grace, born Demetria Garrity of a Greek mother and an Irish father, had been performing since the age of fourteen. Starting as a member of the chorus with a local Greek troupe doing the classics of Aeschylus and Aristophanes, she made the transition to the American theater via readings, avant-garde experiments in back rooms and lofts, off-off Broadway, road shows, and stock. She had climbed virtually line by line to this opportunity of playing the lead role opposite Alfred Cassel. When *Of Light and Dark* opened, she confidently expected that the critics would exclaim that a new star had burst upon the Broadway scene overnight, not knowing or caring what had gone before. She resented Julia Schuyler, not because of her talent and her acquired skills but because Julia Schuyler had thrown away the opportunities Delissa Grace had had to scrabble for. It was a matter of pride with Delissa that she had never used her sex to get a job. When she took a lover, it was because her passion had been aroused. If, on occasion, the lover was also able to assist her in her career—that was fortuitous coincidence.

"Julia could play the pants off that part," Cassel told her with uncompromising candor. "It would be a differ-

37

ent interpretation from yours certainly, but just as valid." He thought about it, envisioned what Julia would bring to the role. "It would have certain underlying values . . . nuances . . ."

"Terrific! Marvelous!" Delissa Grace rose majestically. "She'd give a typical Schuyler performance laced with 'intuitive insights' and 'garnished with pyrotechnics.'" Derisively she quoted some of Julia's best reviews, then added, "If you managed to get her through rehearsals and to the stage on opening night. Assuming you did, she'd give you a triumph, but what would happen the second night? And the night after that for six nights every week and two matinees?"

"That's why you've got the job, dear, and she hasn't."

It was what she'd been waiting to hear, of course, and she calmed instantly. "So what are you going to do?"

"Nothing. Aside from your part in the show, I've got nothing she wants."

"Talk to her. Reason with her. Point out to her that if she accuses you of nonsupport you can accuse her right back of being an alocholic and drinking up whatever you give her."

"You don't mean that."

"I don't mean for you actually to do it, no. Of course, you're not going to do that any more than she's going to take you to court. It's just tit for tat. Threat and counter-threat."

"Pretty spectacle."

"She started it."

For some reason he didn't himself understand, the mild, introspective, and rational man suddenly exploded. "Shut up, Dee! Will you just please shut up! God damn it, shut up!"

"Billy! Billy Zip!"

Mici sprang from her chair and went running to him. They threw their arms around each other and kissed. Then, at arms' length, each examined the other in mutual delight.

"Billy, it's so good to see you."

"You look exactly the same, darling," he told her. "Not a year older, only prettier—if that's possible."

"You haven't changed either." He hadn't, Mici thought. As natty and stylishly turned out as ever in this season's latest, an impractical, cream-colored, linen suit. His hairline had receded, or was that a wiglet he was wearing? It wasn't till she looked closely that she noticed the fretwork of fine lines behind the rose-tinted glasses and at the corners of his smiling mouth.

"I've put on weight," he murmured deprecatingly.

"Who hasn't?" she grinned. "But what's this 'Mr. Zipprodt' bit? When the girl brought your name in, it took me a minute to figure out who was here."

"I'm so impressed with your position, darling. I was trying to live up to it." He smiled back fondly.

"Billy, Billy, you're so good for my ego; you have no idea . . ." She waved him to a chair and then took her own place. "So how are you? What's new? Are you working?"

"You could call it that."

"What are you doing—designing the decor for massage parlors?" she teased.

"Nothing so exciting. I'm stage manager for daytime TV. I've got two soap operas—'Storm of Life' and 'The World We Live In.' "

"But that's marvelous, Billy! Terrific! Do you like it?"

"It's not exactly the fulfillment of my ambitions, but . . . yes, I like it all right. It's steady. It's nice to know there's a paycheck coming in every week." He paused. "I guess you're crazy about your job?"

She shrugged. "Nothing's perfect. So what can I do for you, Mr. Zipprodt? I don't suppose you came down here for a social call. By the way, how did you find me?"

"You remember Julia Schuyler?"

"Who could forget Julia?"

"Julia read about you in the papers, about some case you were prominent in where you helped clear a woman of murder."

"That was a while ago."

"You've turned into a real hotshot investigator, Julia says. She's very impressed."

"That's nice to know. As I recall, she didn't think much of me as a dancer. And she was right." Mici grinned to alleviate the stage manager's embarrassment.

Billy Zip had been an assistant stage manager for the Joffrey Ballet Company when Mici was dancing minor roles. He'd aspired to be a scenic designer but got sidetracked. During the run at the Civic Opera House in Chicago, they were next door to Julia Schuyler at the Civic Theater in *A Streetcar Named Desire.* Mici remembered that she'd thought Cassel miscast in the Brando role, too civilized, too sensitive, but Julia had been absolutely magnificent as Blanche. The stage doors of the two theatres were adjacent, and actors and dancers encountered each other coming and going. There were cast parties; they met at after-the-show hangouts. It wouldn't have happened in New York. Neither Billy Zip nor Mici Anhalt would have met Julia Schuyler or moved in her social circle, but it was different on the road. A company on tour is usually the only show in town. Hitting a city like Chicago, able to support several shows, was like coming back from exile. The casts fraternized, stars and bit players; even when they didn't like each other, the actors mixed and were friendly. Having met Julia Schuyler, Billy was instantly smitten. Julia and Alfred Cassel weren't married then. Mici didn't recall to whom Julia had been married at the time, if anybody. At any rate, she was sure that Billy would have been content to worship the star from afar, but Julia had encouraged him. Whether she'd used Billy to stir Cassel's ardor or whether she was just flattered by his adulation—for he was personable, intelligent, and did have a rather shy charm—Julia and Billy were an item during that Chicago season. When the time came for the Joffrey to move on to the next stand, Billy quit and stayed behind. In due course, Julia got him a job with *Streetcar,* and from then on he worked in every show she did. Unfortunately, they weren't many and the "rest" periods between grew longer and longer. Even after their romance—if there had actually been one—faded and

40

Julia married Cassel, Billy stuck with her. He was her unpaid secretary, companion, errand boy. He saw to it that there was food in the house and even cooked it. He nursed her when she needed nursing. He'd finally had to go out and get himself a real job, but evidently he was still in touch.

"How is Julia these days?" Mici asked. "I don't hear anything about her."

"She's bad, Mici. Terrible."

"I'm sorry. I did hear that Alfred has a new show."

"They're separated."

"Again?"

"This time it's for keeps. You have no idea what they went through. Neither one of them could get work for . . . oh, a couple of years. They sold everything they had—the car, that went first, then the co-op. They moved into a friend's apartment, which was all right, a decent place, but when they couldn't pay the rent he had to ask them to leave. After that they went from one furnished dump to another. It would break your heart. They got down to the clothes on their backs, just about. The furs, the jewels? Forget it—sold or in hock. They never stopped fighting, blaming each other." He shook his head. "They were dragging each other down."

"I'm sorry."

Zipprodt peered at her through the upper half of his tinted bifocals. "So darling, that's why I'm here. I came to ask you to help Julia. Please, for God's sake, help her."

She was completely taken aback. "Billy! What can I do?"

"That's your job, isn't it? To help people? To help the victims of crime?"

"Julia's the victim of a crime? What crime?"

"Assault. He came around and beat her up."

"Who?"

"Alfred."

Mici gasped. "I don't believe it."

"It's true. I saw the bruises."

"Did she say he was responsible?"

"No," Zipprodt admitted, "but it had to be him. I'm

41

not saying she didn't provoke him but . . . Actually, I blame myself. Julia sent me over to see Alfred and to tell him that she needed more money and that if he didn't provide it she would sue for nonsupport. He was very upset, naturally. He claimed he was already giving her every cent he could spare. I suggested he go over and talk with her. In fact, I urged him to go over and see her, reason with her. He said he would. So I suppose one thing led to another and he lost control. Alfred has a temper. Most people don't realize it, but he can get violent."

"I know that they're both highly charged, emotional people, but . . ." Mici shook her head. She tried to forget that these were people she liked and even respected. "Has she had medical attention?"

"I don't think so."

"She ought to see a doctor. How about the police? Has she reported the beating? She should do that, Billy. She should do it within forty-eight hours of the alleged assault."

"Alleged?"

"Manner of speaking, Billy."

"I don't think Julia wants to go to the police."

"It's up to her, of course, but in any case I'm afraid that there's nothing this agency can do. It's a family matter and we can't touch it."

"If she'd been mugged on the street, then could you help her?"

"Yes."

"If she weren't married to Alfred, if they were just living together, then you'd pay?"

"It's not that simple, Billy."

"Sure it is. Sure it is. The present morality is a joke. On the one hand, society looks down on 'cohabitation' and on the other, rewards it. Don't tell me I'm wrong. Two singles living together pay less taxes than a married couple. Senior citizens lose part of their social security if they remarry, and here's a situation where a woman has suffered bodily harm and your wonderful agency refuses even to consider her case because the

42

assailant happens to be her husband." He finished on a rasping note of indignation.

"Don't lay it on me, Billy Zip. I don't make the rules." Mici's indignation matched his.

"From you I expected a little compassion, a little sympathy. . . ." he raged.

"I have all the feeling in the world for Julia Schuyler," she shouted back, then paused, and when she resumed it was with a touch of irony. "Only yesterday my supervisor called me on the carpet for having too much compassion."

"Maybe I should have come over yesterday." William Zipprodt got up and started for the door.

"Billy, come back. Please, come back and listen to me."

He did stop but remained where he was. "She needs help. She's run out of things to sell and friends to mooch off. I give her what I can, but I've got to live, too." He took a breath. "She's even trying to write a book. It's pitiful to see her commercializing her own degradation."

"Is there any interest?"

"In her own story? There have been too many like it. In what she has to say about her father . . . possibly. John Malcolm Schuyler has been gone nine years, but he still pulls the old magic. Of course, nobody's going to give her any kind of advance until she can show something on paper. I'm trying to help her but . . ." He sighed. "She won't work on any kind of regular schedule. She gets muddled, contradicts herself, can't seem to keep her facts straight."

"I suppose her unemployment insurance has long since run out. How about welfare?"

"You want Julia Schuyler to go on welfare?" The stage manager was outraged.

"You came to me and I'm doing the best I can."

"Which is nothing."

"Because there is nothing I can do. I just wish there were."

He stared at her for a long moment. "She's terrified, Mici. She can't sleep at night, she's so scared."

"Of Alfred?"

Once again Zipprodt headed for the door. "Thanks. Thanks for your time."

"Tell her to go to the police," Mici entreated. "Even though he's her husband, she can swear out a complaint. They'll arrest him and put him in jail. The law was passed last September."

"She'd never do that."

"All right then. Let her apply to Family Court for an order of protection. It would enjoin Alfred to stay away from her. If he disobeyed, then he'd be arrested."

"Well, maybe if you explained it to her . . ."

"Me? Billy, I haven't seen Julia in . . . I don't know how many years. I can't just walk in on her and bring up this kind of subject."

"Yes you can. She's expecting you."

"Julia is?"

"Tonight. She sent me to get you."

"She sent you? I—I can't see her tonight." She succumbed without realizing it.

"Tomorrow night then."

"Tomorrow's Friday. I'm going home for the weekend," she protested weakly. "I'd planned to leave right after work."

"Take a later train. You can do that much, can't you?"

The rain started just after 6 P.M. on Friday night. According to the weather bureau, it would do little to alleviate the heat that continued to rise by a few degrees each day, but at least there would be a temporary respite. As far as Officers Ray Emmenecher and Attilio Pace were concerned, it meant that there were fewer people on the street and therefore less work for them. The girls lounged in doorways, but the johns weren't out. Emmenecher half dozed behind the wheel of the parked patrol car. Even Pace was bored.

"It's sure quiet," he complained.

"Mm . . ."

"It's the quietest night we've had. At least since I've been on the job."

"You don't like it?"

"It makes the time go faster when there's action."

Emmenecher didn't bother to comment.

"You think it would be okay for me to go around the corner and get a hamburger?" Pace asked out of restlessness.

"Why not?"

"You want one?"

"Okay." Em didn't want one any more than his partner did; it just offered a break in the monotony. "Medium with plenty of catsup."

Pace had one foot outside the car door and on the pavement when a shrill scream froze him and galvanized Emmenecher into sitting up straight. After the initial split second of paralysis, the two men looked at each other, each with his hand on his gun.

"What was that?" Pace whispered.

"Shut up," the older man snarled.

They listened hard, but the scream was not repeated. They watched. No one came out of any of the buildings within their range of vision. Suddenly, preceded only by a hiss that was like the rushing of a train through a tunnel, the light rain turned into a downpour.

Ray Emmenecher rolled up his window.

Pace heistated; then he pulled in his foot and shut his door. "Shouldn't we do something?"

"What?"

"Find out where it came from?"

"How?"

Pace thought about it. They couldn't ring every doorbell of every apartment in every building. They couldn't check every bar and massage parlor. Unless somebody called 911, and people in that neighborhood weren't inclined to call the police over every scream in the night, there was really nothing they could do. Reluctantly, he rolled his window up too, though he left it open just a bit at the top in case there should be another scream. . . .

"I thought you were going to get us hamburgers?"

"You don't expect me to go out in that, do you, for

Chrissake!" Pace was so frustrated he forgot to be humble.

Emmenecher's shaggy eyebrows shot up.

Both men automatically checked their watches. It was 11:12 P.M.

5

They might not have found her as soon as Monday if her windows hadn't been shut against the rain and the temperature hadn't soared above ninety-five for the third straight day. The sickly odor seeped through the loose frame of the kitchen window into the courtyard where it mixed with all the other noxious fumes from all the apartment and restaurant kitchens, the overflowing garbage cans, the rat and human feces. It filled the apartment; then oozing from under the front door like a viscous liquid, it evaporated back into poison gas that contaminated the second-floor hall and filled the entire stairwell. Inured as they were to the stinks of summer, the tenants passing up and down ignored it. When it was no longer possible to do so, they began to whisper among themselves. On Monday shortly before noon, the tenant of the third-floor front, Bettedene Barber—also known as Barbi or Barbidoll—feeling queasy anyway after a big weekend, nearly gagged on the stench on her way downstairs. But it was the ringing of the telephone inside the apartment from which the foulness emanated, a ringing insistent and somehow desolate, that decided her. When it stopped, unanswered, she went looking for the super.

"I didn't smell a thing," Eddie Manzor insisted.

"How the hell could you? You haven't been in the building in a week."

"I've got other buildings to look after, you know. You

46

got a complaint, you know what you can do with it."

"And I'm doing it," the teenage blonde shot back. "I'm telling you. The smell is sickening."

"Bad for business?" Eddie Manzor leered. He was a slovenly man of indefinable age. Never clean, never shaven, always tired, he shuffled from one tenement to another doing little more than hauling out the garbage; even that he couldn't manage, leaving a trail of spillage in the halls. He knew that none of his various employers was likely to check on him. If any one of them did, for the money he was getting Manzor could tell him to stick it.

Bettedene Barber didn't rise to the bait. In her abbreviated version of the doll's outfit with her cluster of golden curls falling around her shoulders, she was sexy and childish at the same time. At the moment, with her heavily made-up face puckered and her black-mascaraed eyes filled, the childishness predominated. "I'm telling you, Eddie, something's dead in there."

"What do you want me to do?"

"You've got a passkey. Open the door."

What Eddie Manzor did, reluctantly, was to call the police.

A patrolman cleared the way through the ogling crowd for Detective Donald Swell, Homicide Third Division, and he made his way walking jauntily on the balls of his feet like a fighter warming up in his corner of the ring. The people were everywhere—on the sidewalks, in the doorways, on the fire escapes. He ignored them. As far as Detective Donald Swell was concerned, this was your typical crime-scene turnout, a little extra heavy because this was a hot summer's day and nobody in this neighborhood had much to do anyway. The local toughs had congregated right at the top of the stoop blocking the entrance to the building, but at a look from Swell they parted—sullenly, but they parted.

The odor of decomposition hit him as soon as he got inside. Swell merely wrinkled his nose and started up the stairs lightly at a half run, noting with satisfaction

47

that he wasn't even breathing hard when he got to the top. That daily jogging sure paid off.

Inside the apartment was your typical homicide scene, Swell thought—ordered confusion, each man doing his thing with complete disregard for anyone else. Nobody so much as looked up at his entrance, but that didn't bother Donald. He might be only a dick three, but the information these hotshots were laboriously collecting would feed through him and he'd decide what was important and what was not. They were the experts, but he was the boss; he was carrying the case.

At thirty-five, Donald Swell had been a detective third grade for four years, two of them working out of Homicide. He liked the job, the guys, the feeling of belonging. It was like the army except that there was more freedom and one could act independently—within limits. The limits didn't bother Donald. He was a pragmatist; in fact, unconsciously, he found reassurance in the rules. He didn't dwell on the horrors with which he came into daily contact; he'd made his accommodation—they were part of the human condition. Take this room. One look sufficed—the threadbare carpet, dirty, cracked walls, cheap furniture; he'd seen a hundred like it. Unfortunately, the victim required more than a cursory glance. She was on the floor lying across the threshold between living room and kitchen, head in the living room. She lay on her left side, knees partially drawn up as though bunched over her wound. Her back was toward him, so the detective took a couple of steps forward to look more closely, but her hands were clutched over the injury. Her head was down, chin on chest, and her dark hair had fallen forward masking her face, which was probably just as well. The gases inside the body had caused her chest to bloat and burst the white cotton shirt she'd been wearing. If the same had happened to her face, which probably it had, then she would be unrecognizable, eyes bulging, tongue protruding, and the usual mess exuding from nose and mouth. Donald Swell swallowed the bile that rose up to the back of his tongue.

"Officer," he called to the uniformed cop at the door. "I'm Homicide. What've you got?"

Joe Camby, one of the two radio-car patrolmen who'd answered the call put in by Manzor, pulled out his notebook. "Name of the victim is Julia Schuyler." He paused. As the name didn't seem to make an impression, he added diffidently, not wanting to appear snobbish, "She was an actress, sir."

"Yeah? What kind of an actress?"

"Legitimate theatre, sir, though she did appear in some motion pictures years ago."

"Yeah?" Swell was not into the legitimate theatre, or ballet, or any longhair stuff. He wasn't much into movies either unless there was plenty of action involved.

Camby on the other hand was a culture freak. He decided to take one more chance. "Her father was John Malcolm Schuyler."

"Yeah?" Even Donald Swell had heard of him. "So go on, what else?"

"The super called in on a complaint from one of the tenants about the smell. We told him to use his passkey and let us in. The tenant who complained, a Miss Bettedene Barber, is waiting upstairs in her apartment, 3A. The super, Eddie Manzor, is in the hall. My partner's with him and some of the other tenants."

"Any of them notice anything? Have anything to say?" Dumb question; these people made it a way of life *not* to notice anything, but if they were unfortunate enough to do so kept it to themselves. Swell had asked because it was routine.

Officer Camby answered and did so earnestly for the same reason. "No, sir."

"Okay, thanks." Swell prided himself on being courteous to lower-ranking men, but he hadn't taken the trouble to note the officer's name prominently pinned to the front of his blouse. If he should need to get back to him, what the hell, he'd find him.

"Hi, Doc." Swell moved on and greeted the assistant chief medical examiner. "You got an estimate how long she's been dead?"

"You should know better than to ask," Herman Childs grunted without looking up.

He did know better, but again it was routine. "Can't you give me any idea, Doc? A ball-park figure? Unofficially."

The exchange was choreographed down to the grunts and gestures. Childs, a twenty-year veteran, had been in line for the chief's job when the chief retired. He'd taken the exam along with the only other two forensic men qualified and then had sweated out the appointment. With each passing day, week, month, the threshold of his irritability was lowered. It took six months for a decision to be reached and Childs lost out. By then the strain had left permanent scars on his face and temper. "In this heat, with the windows shut tight . . ." He cast a glance at the kitchen window. "What the hell, we had to open it. You'll have to take my word that everying was closed when we came in."

"Hey, Doc!" Swell smiled and spread out his hands in a gesture which said that Child's word was good with him for just about anything. Actually, as there was no discernible movement of air in the apartment, the detective wouldn't have noticed that the window was in fact open if the ME hadn't called attention to it. However, Childs was on the defensive and Donald hurried to take advantage. "So, taking into consideration the heat and humidity, the position of the body, the type and size of the wound, the amount of clothing she was wearing . . ." He listed it all just to let Doc know he wasn't a complete ignoramous.

"I'd say she'd been dead two to three days. Closer to three." Childs made a grudging estimate.

"How was she killed?"

"Stabbed in the heart. Her asailant was facing her. The weapon was some kind of carving knife, very big and very sharp. Apparently the killer took it with him."

"Yeah?"

"It's not around, is it? I don't see it, do you? So unless the killer washed it and wiped it and put it neatly back in a drawer . . ." He shrugged. "You want to take a look?"

"You're kidding, huh, Doc?"

"I never kid," Childs replied.

Swell hesitated. His eyes swept the small kitchen perfunctorily but took note of the empty bottle of Dewar's on the counter. Good brand, he thought. Then, just to be on the safe side, he went through the drawers. "There's no kind of carving knife around," he said.

"Really?" Childs grunted.

Swell still wasn't sure whether he'd been had. He tried to reassert himself as an expert. "If the attack was frontal, then she would have made some kind of attempt to defend herself, wouldn't she? There would have been a struggle, right?"

"Yes," Childs admitted. "There are bruises, but under these conditions it's pretty hard to say exactly when they were inflicted. We'll have to see."

"There could be skin particles from the perpetrator under her fingernails, huh, Doc? Traces of his blood and like that. So you'll let me know, right, Doc? First chance." Considering that he had evened the score, Swell thought it was time to get out. "Where's the officer who caught the squeal?" he boomed.

Camby stuck his head in from the hall.

"How about those witnesses?" Swell demanded. "Where are they?"

Camby forebore to remind the detective that he'd already been informed of their whereabouts. "Waiting for you, sir."

"Fine, fine. I'll see the super first."

Camby hesitated and Swell realized why; the place was swarming with technicians and cluttered with their equipment. "In the bedroom, of course. I'll talk to him in the bedroom." Swell sauntered off as though that had been his intention from the first.

The sagging bed took up most of the space; pushed up against one wall, it left barely room enough to get to the closet. It was covered by a chenille bedspread and apparently had not been slept in. The room was so small that the only other piece of furniture, a scarred bureau, partially blocked the single dirty window. Julia Schuyler couldn't have been much if she had lived like

51

this, Swell mused. The father now, John Malcolm Schuyler, his name was legend. He'd come from a long line of distinguished actors—father, mother, uncles, aunts—but John Malcolm had been the brightest star of them all. He'd also become a hopeless alcoholic. He'd drink anything he could get his hands on, including—once when he'd been out at sea on a private yacht for the express purpose of drying out—the alcohol used to heat his wife's curling iron. Donald ranked actors in two categories: those who made it and those who didn't. The former he regarded as superior human beings, the latter as bums too lazy to go out and get regular work. It looked as if Julia Schuyler had been one of the bums.

Swell sat down on the edge of the bed because there wasn't anywhere else. "You the super?" he asked the bleary-eyed, unshaven man in soiled work clothes who presented himself at the door.

"Yes, sir."

"Well, what are you waiting for? Come on in. What's your name?"

"Manzor. Eddie Manzor." He crept in along the wall.

"Well, Mr. Manzor, how come it took you so long to call us?"

Manzor flinched. "Uh . . . well, you see . . ."

"According to the officer, you called only because one of your tenants insisted. How's that?"

Manzor was defensive. "I didn't know she was dead. I mean, how could I know?"

"She's been dead for close to three days, Mr. Manzor." Swell's tone was cutting. "You've got a nose, haven't you? Just like Miss Barber upstairs?" He hadn't needed to consult his notes for the name; Donald Swell remembered what he needed to remember. "So why did you wait? Why did Miss Barber have to go looking for you?"

"I don't live in the building."

"This is Monday. Don't you come around on Mondays anyway to put out the garbage?"

Manzor looked down at his matted, stained shoes. "I was here. But I didn't come upstairs. They're supposed

52

to bring their garbage down to the back door for me to put out. I mean, this ain't the Ritz."

"You don't say? When was the last time you saw Miss Schuyler alive?"

"I don't know." Manzor shrugged, but the look Swell shot him made him add quickly, "I don't remember."

"When was the last time you were in this apartment? Come on, Mr. Manzor. I asked you a question."

"I was never in here. Never."

Swell looked his disbelief. "You never came in here to fix anything? She never called you to repair a leaky faucet, or unstick a window, or any damn thing?"

"Oh, you mean like that? Well, sure, naturally."

"How did you think I meant?"

"Her bathroom sink got clogged once. Hair balled up in the drain. I warned her about that. Dirty habit."

"When? When did you clean the bathroom sink?"

"Uh . . . maybe a week ago?"

"Are you asking me?"

"No. It was a week ago."

"You're sure? You remember now?"

"Yes, sir. I remember."

"Good. Was she alone?"

Too late Manzor saw the trap. The sweat stood out on his grimy forehead. "Yeah."

"What are you so nervous about?"

"I'm not nervous. Why should I be nervous?"

"That's what I was wondering," Swell replied blandly. "If nothing happened."

Manzor raised his squinty eyes up to the ceiling but found no help there. "She invited me to have a drink with her, but I said no. I know better than to get involved with a lush. No. No. I didn't mean that. I swear I didn't. What I meant . . . she was a nice woman, a lady—when she was sober. But she's been real lonely since her husband walked out and ready to grab out for anybody . . . Oh, God!" He realized, again too late, that he was making the situation worse.

"When did her husband leave?"

"Four, five months ago? I don't know. I mean, after a

53

while I just kind of realized he wasn't around any more. He's an actor too, Alfred Cassel. Maybe you heard of him?" Manzor was eager now, eager to talk as long as it wasn't about himself. In fact, in order to divert attention from himself, the super was anxious to tell everything he knew or had ever heard—just as Swell had intended. "He's been in the movies and on TV, and I hear he's gonna star in a big, new Broadway show. According to Ms. Schuyler, she threw him out on account of he had a girl friend. I guess she was sorry when she found out he had this good job. I guess she tried to get him back, but it was no go."

"How do you know that?"

"I seen him coming out of the building a couple of times. What was he doing here if not visiting her?"

"How do you figure it was no go?"

The super shrugged. "He didn't move back in, did he? Besides, every time he showed up, the next couple of days she was really knocking back the booze." This time he anticipated the question. "I could tell from the trash—the empties. You can tell a lot from people's trash," he went on. "Like Ms. Schuyler and Mr. Cassel—used to be Chivas Regal empties I found in their can; then it went down to house brands in quarts and half gallons; now it's mostly beer cans. Or was," he corrected himself.

"So when was the last time you saw Alfred Cassel?" Manzor considered. "Thursday for sure."

"What do you mean—for sure?"

"I spoke to him on Thursday, but on Friday . . . It was a lousy night. I'd had a few at the corner bar and when I come home I thought I spotted him coming into the building. I thought it was him, but like I say . . . I'd had a few."

The ME estimated she'd been dead close to three days. Swell did some mental figuring. "What time Friday?"

"I couldn't tell you."

"Try."

Manzor shook his head. "Eleven? A little before, a little after." Swell's look scared the hapless man into

54

the ultimate sacrifice. "If you want, I'll ask the wife what time I got home. She'll remember, believe me."

"I'll ask her myself," Swell told him. *I'll also ask the bartender what time you left, Buster, and if there's a gap—God help you!* the detective thought, but spoke with deceptive mildness. "This man you saw entering the building—what made you think it was Cassel?"

"The raincoat. Cassel had this raincoat, black with a cape around the shoulders. How many of those do you see around?"

"Policemen have them," Swell observed.

"No, no. I mean, those are like a rubber material; this was more like cloth. It didn't shine."

Swell nodded. "Was the rent getting paid?"

"Sooner or later."

"Who paid? Her or him?"

"How should I know?" Thinking he was off the hook, Manzor reverted to his normal truculence.

"She didn't mention it?" Swell asked pleasantly. "What did you talk about while you were drinking together?"

"We weren't drinking together! Never. I swear." The sweat glistened in the creases of his dirty face and his whole body gave off a smell so rank it was noticeable even in that fetid atmosphere. "Listen, I'm a married man. I've got a kid. I know better than to . . ." He stopped, grimaced, groaned, and gave up. "Okay. All right. So I had a beer with her. One beer, once. I felt sorry for her and I had a beer with her and I let her tell me all about how big she used to be in the business, the jobs her agent was lining up for her, the book she was writing. But she was dreamin'. All she wanted was for somebody to listen."

"Where's Cassel now?"

Instinct prompted a flip reply, but Manzor caught himself. "I don't know, Officer." He waited and watched anxiously as the detective got up and began poking through the bureau drawers, examining the closet which was half empty. "Say, uh, Officer . . ." Manzor cleared his throat. "You through with me? Can I go now?"

Swell turned as though he'd forgotten all about the super. "Oh, sure. Go ahead. And say, thanks for your help, Mr. Manzor." He was breezy and friendly and sent Manzor off in a state of bewilderment.

On the shelf above the clothes rod of Julia Schuyler's closet were a couple of good-quality but badly worn handbags. By hefting each one, Swell determined which had been in current use. The contents were the usual wallet with a couple of dollars in it, credit cards driver's license but no vehicle registration, and check book showing a balance of eleven dollars and two cents. There was also a small, red-leather address book. Swell flipped through it cursorily. A name caught his eye then another. He took the book over to the window as though the bit of extra light would make the difference.

A big grin transformed Detective Donald Swell's tough-guy face into that of a happy schoolboy. Names, names, names he recognized! Big important names of famous people in show business, sports, the jet set God! The only one missing was Jackie Onassis.

He'd hit it lucky—at last. You needed the breaks to get ahead in the police department the same as anywhere else. He'd had his share; he couldn't deny it. The first had come when he'd been in the force only three years. He'd been parked in his radio car across from the New York Medical Center—his partner was making a pit stop—when he noticed a couple of orderlies strolling out of the main building. It was January and a real cold day and they weren't wearing coats. That made him suspicious. They sauntered down the U-shaped drive to the street awful slow for guys without coats, he'd thought, and then he heard the faint sound of the alarm. They heard it too and made a run for it, but he collared one of them. The other was picked up in due course through his buddy's turning state evidence. The haul was over $200,000 worth of drugs which they'd hidden in special holders taped under their shirts. That was what had kept them warm. The bust had put Donald into plain clothes.

Two years later he was once again in the right place

at the right time. He and his partner walked in on a robbery in progress in a liquor store. It'd looked like a one-man job, and they'd disarmed the prepetrator and were cuffing him when his accomplice came up from behind the counter. Swell spotted him and fired first. Damn near killed the guy, but probably saved his partner's life, not to mention his own and that of the proprietor. That got him the gold shield. The PC himself pinned it on Donald. He was a hero—for a couple of days, anyway.

That had been four years ago. For four long years he'd been stuck in his present grade doing the most routine kind of leg work. When he thought back to the two incidents, which he did more and more often lately, Donald was honest enough to admit that he'd acted more out of instinct than bravery. He wondered whether he'd act so quickly now if the opportunity arose. He was older and smarter. He'd weigh the consequences— the mandatory Internal Affairs investigation into any shooting by a police officer, possible charges by the perpetrator, the reactions of bystanders which could be ugly—and the moment would pass him by. But there was no instant stress in this particular situation.

The little red book in his hands, Detective Third Grade Donald Swell stared out the unwashed window at the other unwashed windows overlooking the steamy courtyard. Brown eyes narrowed, pudgy face puckered, Swell considered how best to make use of the case that had been handed to him. Though herself a has-been, as her father's daughter Julia Schuyler had publicity value which was much enhanced by the circles in which she'd moved—never mind how long ago. As for Alfred Cassel, if he had been on TV and was now due to star in a new Broadway show, then the case would hit the headlines for sure. And if Swell could break the case, it could mean making second grade.

The grin returned, very broad, turning him back into the chubby schoolboy. Depending on who the killer turned out to be—maybe he could make first grade! Donald Swell daydreamed.

6

On Sunday night Mici Anhalt returned from her weekend at home. She was much calmer. She'd decided that she had overreacted to Adam's lecture, but that he too had overreacted to the situation because he was tired, overworked, and dragged out by the heat. She admitted that she did have a tendency to slough off the dull, routine cases, to neglect paperwork, and to crow over her successes. In the future she would allot equal time and attention to all and maintain a low profile with her colleagues. As for Julia Schuyler, the image of the actress had haunted Mici through most of the weekend. Though forewarned, she hadn't been prepared for the squalor in which she found Julia living or for her emotional state. Regardless of Adam's recent strictures, nothing could be done for Julia under the program. The truth was that nothing could be done for Julia except by Julia herself. Mici kept thinking of the once glamorous actress as she had left her on Friday—asleep on that hard, sleazy couch, mouth open and snoring like a day laborer—and she couldn't shake off a sense of responsibility toward her.

Several times on Monday morning Mici reached for the telephone to call Julia but it was always too early—Julia Schuyler wouldn't be fit to talk till at least noon. Not that Mici had anything special to say; she just felt the need to contact the actress once more and to make sure she understood the options that were available to her. At noon, while the number was ringing, Clay Marin appeared on the threshold of Mici's office. She had to put the receiver down. The blind man's visits always tried her patience. Today, his arrival would put her recent good resolutions to the test.

Dowd's secretary, Mrs. Jarrett, had escorted the blind man this far. Though she knew that he couldn't see it, Mici forced a bright smile and ran over to take him from Fran and guide him the short distance to the chair beside her desk. With a sweep of his cane that stopped just short of hitting her, he made his own way. Mici jumped aside but didn't say anything. She was sure he'd done it on purpose. She was glad that his mobility was improving; too bad the same couldn't be said for his disposition. She stifled a sigh and spoke with that false, loud cheeriness reserved for invalids.

"It's good to see you, Mr. Marin. You're looking fine, just fine." He wasn't. He was badly shaved, wearing a rumpled suit, a stained tie, mismatched socks. It was his way of pointing up his affliction. There had been a time, she well remembered, when Clay Marin had done everything possible to hide it.

"You stood me up last Wednesday," he accused.

Apparently he was in an exceptionally sour mood, even for him. "I'm sorry about that, Mr. Marin. It couldn't be helped."

"Do you realize the effort I have to make to get here?"

"Yes, I certainly do, and I'm really very sorry . . ."

"I depend on the charity of neighbors to bring me. My wife, what the hell does she care? She can't be bothered. We don't sleep together any more, did you know that? Sleep together? Hell, we hardly talk any more."

"I was at fault on Wednesday, Mr. Marin, completely at fault. Please forgive me."

"Nobody had any idea where you were," he whined. "Nobody had any idea when you'd be back. I didn't know whether I should wait around for you or what."

Mici was getting tired of apologizing, "I understand that Mr. Lischner took care of you."

"Mr. Lischner was very sympathetic, but what could he do? He didn't have access to the recent medical reports. He went through your desk, but he couldn't find them."

Mici frowned. Wally sympathetic? That wasn't his style with clients. Wally going through her desk? She didn't like that. She didn't like his telling Marin that he couldn't find the reports; they were right there in the bottom drawer. Why had he lied? Unless it was a way of getting rid of Marin. That was it, of course. Unfortunately, she couldn't do the same.

"He didn't know where to look," she offered as cheerfully as she could. "But here they are. If you'll just give me a moment to look them over once more . . ."

She felt sorry for Clay Marin. One year and four months ago he had interrupted a rape. Coming home at dusk, he had parked his car in his own driveway on Dartmouth Street in Forest Hills, got out, and was just approaching his front door when he heard a woman screaming. The screams came from an empty lot at the corner. Marin—in his early forties but in excellent physical condition from daily workouts at the prestigious West Side Tennis Club further down the street—ran to investigate. The trees, one of the beauties of the privileged "Gardens" enclave, were in full leaf, further cutting down the light from the street lamps, replicas of old-fashioned gaslights which gave almost as poor illumination as the originals. Marin could barely make out shapes down among the tall grasses at the back of the lot.

The woman screamed again and then she began to sob and whimper. "No, no . . . please . . . oh please . . ."

For a moment, Marin froze. He didn't know what he faced. Was the assailant armed? Did he have a gun or a knife? Was he young, old, big, strong? There were apartment buildings across the street overlooking the lot; had anyone there called the police? When would the police arrive? Meanwhile his eyes adjusted to the shadows and he could make out an amorphous mass writhing and heaving on the ground.

"Say, you! What are you doing? Let her go! Let that woman go!"

The movement stopped; the mass separated into two parts, and the rapist rose from his victim to look

60

around. Surprised and encouraged and sure now that the man was not armed, Marin pushed through the dew-heavy grass, lunged, and grabbed the assailant by the shirt collar.

"Run!" he yelled to the woman. "Run! Get the police!"

In the effort to pull loose, the attacker turned and for a couple of seconds he and Marin were face to face. Then the attacker, younger and stronger and more desperate, literally tore free and fled, leaving Marin with the ripped shirt collar in his hand.

Later that night a suspect was apprehended. The victim was willing to press charges, not always the case in such crimes, but she had not seen her assailant clearly and could not make a positive identification. But Marin could.

Clay Marin had a strong sense of duty and of confidence in ultimate justice. He was further motivated by the fact that the victim turned out to be the nineteen-year-old daughter of a neighbor. All this combined to make him an excellent witness. He picked the suspect out of the lineup without indecision of any kind and agreed to testify at the trial. Both the police and the prosecutor were delighted. Marin was a hero at home, at his club, throughout the neighborhood. And when the story appeared in the newspapers, his name and address were given.

The threats began: letters, phone calls, a dead cat thrown on the doorstep. His children—Rosalie, twelve, and Kenny, six, cried; his wife was frightened; but Clay Marin refused to be intimidated. As the time of the trial drew near, the harassment stopped abruptly.

"They know they can't scare me," Marin told his wife smugly, and Sandra Marin smiled and prayed to God that he was right.

On the night before he was due to testify, with the children sleeping soundly upstairs, he and Sandra were watching the late news before turning in. Each was thinking that by that time the next night the ordeal would be over, the suspect convicted and behind bars for good—well, for several years at least. Then the front doorbell rang. Marin, assuming it was one of the patrol officers assigned to keep a special eye on the house, got up automatically to answer. Sandra Marin stayed where she was, expecting to hear only a murmur of voices as her husband and the cop exchanged good nights. What she heard was her husband's shriek of pain. She got up and ran out to the hall in time to see him stagger back from the door, hands clutching at his eyes.

"Water! Water! Get me some water!"

Clay Marin did not appear in court the next day to make the identification: you can't identify somebody you can't see. The acid thrown in his face had blinded him.

Early medical opinions were cautious. There was hope; he could distinguish light from dark. There was hope. Wait and see. That was all they could say. Or would.

Mici had handled the case from the start and she remembered Clay Marin when he first came in—an angry, proud man, determined to beat the disability and to punish the criminal who had caused it. His claim was approved under the Good Samaritan provision. In case of death this would have meant larger benefits for the surviving family but in Marin's situation entitled him to reimbursement for loss of earning power for a longer than usual period. All the victims who qualified were entitled to unlimited medical assistance. Every possible avenue of treatment was investigated for Marin and passed on to J. Hammond Cornelius with Mici's and Dowd's recommendation for approval. In each instance, Cornelius had given his final okay.

As the months passed and the medical reports turned pessimistic, Marin turned bitter. Who could blame him? But the more that was done for him, the less he did for himself. He had started eager to become self-sufficient and taken mobility training at the Lighthouse for the Blind. The board okayed the purchase of a C5 Laser cane at a cost of $2,000, instead of the usual,

62

conventional cane. In this costlier device, the laser beam is converted into sound of varying pitch by which the user can judge the relative height and distance of the obstacle in his path. It gives protection to the entire body, where other devices—the sonic glasses, for instance—cover only the area above the waist. According to his instructor, Marin had learned to handle his can proficiently, yet, so far as anybody at the board offices knew, he seldom used it except when he came in to recite his woes and ask for more benefits. He was a salesman of commercial real estate and the company for which he'd worked offered him his old job back, reasoning that most of the properties had been listed before Marin's blindness and that he could be briefed on any new ones. According to Marin, to show what he couldn't see would be playing on the clients' pity. He refused. He also refused vocational training, claiming that the jobs available were menial and beneath his talents.

He was getting to be a pain.

Psychiatric treatment was arranged for him. It didn't help. The deterioration, physical and psychological, accelerated. It was downhill all the way.

Having started by admiring him, Mici now dreaded Clay Marin's visits. Everybody in the office did. As Adam had said, he was a whiner and a complainer, but nobody would turn his back on Clay Marin.

Privately, Mici thought he would adjust to his disability if he weren't still hoping to regain his sight. For a while he had been able to perceive shapes, and the Eye Research Institute of the Retina Foundation in Boston had advised patience in the hope that nature would do her own healing. For a period that appeared to be happening. But the improvement had only been minor, followed by further deterioration.

Marin had heard of a new surgical procedure to replace the vitreous, jelly-like filling of the eyeball, and he was convinced this would restore his sight. Of course, he was sent for examination to the specialist who had developed the procedure. It was that specialist's

63

report which Mici was now reviewing. Finished, she looked up to meet the dark glasses through which her client could not see.

"Did Dr. Harden discuss his conclusion with you?"

"He told me he didn't believe that a vitrectomy could help me."

"That's what he says in his report. I'm sorry, Mr. Marin."

"He said I could always get another opinion."

"Dr. Louis Harden is the authority on the subject. I doubt that another opinion would contradict his."

"I want it. I'm entitled to it."

"I understand how you feel, Mr. Marin but . . ."

"The hell you do! You haven't the faintest idea of how I feel or what my life has become!"

"You're right, of course," Mici admitted. "At the same time . . ."

"I want another opinion! I demand it!" He was shaking with rage and frustration. His long, dour face contorted, sweat glistened amid the stubble on his chin.

"I'll put through your request, Mr. Marin." Mici hesitated. In the past Marin had been handled too carefully, shielded too much, given false hope. She decided to be frank with him. "But under the circumstances I don't think the request will be granted." She waited for the outburst.

He took it quietly. In fact, he took it very well. "You've always been honest with me, Miss Anhalt. I appreciate that."

Surprise, what a surprise! "Thank you."

"I know you want to help me."

"I do, Mr. Marin."

"Well then, what could be simpler than to say that Dr. Harden has suggested another opinion?"

"But what about the report?"

"You could hold that back."

Slowly she shook her head. Remembering that he couldn't see, she murmured, "I'm sorry, no. I can't do that."

"You mean you won't."

"All right, I won't. It wouldn't do you any good. The second man might discuss the matter with Dr. Harden and the whole thing would come out."

"Not if you explain the situation to him."

Tired of his importuning, Mici cut Marin short. "Forget it, Mr. Marin. I'll put through your request along with Dr. Harden's report in the usual way."

"You women are all alike. All alike. You're sweet, willing to help as long as it's done your way, your way. Well, I don't need you and I don't need her. Forget it." Shaking, he got to his feet and, using his cane, expertly pointed himself toward the door.

Automatically Mici rose and went around to put a hand on his arm.

He shook her off. "I can find my own way."

He could and did, leaving Mici's office and heading through the big main room toward the exit while the various secretaries and clerks stopped to watch in amazement.

So, Mici thought, what Clay Spoiled Rotten Marin needed was not sympathy but a kick in the pants.

Suddenly she thought of Julia Schuyler. A swift kick wouldn't do her any harm either. But not on the telephone. The best thing would be to run up there. It shouldn't take too long. Mici grabbed her handbag, threw a light jacket over her arm in case she happened to get an air-conditioned subway car—what a hope—and sped out of her office.

"Leaving early?"

Wally Lischner just happened to look up as she passed his open door.

She paused guiltily and glanced at her watch. "Going out for a late lunch."

"Sure."

Their eyes met. He winked. "I'll cover for you."

"Thanks," she smiled. *Nuts,* she murmured under her breath.

By the time Mici Anhalt got uptown the block of Forty-fifth between Eighth and Ninth Avenues was pretty nearly back to normal. The official cars were gone. No one stopped her from entering the building. It wasn't until she climbed to the second floor that she spotted the uniformed officer, and the vague dread she'd been suppressing since Friday night rose up to choke her.

"What happened?"

"Homicide, ma'am."

"Who? Who was killed?"

"The woman who lived in this apartment, ma'am."

God! Ice-cold sweat broke out all over her body. "When? When did it happen?"

"I don't know, ma'am. I don't know anything about it."

If he did, he wouldn't tell her. "I'd like to talk to the person in charge."

"There's nobody here, ma'am. They're all gone." Because she seemed genuinely distressed, he added, "You could try the precinct, ma'am. Midtown South; that's 357 West 35th Street. Talk to the desk sergeant, ma'am."

"That's being handled by the Third Homicide Division, ma'am," the desk sergeant informed Mici. "If you want to leave your name I'll see to it that . . ."

Mici had a good idea what leaving her name would mean; a couple of days from now, a week from now, when he had nothing better to do, some detective on the fringes of the case would get around to calling her. She was jittery; she felt like pounding on the sergeant's desk and it took considerable effort to smile sweetly instead. "If you could just tell me who's in charge of the case, Sergeant. I need to talk to him. The victim was a friend . . ." Her voice broke. It wasn't put on. All Mici was doing that she wouldn't ordinarily do was let her feelings show.

Sergeant Eugene Crance, faithful husband, devoted father, dedicated deep-sea fisherman, still appreciated a pretty woman and not many like this redhead walked up to his desk. Procedure was to take her name and pass it on but . . . what the hell! Unaware that he was licking his lips, Crance reached for the telephone.

"This is Sergeant Crance at Midtown South . . . oh, is

66

that you, Vito? How are the blues running? ... Way out there, huh? Yeah, I'm going to try to make it on Wednesday. Say, who's carrying the Schuyler homicide? ... Today on Forty-fifth, that's the one, right. ..." He covered the mouthpiece and spoke to Mici. "He's checking. ... Yeah, Vito? Okay. Thanks, pal." Feeling Mici's eyes on him, he added, "Is he there now? ... So when's he coming in? I've got a witness here with important information. ... Sure, I'll tell her." Crance hung up, pushed the piece of paper on which he'd written over to Mici. "You want Detective Swell. He's off duty; you should call in the morning. I've put the number down."

Mici sighed. "Thanks, Sergeant."

Crance watched the sway of her hips as she headed for the door; then he noticed the slouch of her shoulders.

"Miss?" He beckoned her back. "No guy on a hot homicide is going home at the end of his shift—not if he knows what's good for him." He winked.

Maybe Detective Donald Swell knew better than to quit at the end of his tour, but wherever he was and whatever he was doing nobody in the squad room on East 51st Street knew anything about it. Mici decided there was no point in going back to her office. She could only hope that nobody besides Wally had noticed that she was gone. She had the uneasy feeling that if he tried to cover for her, Wally would only succeed in making matter worse. She wished now that she'd challenged his offer. Hell! The damage was done; she might as well sit it out here.

Every time anybody new walked through the door, Mici looked up hopefully, but it was never the man she wanted. By eight, too dispirited to be hungry, she gave up. She wrote a note and asked one of the detectives, the one with the black patent-leather hair who had been making a play for her between phone calls and trips to the cooler, to put it on Swell's desk. On her way out, she also left her name with the desk sergeant downstairs. Then she bought all the late papers at the stand outside the subway and started reading them on the ride uptown.

Donald Swell had more urgent things to do than hang around the squad room. He had important people to see, the first being the victim's estranged husband.

As soon as he walked into the actor's suite, Swell sensed that the scare technique he had used on Eddie Manzor was not going to serve. The actor puzzled the detective. Economically, Swell knew that Alfred Cassel was in bad shape, worse off than the detective himself, that the suite in the old-fashioned but prestigious hotel had to be all front. So the respectful routine was inappropriate. But socially, Cassel was way up there in a stratum Swell could never hope to reach. Therefore the buddy-buddy bit wasn't right, either. What was left? Man-to-man, Swell decided; he'd adopt the forthright, straight-from-the-shoulder approach.

But Cassel was a better actor than the detective; the skill of the professional all but swamped the amateur. Swell arrived before the news of Julia Schuyler's death hit the radio or the newspapers; Cassel received it with a convincing demonstration of shock and sorrow.

"When?" he asked. "When did it happen?"

"It's hard to say. She wasn't discovered till this morning, and several matters have to be taken into consideration in estimating how long . . ."

"Ahh . . ." Cassel looked sick. He turned aside for a few moments, and when he faced the detective again he was at least three shades paler. "Have you any idea who did it?"

"I was hoping you might have, sir." Swell frowned; he hadn't meant to add the sir.

Cassel shook his head. "We weren't living together. Well, you know that. In fact, I wanted a divorce which she refused to give me. I might as well tell you; you'll find out soon enough. I called her, wrote her, I asked mutual friends to intercede, but she was obdurate." He paused, apparently lost in a reverie. With a slight start, he came out of it and observed. "You don't kill a woman because she won't give you a divorce, not in our

68

day, anyway. There is someone else, a lady I would like to marry but ... if we can't ... that's no big thing nowadays, either. And, of course, we can now, can't we?" The performance was disarming, as intended. "Julia was badmouthing me around town; you'll find that out too. But in this business if you went around killing everybody who took a crack at you, you wouldn't have any friends left."

"When did you last see Miss Schuyler?"

The slightest hesitation, the first touch of uncertainty was in his reply. "Thursday, I think. Yes, last Thursday. Frankly, it was an unpleasant meeting. I didn't want to go, but I was strongly urged by several friends to try to reason with her. Of course, I should have known better. Nobody can ever—could ever—reason with Julia even when she was sober, and last Thursday she was very, very drunk. It ended in a yelling match and Julia always won those. I guess the whole house must have heard us."

Which is why you're so forthcoming, Buster, Swell thought. "Would you mind accounting for your time over the weekend, Mr. Cassel? Say from Friday noon to Sunday night? Just routine."

"Is that when she was killed?"

"As I told you, sir, we don't know for sure."

Cassel sighed. "I spent the weekend with the lady I mentioned."

"Her name, please."

"Miss Grace. Delissa Grace."

Dutifully, Swell wrote it down. "You were together the whole time?"

"Just about."

Swell let it go. This was a preliminary interrogation. He'd be back.

Delissa Grace was one gorgeous doll, Donald thought as he looked her over with great appreciation. Unfortunately, the macho approach didn't impress the lady. She kept her cool and backed her boyfriend right down the line. According to her, the only time they were apart during the whole weekend was when one or the other of them went to the john.

Swell wasn't discouraged, not at all. In fact, he was elated. These people were a whole new breed to him, a challenge. Everything was proceeding satisfactorily. Julia Schuyler's death made a bigger splash in the papers than Swell had anticipated, in fact bigger than he had dared to hope. Either hard news was scarce or Schuyler had been a real star. Just as the publicity was dying out, the autopsy report was ready. According to the report, there was a heavy percentage of alcohol in the dead actress's blood. There were indications that she'd been severely beaten sometime before her death and also that she'd had sexual intercourse just prior to the stabbing. Zoom! The coverage shot right up again.

As it turned out, the case got *too* big, from Swell's point of view. The brass began to take an interest, and as they did, naturally, so did Swell's lieut and his captain. The whole thing was too rich for a mere dick three. Swell was eased out. Oh sure, technically Donald Swell was still carrying—that was procedure—but it was the big guys who gave out the progress reports, stood in front of the TV news cameras squinting in the glare of the spotlight, got their pictures on page two or three of the dailies—page one was reserved for crime bosses and theatrical personalities. A task force of twenty men was thrown in to canvass the neighborhood in which Schuyler had lived the last months of her life, and Swell was one of the troops. Specifically, he was to interrogate the tenants of her building. He was okay for that, but not for celebrities. Donald Swell saw his big chance slipping away and he didn't know what to do about it.

He'd gotten the message from the desk sergeant that a woman had been around to see him regarding the Schuyler case. M. Anhalt. The name didn't mean anything, but he knew enough to check Julia's little red book. Not listed. Forget it. By the time Donald sat down at his desk, Mici's note put there by her detective admirer was down at the bottom of the pile Donald swept aside as he prepared to write his report.

7

For forty minutes in the morning usually starting around eleven—beginning later and lasting for a shorter duration during the winter—the sun found its way between two buildings to the east and entered the window of Bettedene Barber's kitchen. This morning there were about ten minutes to go before it disappeared behind the water tower two blocks to the west when Mici Anhalt rang the doorbell.

By permitting him to think he was making headway, Mici had prevailed on her friend at the Third Division to divulge that Detective Swell would be at the Schuyler address for most of the day conducting interrogations. It was forty-eight hours since the discovery of Julia's abused and partially decomposed body and one hundred and eight hours or four and a half days since the earliest estimate of the time of her death.

"I'm sorry to bother you," Mici apologized to the wispy teenager with the dark circles under her eyes. "I'm looking for Detective Swell. Is he here?"

The girl nodded. "Somebody for you," she called and stepped back so Mici could pass.

Mici entered through a dingy, dark living room into the sunny kitchen, its tenement rawness camouflaged by checked-gingham curtains, scalloped edging on the shelves, decals of fruits and animals on the walls. The cheap pots hanging over the stove had been burnished bright, the antiquated refrigerator sprayed a daffodil yellow.

Swell, jacket off, tie loosened, and collar opened, was sitting at the kitchen table having a beer. "Who wants me?"

"My name is Anhalt."

71

He frowned. He remembered. "Oh yeah, M. Anhalt. You left a message."

The sun hit Mici like a spotlight, highlighting her red-gold hair so that it threw off rainbow sparks. Her tanned arms and shoulders, covered with a thin film of sweat from the exertion of climbing three flights in the heat, looked as though she'd just put on suntan oil. She was wearing a loose but clingy cotton knit, and every curve of her knockout figure was delineated. Swell put the beer can down, got to his feet, and took a step towards her. Looking into her clear blue eyes, he sucked in his breath. He didn't miss the fine lines around the eyes nor at the corners of her nice, wide mouth. He judged that M. Anhalt was in her early thirties, a little mature for his taste but by no means over the hill. What the hell! Like the ad said: *you're not getting older, darling; you're getting better.* He buttoned his collar and pulled up the knot of his tie.

"Sorry I didn't have a chance to get back to you." He started to put on his jacket but decided that was overdoing it.

"I left several messages."

"I've had my hands full."

"I can see that." She glanced at the beer can on the table.

"What can I do for you, Miss Anhalt?"

Mici had taken her own inventory of Swell and formed her own opinion. Donald Swell was flashy, overconfident, overweight, but—with his rumpled sandy hair, boyish yet rugged face, and blue eyes—not unattractive. Not that it mattered; she wasn't here either to put him down or to try to make points with him. "I have what may be important information about Julia Schuyler. I saw her on Friday night. She told me something which may or may not be true, but which I feel I must pass on."

"Where did you see Miss Schuyler?"

"Here. That is, downstairs in her apartment."

"What time?"

"I came a little after seven-thirty P.M. and left by eight."

72

Swell's eyes narrowed; his lips formed a silent whistle.

"You could be the last person to have seen her alive."

Mici waited till they were alone.

"Except for the killer," she said, correcting the detective's statement.

The sun had passed on and in shadow the little kitchen looked sad despite its cheery decor. Bettedene Barber had not taken kindly to being sent out of her own home, but Swell had handed her a couple of dollars and told her to go out and buy herself lunch. Barbidoll had already eaten but knew when to do a cop a favor.

Mici, resenting Swell's arrogance toward the girl, was testy. "I may have been the last person to see Julia alive except for the killer."

"Of course, sure, that's what I meant."

"Thank you." She frowned. What she had to say was a heavy weight on her conscience, and she was treading cautiously. "Do you have a suspect?"

"Now Miss Anhalt, you came to tell me something, remember?" Donald was almost coy. "You say you visited Miss Schuyler on Friday night and were with her for half an hour. How was she when you left?"

"Sleeping."

"Sleeping?"

"All right, passed out."

"Ah . . ." He nodded. "And you walked out and left her like that?"

"What else could I do? You've got to understand that it wasn't the first time I'd seen Julia drunk and passed out. She was liable to get that way at any time. At a party. She'd just lie down on the floor and go to sleep and people would just step around her, over her if necessary."

"This wasn't a party, was it?"

"No."

"You just walked out and left her?"

"I had a train to catch. I was going away for the weekend."

"Sure. You were in a hurry."

73

"Look," Mici pointed a finger at him and was mortified to note that it was trembling and she couldn't make it stop. She clenched her fist and put it down into her lap. "Don't you try to lay any guilt trip on me, Detective Swell."

"You've already done that yourself, lady."

"When I left Julia Schuyler, she was sleeping as peacefully as a baby. I expected she'd wake up in a couple of hours and probably start drinking again. The same as all the other times."

"So you left her alone with the door unlocked."

Mici was genuinely shocked. "Are you telling me that somebody just happened to try her door, found it unlocked, walked in, and killed her? A stranger?"

Swell hesitated. He had her on the defensive. He could hit hard, make her feel responsible for leaving that door unlocked, and maybe break her. Swell was shrewd and he sensed two things about Mici Anhalt: one, that kind of attack could have the opposite effect and cause her to clam up; two, she was a friend of the dead woman and might prove useful it he had her on his side. Besides, she was the type of witness it would be fun to cozy up to.

"Why don't you just tell me what happened, Miss Anhalt?" He offered an engaging smile.

"That was the original idea," she reminded him, then mused ruefully that she wasn't used to being on this end of an interrogation. So she smiled back. "I was a dancer at one time, and I knew Julia Schuyler from my show-business days. I hadn't seen her in . . . oh, seven or eight years. Thursday afternoon a mutual friend, William Zipprodt, came to my office. Julia sent him to say she wanted me to help her."

"Why didn't she call you herself?"

Mici shrugged. "Julia never did anything herself that she could get someone else to do for her."

Swell's eyebrows went up. "What did she want?"

"Money. Financial help. She knew that I work for the Crime Victims Compensation Board, and she wanted to file a claim."

"She was a victim of a crime? What crime?" Another

74

hit, Swell thought. This was his case, no doubt about it.

"Assault."

Swell's excitement mounted; he was going to get the answer the autopsy had not been able to supply—how long before death the bruises had been inflicted. "When? When was she assaulted?"

"She didn't say. She had all kinds of marks on her arms and legs. They were various shades, as though the results of several beatings."

Swell was disappointed. "Did she file a complaint?"

"No."

"Why the hell not?" He was almost personally affronted.

"She didn't think the police would do anything for her."

"Why should she think that?" he demanded, and then he got it. All at once he got the whole picture. "Who did she say did it to her?"

"Her husband."

"Ah ha." A tight, smug smile was in direct contrast to the caution with which he spoke. "Alfred Cassel moved out four months ago."

"He still had a key and showed up whenever he felt like it."

Still playing devil's advocate, Swell continued his objections. "The way I heard it, Cassel's got himself somebody new—his leading lady."

"I'm telling you what Julia told me; I'm not saying I believe it."

Swell didn't like that. "Go on."

"That's all, really, I urged her to file a complaint, but she said the police didn't consider wife-beating a crime."

"There's a new law . . ."

"I'm familiar with it. I told her about it. She didn't want to go that route. She didn't want to humiliate herself."

"So what did you do? Did you agree to file a claim for her?"

"How could I? We don't cover crimes within the family, not to the third order on consanguinity," she quoted with some asperity; he should have known.

75

"Yeah, well listen, don't feel bad. We've all got to say no sometime." He put a hand on her shoulder. "Hey, you want some coffee? I could fix us some." He looked around vaguely.

Mici shook her head. "All I could advise her to do was to go to Family Court and seek an Order of Protection. She turned that down, too. So then all I could do was tell her to change the lock on her door." Mici bit her lip.

"Don't blame yourself, Miss Anhalt. I can certainly understand how troubled you've been about this, but actually your being there on the night she was murdered was just a coincidence." While he was offering solace, Swell was inwardly exulting. A battered-wife case involving show-business personalities. Terrific! And he was right in the thick of it. The thing was to play it cool with the chick. He had to handle the redhead just right; she wasn't exactly hostile, but . . . call it reluctant. "You've shown integrity coming forward like this, Miss Anhalt, and I'm very sorry that I put you to so much trouble in finding me."

"That's okay."

"So let's just review what we've got. Julia Schuyler asked you to come to see her, and in the course of the conversation she accused her estranged husband, Alfred Cassel, of beating her."

"That's what she said."

"I understand. Now, I get the impression that this was something new. In other words, that he hadn't been in the habit of beating her while they were living together."

"Never. I never heard of it. Nobody ever heard of it. There was no indication of such a thing."

"Hm." Swell pursed his lips. "If it's in a man's character to commit this kind of violence, he doesn't wait long to start."

He was perceptive, Mici thought, and for the first time during the interview she felt a surge of optimism.

"I gather the marriage was tempestuous," Swell continued. "Yet Cassel only got violent after the separation. Why? Did she say why he suddenly started to beat her?"

"No."

Swell moistened his lips and thrust them forward while he thought. "The divorce. He wanted a divorce and she wouldn't give it to him. He came over to plead with her and ended up losing his temper."

"I could see that happening once," Mici agreed. "Not more than once. Not time after time."

"Describe the bruises."

Mici sighed. "As I told you, some seemed more recent than others. Some were turning yellow, and some were black and red. She had one big, ugly, black mark on her upper right arm, as though she'd raised that arm to shield her face and he'd grabbed it and tried to pull it away."

The detective had a list of the salient facts of the autopsy, among them the type and location of the various bruises. "How about her face? Was it badly marked?"

"There was a cut on her left cheek and her lower lip was swollen. Those marks didn't seem as recent as the one on her arm."

"How about her eyes?"

"Nothing wrong with either one of her eyes."

"You're sure?"

"Absolutely."

According to the autopsy findings, the victim's right eye had been blackened long enough before death to be distinguishable in spite of the postmortem bloat. He underscored the word *eye* in his notes and put a big question mark beside it. "So you advised Miss Schuyler to swear out a warrant against Cassel, but she refused, even though you explained to her that the new law was supportive of the claims of battered wives."

Mici nodded.

"Was she afraid that swearing out a warrant would affect his earning power, or was she afraid he'd come back and give her a worse beating?"

"I don't know."

"You must have formed an impression," he suggested, still handling her carefully.

"She was pretty well loaded by then. I have to take that into account."

77

"You mean she'd been drinking through the interview?"

"Steadily. Opening one can of beer after another."

"Beer?"

"That's right. That's one of the reasons I didn't worry too much about leaving her. I figured since it was only beer she'd been drinking that she'd come out of it in a couple of hours at the most."

"Unfortunately, she'd also had a few belts of scotch, but of course you couldn't know that. Or maybe," he mused aloud, "maybe she had the scotch later."

"No, no to both. She didn't have any hard liquor in the house. She told me. She offered me a drink when I first arrived and apologized that it had to be beer as that was all she had. She said she wasn't drinking anything else because she was trying to cut down, but we both knew it was because she couldn't afford anything else."

"According to the autopsy report, there was a heavy concentration of scotch whiskey in her blood." Swell scowled. According to the super, there hadn't been anything but beer empties in Schuyler's trash recently, which supported the redhead's evidence. "So where did she get the booze?" he asked aloud. "According to you, she wasn't in any shape to go out for it, and she didn't have the money to pay for it, either. She had no credit, not in any of the local taverns or liquor stores; I checked that. So somebody had to bring it to her."

"Not Alfred. Alfred would never bring Julia anything to drink; he'd spent too many years and worked too hard trying to get her off the sauce."

"That was before he'd given up on her, while he was still trying to salvage their marriage and their careers. Now she was proving hard to shake, and maybe he saw the booze as a way to get rid of her."

"I knew it!" Mici exclaimed. "I knew this would happen."

"What?" The outburst surprised Swell.

"You're taking Alfred's guilt for granted. The husband did it. Right? I know; I know the figures: sixty-five percent of all homicides are committed by a member of the victim's immediate family. What percentage of those are committed by the husband or wife? Never mind, it doesn't matter. What does matter is that those are the cases the police solve. The others are *mysteries*. How many mysteries a year do you solve, Detective Swell?"

"Hey, wait a minute . . ."

"Mighty few. Why? Because you don't pursue the mysteries. It's so much easier to rack up a good score in the husband or wife cases."

"Hold it. Just hold it . . ."

"The person who beat Julia wasn't necessarily the one who killed her. Did you ever think of that?"

"As a matter of fact . . ."

"She didn't die as a result of the beating, did she? She wasn't hit in such a way that she fell and suffered a fatal injury. No. She was stabbed, a different method entirely. To me it suggests different attacks by different persons."

Swell was impressed by her logic, but he had no intention of letting her know it. "So! The husband walks in, knocks her around, walks out again. The next guy walks in, boozes her up, and sticks a knife in her heart. With which one did she have intercourse?" He paused. "I guess you read about that in the papers?"

"Why does it have to be either one?"

"You're suggesting a third party? She sure was a busy lady."

"And you don't like that because it makes it tough for you."

"If true, it would."

The ready answer and the grin that went with it were disarming. "I'm sorry," Mici sighed. "I've been uptight about this. In spite of everything, I liked Julia Schuyler and I admire Alfred Cassel." She got up. "That's all I came to say. If you need me for anything more, you've got my number on those messages on your desk."

"Miss Anhalt?" He called her back from the door. "Can I ask you something? Every one of those messages was signed M. Anhalt. What does the M. stand for?"

79

"Mici."

"So, Mici, do you have a boyfriend?"

Her blue eyes widened. "Yes, I do."

"Steady?"

"More or less."

"That means less."

"How about you? Do you have a girlfriend?"

"Nope."

"Why is that?"

"Can't find anybody who'll have me."

"Really?"

"Can I call you for dinner sometime?"

Mici took a breath and looked straight at him. "I don't think you're going to want to, not when you find out where I'm going right after I leave here."

He waited.

"I'm going to see Alfred Cassel. I'm going to tell him everything I've told you. It's only fair."

"You're a private citizen, you can do what you want. What's that got to do with having dinner?"

"I swear to God I never laid a hand on her."

Alfred Cassel reacted to the accusation with a mixture of sadness and indignation. He got up out of his chair and immediately regretted it; his right knee started to jerk spasmodically and he couldn't make it stop. It was like one of his rare, but nightmarish attacks of stage fright. The knee was merely the prelude of worse to follow—a tremor that would creep upward and possess the rest of his body, freeze his vocal chords, and culminate in a disorientation that would wipe out every line and bit of business laboriously worked out and learned and repeated during four weeks of rehearsal. Unconsciously, Cassel turned away from Mici Anhalt as though he were indeed on the stage and the young woman—whom he had known as a dancer and was now some kind of investigator—were the audience from which he was trying to hide his affliction.

"I swear that I never laid a hand on her," he repeated. "I knew that she was circulating some wild rumors

80

about me, but this . . . this is ridiculous. Well, no, I don't mean ridiculous, of course not." At this point, the actor was more concerned with controlling himself as an instrument than in refuting his dead wife's charges. "I just wish you'd come to me before the police," he said.

"I couldn't."

"No, I suppose not. Actually, I have to thank you for coming at all. I hope that means you don't really believe that I hurt Julia."

"She showed me the bruises."

"You'd seen her with bruises before."

"Not like these."

The actor's knee began to twitch again. "If she'd been drinking heavily as you say . . ."

"I don't think she could have gotten those bruises from falling down drunk. And according to the autopsy, she had a black eye. I don't see how she could get that accidentally."

Cassel's pale face looked as though all the blood had been drained out of it; his full, sensuous lips were blue to match the thick vein pulsing at his temple. A vise of fear tightened across his chest as the full force of his peril hit him. The accusation in itself was ugly enough and since the accuser was in her grave there was no possibility of retraction, but the fact that it could lead to a charge of murder shocked him out of his fantasy world. The knee stopped jerking; the sweat on his body dried.

"I need a drink. How about you?"

Mici nodded gratefully. The two interviews had both depressed and depleted her.

When he fixed the drinks, Cassel came over and sat down beside Mici. "Even in the old days, when things were going well, Julia had those drinking bouts and got herself knocked up."

"She never blamed anybody then. Why should she now?"

His reply was short and bitter. "Blackmail."

Mici just looked at him.

"I wanted a divorce. She wanted the lead in my new

81

show. Of course, I couldn't trade. So then she called Oscar Brumleve and accused me of nonsupport and ordered him to take me to court. Well, that didn't get her the part, either. So I suppose accusing me of wife-beating was the next step."

"But why go through me? Why not go to the police?"

"And land me in jail? I might lose the show then, and if I did I couldn't help her even if I wanted to. I'm afraid she tried to use you, Mici, just as she did me."

"I turned her down. I told her I couldn't file a claim for her."

"Dear girl." Cassel gave her an avuncular smile which managed, nevertheless, to convey plenty of sex appeal. "She was just using you to get the message through to me."

"She didn't ask me to talk to you."

"She wouldn't be that obvious. She'd have waited a few days; then if you didn't make the move on your own she'd have given you another little goose. Be honest, hadn't it occurred to you to get in touch with me?"

Mici frowned. "It seems so devious . . ."

"Ah well, she was devious, our Julia." Cassel sighed. "I don't know, maybe she did think she could get money through you—though she wasn't all that hard up. She didn't have to stay in that fleabag. I gave her enough to get out; it's not my fault if she drank it up instead. I did my best for her and I would have gone on doing my best for her. I would never have abandoned her. Never. That's the truth, and she knew it."

The actor's face softened. "When I first met Julia Schuyler, she had all the promise of her heritage, her youth, and her desire. She was a rising star, going up fast, too fast. They were exploiting her out in Hollywood, putting her into parts for which she wasn't ready, but she didn't know it. I was making a picture with her; we had scenes together, and it struck me right away that she wasn't getting any direction, any help from anybody. At first I figured she didn't want it, then that they thought she didn't need it. But she did. She had inherited some of John Malcolm's talent, but not his greatness. She tried so hard to imitate him instead of trying to create her own style, to find her own truth. I don't know where I got the nerve—maybe it was selfishness because I wasn't getting anything from her and my own work was suffering as a result—but I offered her a few suggestions. She was pathetically grateful and eager and willing to try them. They helped some, but she gave me too much credit. She thought of me as a Svengali. Oh, she improved, but not to the extent she'd expected and so in the long run she was more disheartened. She turned down the light, easy roles for which she was suited and took on—well, Hedda, for God's sake! Fell on her face, of course." His smile had long since vanished. "And the Medea—that was a disaster that nearly drove *me* to drink."

He finished what was left in his glass, got up, but didn't appear to want a refill. "We produced the Medea ourselves and it wiped us out financially. Worse, it destroyed what was left of Julia's confidence. I understood what she was going through. John Malcolm Schuyler had been an idol of mine, too, at one time, and I'd patterned myself on his grandiose, swashbuckling, larger-than-life delivery. I went around dressed in somber suits, wore my hair long when it wasn't in fashion, and listened to the sound of my own voice till I realized it wasn't right for me. But Julia refused to learn. When she couldn't match John Malcolm on the stage, she set out to do it in real life."

"She was his daughter."

"True." Cassel nodded. "But she couldn't even destroy herself with his style. It took Schuyler years of profligate living to die. He played out his tragedy as he had played out his triumphs—in the grand manner, on private yachts belonging to Greek tycoons, in Beverly Hills mansions with the jet set for his audience. Julia went fast; she went in squalor, and she went alone. In the end, she blamed me."

Mici thought back to that final visit with the murdered actress and remembered that there had been little rancor in Julia's accusation of her estranged husband. In fact, Julia had been almost tender when she spoke of him. If Mici hadn't been so shocked by the nature of the

83

charge, she would have been more sensitive at the time.

"No, she didn't blame you."

"We didn't have a marriage; we had a professional alliance," Cassel continued. "Each failed the other. I didn't bring out her talent, and being married to her didn't automatically make my name a household word. She didn't refuse me the divorce because she loved me, but because I was finally and at last on my way up and she had to hang on to my coattails. I understood that. I would have helped her if I could, but the producers wouldn't touch her. Who could blame them? Ultimately, she would have agreed to the divorce, and I would have been able to do something for her in some other show or movie or something. She knew that. There was no real antagonism between us. It was all an act on her part."

And how much of this was an act on his part? Mici wondered. How much was he selling her? How much was he selling himself?

"I'm sorry that I had to go to the police," she said.

"You did what you had to do."

"Will you postpone the opening?"

He was amazed that she should ask. "Our out-of-town bookings are set. We've got a Broadway house. We might not get another till the end of the season. That wouldn't be fair to the cast or to the backers. And what good would it do?"

"Have you any idea who killed her?"

"I haven't slept asking myself that question. Julia wasn't a bad person. In spite of her tantrums, her drinking, she never hurt anybody. On the contrary, she tried to help whenever she could. You know that."

"Yes."

"Everybody wanted something from her. Everybody used her."

Mici knew he was including himself. "Except Billy Zip," she noted.

"Maybe." The actor paused for a few moments. "The only thing I can think of is that some psycho broke in and attacked her. She tried to defend herself, but she

84

was too weak and boozed up. So he killed her. It happens. My God! Nowadays it happens all the time. Not two weeks ago there was a woman up in the Bronx, eighty-five years old, stripped and beaten to death." He covered his face with his hands, and his hands were trembling.

Mici trembled, too. She had just about succeeded in convincing herself that Julia's death was the result of what she was and how she'd lived, and now Cassel had reawakened her sense of guilt for having left Julia sleeping behind an unlocked door.

Assume, she said to herself, walking the tawdry streets of Times Square after she left Cassel's suite at the Algonquin, that some creep sheltering from the storm entered the building and tried the doors till he found one that was open and slipped inside. Julia awakens; she's groggy, half conscious; she screams. He beats her, assaults her sexually, kills her. Maybe the creep had the knife on him and so he took it away with him. But how about the booze? No way some creep trying doors in a storm would have a bottle of expensive scotch with him and then share it with his victim prior to the attack. No way.

So it had not been a crime of opportunity. Mici felt tremendous relief. Passing the pocket park between Forty-fifth and Forty-sixth Streets just off Sixth Avenue, she went in to sit down. Thank God! she thought. Not till that moment when she was free of it did she realize how heavy a burden of guilt she'd been carrying. The liquor was the key, she thought. Someone had brought Julia Schuyler the scotch—not a friend, no friend would bring her booze. . . . Hold it. Wrong. This friend had brought the scotch knowing the effect it would have on her. Purposely.

It could also have been somebody from the neighborhood, a casual acquaintance, somebody Julia had talked to in a bar, a pickup. Maybe he'd come looking for her with his bottle of scotch and she welcomed him and drank his scotch and then repulsed him. He was drunk himself and angry at being denied. He beat her up first, then killed her.

85

Though she'd taunted Detective Swell for looking for the easy solution, Mici couldn't blame him if he shied from this one. To find a killer with so little prior connection to the victim was one of the toughest jobs in a criminal investigation. In this instance, the problem was made more difficult by the uncertainty regarding the time of death. If the time of death could be narrowed down somehow . . .

8

Mici called Donald Swell to tell him about the patrol car she'd noticed on the block near Julia's house the night of the murder. She mentioned that the car was there when she went in and still there when she came out. True, that was only a period of half an hour. Still, if that was a regular post, the officers might have noted the comings and goings from Julia's building unaware of the significance of what they'd seen.

Donald wasn't impressed, but he said he'd look into it.

He only did it because he'd covered every other possible angle and had nowhere else to go. There was no difficulty in locating the two men who had been on duty that night in that location. When he learned that Raymond Emmenecher and Attilio Pace had heard a scream late Friday night, Swell blew his stack. Not because they hadn't gotten out of the car to investigate. It had been a lousy night; they were on another job; there had been one single scream and no way for them to know where it came from. Their rationale for doing nothing held as far as he was concerned. If Donald had been sitting in the squad car himself that night, he would have reacted in the same way. What teed him off was that they hadn't reported it later.

"You must have heard about the homicide? Read about it in the papers, maybe?" Donald was heavy on the sarcasm. Sure, he knew why they hadn't come forward, scared of getting blasted. Well, now they'd get it worse from him, the lieut, maybe even from the captain. "I hope you noted the time at least."

"Look, sir, what's unusual in one neighborhood is just background noise in another." Emmenecher strove to justify their apparent lack of concern.

But Attilio Pace had his notebook out and was clearing his throat. "Yes, sir, yes, sir, I made a note. It was 11:12, exactly 11:12 P.M. when the scream occurred."

Emmenecher looked the way he felt—sour. After all these years, he thought, to get hung up on a lousy thing like this. And the twerp wasn't helping; he gritted his teeth and glared at his partner. "What were we supposed to do, sir? Go ringing doorbells in every building?"

"It was 11:12 exactly," Pace repeated, waiting for a word of commendation.

Swell ignored him. "You should have reported it," he berated Emmenecher who was the senior man. "How do you think it looks getting the information through a civilian?"

That was neither accurate nor fair, and Emmenecher wasn't taking it. "If we reported every scream . . ."

"Nothing moved on the whole block, Detective Swell." Pace was still seeking favor. "We were there another fifteen minutes, sir. It was a regular cloudburst and nobody came out of any of the buildings."

"What does that prove?" Swell demanded.

"I don't know, sir." Pace was finally squelched.

"We don't know that the scream was from your homicide victim, sir," Emmenecher pointed out.

"Yeah, yeah, yeah." Swell waved them off and slumped low into his chair. Emmenecher was right, of course. He'd already interrogated everybody in the damned building and nobody had mentioned any scream. Maybe now that he had a specific time to home in on . . . He reached for his hat and jacket. It was better than sitting around on his butt.

Three hours later, jacket and tie dragging in one hand, collar wilted, shirt plastered to his back, Swell returned to the squad room. You could get more cooperation from inmates of a deaf-and-dumb institution, he thought, than those damn tenants, That kid prostie on the third floor, she knew something for sure. He should have brought her in, sweated her. So, it wasn't too late to go back and get her.

"Say, Don," Reiseberg at the next desk looked up. "LaRock wants you. Now."

"Yeah?"

Swell had no idea why the lieut wanted him, but he wasn't worried. Actually, he was glad of the summons. He was now convinced that the scream heard by the two patrols cops at 11:12 had actually come from the Schuyler apartment. The woman two floors up in 4A had admitted hearing a scream, but she thought it wasn't anything out of the ordinary. Of course, she'd had her TV on. The kid prostie, one floor closer, had absolutely denied hearing anything. To Donald's way of thinking, that made it more interesting than if they'd both agreed. So while Swell didn't exactly swagger into Lieutenant John LaRock's office, he pranced lightly, weight forward, confidence high. He was going in with what could turn out to be a significant break in the case—the time of the attack. Never mind how he'd got it.

"Where the hell have you been?" LaRock blasted him before he was through the door.

At forty-eight, a high-school football player who hadn't made it in college, gone to fat and given to double-breasted suits that emphasized his girth, John Willard LaRock could pass for the typical middle-echelon executive who had risen as far as he ever would in the company and knew it. All LaRock was interested in now was in keeping what he had. It wasn't so bad: a nice house in Massapequa five minutes from the town beach; two cars; a satisfactory marriage. How many could say that? All provided by his job, a job with dignity and authority. True, compared with the real brass up at the top he wasn't much and sometimes, as now, the pressure came down pretty heavy. Still, he had men under him on whom he could unload.

"What the hell do you think you're doing?" LaRock demanded.

Swell didn't get a chance to speak, not that he would have known what to say, before getting hit with the next barrage.

"What do you know about this?" LaRock snatched up a late edition of the *News* and an early edition of the *Post,* waving each briefly in front of Swell so that he had only a glimpse of the black scare headlines. A glimpse was more than enough.

COPS IGNORE DYING WOMAN'S SCREAM
COOPING COPS COLD TO CRY FOR HELP

A cramp knotted Swell's intestines. It was all he could do to keep from doubling over. "I was just coming to tell you about it, Lieutenant."

"Oh, you were, were you? Isn't that nice? Thank you, Detective Swell. Thank you so much."

Bad, this was real bad, Swell thought. "What I mean, sir, is that I was following up the lead before bothering you in case it should turn out . . . uh . . ." The corner of his mouth developed a nervous tick. "Uh . . . in case it didn't amount to anything."

"How considerate."

Paralyzed except for the humiliating, betraying tick, it took what seemed an interminable period but was actually only a couple of seconds for the reason for the lieut's ire to filter through to Donald. "Oh, my God! No, sir, it wasn't me. I didn't release it to the press. My God, Lieutenant, I wouldn't do a thing like that."

"Then who did?"

"I don't know. I haven't the vaguest idea." The lieut was waiting and he had to come up with something. "Maybe Emmenecher or Pace?"

LaRock snatched up the *National Enquirer* and read

89

with dripping bitterness: "COPS STAY COZY IN PA-
TROL CAR WHILE WOMAN FIGHTS FOR LIFE.
You think they gave that out?"

"No, sir."

The lieutenant continued to read. "This reporter
learned today that Detective Third Grade Donald Swell
who is carrying the Schuyler case has been canvassing
all officers on patrol in the Times Square area on the
night of the murder. He discovered that two men
assisting the Pimp and Prostitution Squad were staked
out on the very block of the tenement in which the
homicide occurred."

"I didn't give out that story."

"Story! What story?" LaRock's voice vibrated with
indignation. "There is no story. Officers Emmenecher
and Pace are a lot smarter than you, Detective Third
Grade Swell. They didn't report anything because
nothing happened. On Friday night at 11:12 some
woman somewhere in the neighborhood screamed—
once. So what? You've made the whole uniformed division look like shit, Swell, and the bureau like a bunch
of morons."

This was not the moment to discuss his latest canvass of the tenants. "It wasn't me, sir. I didn't leak the
sto . . . the information."

"Then who did?"

They were back to that. At least the initial shock had
worn off and Donald's mind was beginning to function
again. Reporters were in and out of the station house
day and night; they hung around the sergeant's desk,
the corridors, the squad rooms picking up snatches of
conversation and they were expert at piecing the parts
together. That was probably how they'd got hold of
this, but it would not satisfy LaRock, not in his present
mood. Swell took a breath. "Actually, Lieutenant, I got
the tip about Emmenecher and Pace being parked on
the block from a witness. She spotted the squad car on
the night of the crime."

"What witness?"

"Miss Anhalt. The woman from the Crime Victims
Compensation Board. The one who was with Julia

Schuyler on Friday night and who claimes that Schuyler accused her husband of beating her up."

"Oh, that one. Uh huh. You think she could have tipped the reporters?"

Swell hesitated, but not for long. It couldn't hurt Mici Anhalt. How could it hurt her? Probably she'd never even find out. He cleared his throat. "Who else?"

LaRock considered then discarded it. "Her name wasn't even mentioned in the stories."

"Well . . ." Swell hedged. "She wouldn't have done it for the publicity. She wants to see justice done—she says. She thinks that Cassel is innocent but that we're not giving him a fair shake."

"But she's the one who put the finger on him."

"That's probably why she feels responsible."

"Amateurs," the lieutenant grunted. "They screw up every time." Swell knew he was off the hook.

"There's good news and there's bad news," Adam Dowd told Mici.

It was the sixth day of the heat wave and, though the air conditioning was on full, the torpor that lay over the city affected them both physically and in spirit. There was tension left over from their last meeting and so they looked each other over warily.

Mici was depressed because she knew that she had not made the change in attitude which she'd tacitly promised. At this point, she wasn't sure she could. In essence, what Dowd wanted was for her to process claims without getting emotionally involved, by simply totting up the figures like an accountant. It wasn't the job she'd signed on for, and if that was what it had become then she wasn't sure she wanted to continue with it. She liked and respected Adam Dowd, had had a good rapport with him in the past, and knew he'd had the same concept of the program that she did. That he was now asking her to turn her back on their ideals and behave like a bureaucrat had to mean that he was himself under pressure.

On his part, Dowd was depressed because he was about to hand an investigator he regarded highly a heavy disappointment, and he wasn't sure how she would take it.

"It's about the Spychalski claim," he began.

"Oh?" Her eyebrows went up. "Let me guess. The Geramita boys were cleared of the arson charges."

"Right."

"Well, we expected that, didn't we? I don't suppose any of the neighbors came forward? Too scared."

"There was one old lady, a Mrs. Feirick. She claimed she saw the boys prowling around the house a short time before the fire started."

"But they wrote her off."

Dowd didn't ask how she knew. "The attorney for the boys got Mrs. Feirick started on the subject of religion."

Mici sighed. "I don't know how much of what she babbles she really believes and how much is for effect. Either way, I realize it doesn't enhance her credibility as a witness. What's the good news?"

"The arson investigators have come to the conclusion that the fire was deliberately set."

"Great!" A big smile replaced Mici's frown. "So now we can go ahead and process the claim. Poor Mr. Spychalski and his wife need all the help they can get. The cost of medical care . . ."

"Not so fast; you haven't heard it all," Dowd interrupted Mici's euphoric prattling. "Since the fire was of deliberate origin and since the Geramita boys have been exonerated, the insurance company is holding up payment on Mr. Spychalski's policy."

"Why?"

"Karl Spychalski is the most likely suspect to have set the fire, isn't he?"

"No. Absolutely not." Mici hotly defended her client. "Anyhow, Karl Spychalski has an alibi. He was down at the hiring hall at the time."

"No, he wasn't." Dowd's homely, pitted face was grave. "He reported early in the morning, but he left before lunch and didn't go back."

Mici was stunned. "I don't believe it. There's some mistake. His two girls were killed in that fire. His wife

92

nearly died trying to save them. She's burned over sixty percent of her body. She's in excruciating pain . . ."

"The house was supposed to have been empty at the time. The two kids should have been in school and Rose Spychalski usually went to the market for the week's shopping on Wednesday afternoon."

"No, no," Mici muttered doggedly. "Karl Spychalski loved that house. It represented the security he'd built for himself and his family. It wasn't just a place to live. You have to understand how Europeans feel about the land . . ."

"He was also unemployed, with benefits running out and no job in sight. The insurance money could keep him going a long time."

"Naturally that's the view the insurance company would take; that way they don't have to pay off," Mici argued. "What we're concerned about is whether or not there was arson. Okay, the police now say yes, there was. Mrs. Spychalski and the two girls were victims. That's it. It doesn't matter who set the fire."

"Unless it was Spychalski."

"Can anybody prove he did it? Can anybody place him at the scene?" Dowd shook his head. "I thought a man was supposed to be innocent till proved guilty."

"We're not throwing out the claim."

"Just filing it," Mici commented bitterly.

"I feel just as sorry for the Spychalskis as you do, but rules are rules. We have only so much money at our disposal and it has to go to those whose claims are unclouded."

Mici was silent.

"All the man has to do is say where he was at the time of the fire and he's in the clear; the insurance company pays off; we process the claim."

"He won't say?"

"He insists he was at the hiring hall."

"Nuts." Mici got up. "I'll talk to him."

"I did not kill my children. I did not burn my wife. I did not destroy my home and everything that I love. It was those boys."

"Forget about them, Mr. Spychalski," Mici advised, keeping her manner brisk and impersonal. "They have been exonerated. It doesn't matter who set the fire as long as it wasn't you."

"Doesn't matter!" Spychalski, a burly man accustomed to hard labor and danger, had wasted physically in the past months as a result of loss of courage and pride, but at this moment rage sustained him. Anger struggled with sorrow and the result was tears that welled in his deep-set, tired eyes. "Nobody came forward at the trial. Nobody was willing to speak for us against those boys except one crazy old woman."

"I know how you feel, Mr. Spychalski . . ."

"It matters to me!"

"What matters is for the insurance company to pay your claim and for the Compensation Board to approve medical care for your wife."

"They will pay. They must. They cannot prove I did this terrible thing. They cannot prove it because I am innocent. So in the end they must pay."

He sounded very sure. "Maybe," Mici said. "But it will take a very long time. You could shorten that time if you'll just say where you were the afternoon of the fire."

"I was at the hiring hall."

"The men say no. They say you left before lunch and did not return."

"I brought my lunch and I had it there as always. They're mixed up. Or maybe the insurance company is paying them to lie."

"You don't really believe that, Mr. Spychalski."

He turned aside and shrugged.

"Wherever you were, whatever you were doing that Wednesday afternoon at two-thirty, nobody is going to blame you. If you were having a few drinks in a bar, or you were out at the ball game to forget your troubles for a few hours, nobody is going to hold it against you." Mici was watching him carefully. In profile his expression remained set; only dried streaks on his sunken cheeks were reminders that he had very recently been weeping.

94

She had to tread carefully, but she couldn't leave any possibility unexplored. "Even if you were with some-one . . . If that person were to step forward . . . I'm sure it wouldn't be necessary for Mrs. Spychalski to know."

She expected Spychalski to rail at her, to order her out, but he didn't deign to answer. He simply stood in the cramped, hot living room of the apartment where they were staying with his wife's relatives and looked out the window over the low roofs of the other row houses toward the big gas tanks in the distance. There was nothing for Mici to do but to leave.

She had shown him the way, she thought, as the subway hurtled its noisy way back to Manhattan. Now it was up to him. One thing, a bitter smile twisted her soft, full lips, nobody could say her cases were gaining automatic approval now. The Spychalski claim would be set aside indefinitely. The Marin benefits were drawing to an end. She thought again of the blind man's suggestion that she suppress Dr. Harden's report. Maybe she should have agreed and given him one more chance? No, of course not! She was not the arbiter of the fate of every man and woman who walked into her office and sat down at her desk. Her job was to investigate and write a report. Dispositions were made by others.

For once the lithe ex-dancer didn't sprint up the stairs to the second floor but waited sedately for the elevator. She squeezed in, wriggled out, and stopped short when she opened the door of the reception room to find Detective Swell comfortably sprawled on the blue-tweed settee.

"Hi." He unfolded himself and rose to greet her.

"What are you doing here?"

"I came to take you to lunch."

"Oh? I've already had lunch. I'm sorry." That wasn't true, but Mici was neither hungry nor in the mood for conversational sparring. "Thanks anyway."

"Dinner then."

She hesitated. "What's up?"

"Nothing's up." He stepped in close. "I just want to see you."

About to answer, she was suddenly aware that they were being observed. She moved back. "I'm sorry if I got those two officers in trouble. Or you."

He shrugged. "What trouble? The press exaggerates everything. The lieut knows that. He didn't pay any attention."

"I'm glad. So does that mean you've been able to fix the time of death?"

"Hey! First we've got to prove that what those two cops heard was in fact Julia Schuyler screaming. So far we haven't been able to do that."

"I see."

"But your buddy, Cassel, is in the clear. His girlfriend backs up his alibi." He moved in again, closer. "So . . . about dinner. I'll pick you up at seven. Be ready."

"For what?"

"That's up to you, babe."

9

Why had Donald Swell gone out of his way to inform her that Cassel had an alibi? Swell seemed so easygoing, without professional jealousy, but Mici knew he looked out for number one. He could have called her for a date for lunch or dinner but had appeared in person instead. She was convinced that he had come specifically to tell her about Cassel and to observe her reaction. Also, there was the business about the alleged dying scream. There'd been plenty of flak over the police reaction, or rather lack of it. Donald had been too casual. It didn't ring true. Maybe he didn't want her meddling any more. Maybe he thought that if he offered her assurance that Cassel was no longer under suspicion she'd lose interest.

It had the opposite effect.

Flashing her credentials, which most people considered on a par with a police card, and which certainly was not the case, Mici Anhalt had no trouble getting the address she wanted from Actors' Equity Association. As she'd expected, it wasn't far outside the theatrical hub and she treated herself to a taxi ride over to the old-fashioned but well-maintained building on Fifty-fifth Street across from the City Center.

Delissa Grace was as impressed with Miss Anhalt's ID as the people at the actors' union. Usually Mici took care to point out that answers were purely voluntary. This time she didn't. She let Delissa Grace take a good look at her card and draw her own conclusions.

The actress scanned it quickly but thoroughly, as she would a script before an audition, to assess what was in it for her and what she could make of it.

"I've already spoken with Alfred," Mici prompted.

Delissa Grace hesitated before picking up the cue. "Yes, I know." Now she was committed to playing the scene a certain way.

Mici was glad; it saved trouble. "Then you know that I used to be in the theater myself and that I knew both Alfred and Julia."

"He told me."

She presented a striking figure with that wild mass of tightly curled ringlets in a dark cloud around her head, hazel eyes flashing, creamy, flawless skin, and lips that were a lustrous maroon without the aid of lipstick. She didn't need the drama of the dark-green velvet caftan trimmed in gold and the row of gold bracelets on her right arm. She was about the same age as Julia had been, but she was just reaching her peak.

"Did Alfred tell you what we talked about?" Mici asked.

"He said that Julia had accused him of beating her. That was a lie! They fought like cat and dog; they screamed and yelled at each other, but there was never any physical violence. Never. He never laid a hand on her. He couldn't. Alfred isn't that kind of person."

"I was repeating what Julia told me. I had to make a statement to the police and sign it. If they decide to regard what Julia said as a dying declaration, it would carry a lot of weight."

"Since she wasn't dying at the time and she didn't expect to die, how can it be a dying declaration?" Delissa Grace was very sure on this point.

"I see you've had legal advice."

"That's just common sense."

"Nevertheless, an accusation like that can be damning."

"What can we do? We can't accuse a dead woman of deliberately lying. We can't malign her character, but we can't let her destroy us either."

"Have you any idea who might have killed her?"

"No." Delissa Grace raised a slender hand to her forehead as though to wipe away a headache; her bracelets made a jangling accompaniment to the gesture. "Who would want to hurt Julia? I mean, why? Those wild stories she made up, they were embarrassing but nobody took them seriously. At least not while she was alive. Now that she's dead—they're damning, as you say. You can see that as far as Alfred and I are concerned, it would be better if she were still alive."

Shrewd, Mici thought, but was it sincere?

"Julia was finished. She'd had everything and thrown it away. You couldn't help but feel sorry for her," Delissa Grace observed.

"Did you feel sorry for her?"

Up to now the performance had been a tightly woven skein of fact and expediency, now Delissa Grace permitted herself one moment of raw truth. "She brought it on herself."

"You mean her death?"

"I mean everything. How much longer could she have lasted the way she was going?"

"And how did Julia feel about you?"

The actress assayed a wry smile. "You couldn't expect her to love me. I've got the part she wanted and that could have meant a comeback for her, except that she couldn't possibly have handled it."

"And her husband. You've got him, too."

98

"She'd thrown Alfred away along with everything else long before I came on the scene."

"So then why did she refuse the divorce?"

"General orneriness. To bleed us for as much and as long as she could."

"Bleed?"

"I don't know about your financial situation, Miss Anhalt, but for me ten thousand dollars is a lot of money. That's what she wanted to agree to the divorce. Oh, she didn't ask Alfred for it; she knew he couldn't get it. But I've managed to put a little something aside, and she knew it and she wanted it. Well, I wasn't about to let her clean me out so I stalled. I gave her a few hundred every now and then to keep her quiet."

Mici caught it immediately. She looked hard at the beautiful woman. "Keep her quiet about what?"

Too late Delissa Grace realized the slip. "To keep her from bad-mouthing Alfred."

"What did she know about you?"

"Nothing. It's a manner of speaking, for God's sake. I paid her so she'd stop bugging Alfred."

"What did she know about Alfred?"

The actress reached for a cigarette from a sterling-silver box on the cocktail table. She lit it with a trembling hand, then with an effort thrust herself forward and out of the depths of the black-velvet sofa and began circling around it.

"You said Julia's stories were wild and couldn't hurt him," Mici reminded her.

"That's right. We just didn't want that kind of publicity."

"What kind?"

"That Alfred wasn't contributing to her support, that he was beating her . . ."

"She hadn't actually circulated those stories?"

"She was threatening to."

"And so you paid her to keep quiet. Blackmail. That's what it amounts to, Miss Grace. And it makes you a suspect as well as Alfred."

"Alfred and I were together the whole weekend.

Whether Julia was killed Friday, Saturday, or Sunday, we were never out of each other's sight."

"That doesn't eliminate either one of you; it makes you accomplices."

"No. Neither one of us killed her, singly or together." Her eyes glowed with intensity, her soft voice that could carry up to the second balcony without aid of a microphone quivered. "There's no way you or anybody else can prove we did."

"Why were you paying her?"

"I told you."

"It's not good enough."

"That's all I'm going to say."

"Then I'll ask Alfred." Mici picked up her handbag, slung it over her shoulder, rose, and started for the door. It seemed as if Delissa Grace would let her go, then at the very last moment she called out.

"Alfred doesn't know. He doesn't know I was paying Julia off."

Mici turned.

"When I first started out, when I was making the transition from the Greek theater to the American stage I had . . . a friend. He was a big shot in organized crime. I didn't know. I was young. He told me he was in the construction business. I didn't question it. They got him for tax evasion, what else? He's in the federal penitentiary. Julia threatened to make a big thing out of it. My friend wouldn't have appreciated that."

"But if he's in jail . . ."

"You don't understand. My friend put up some money for the show." She paused, sighed. "He put up all of it."

"You mean he would have pulled out?"

"No, no." Delissa Grace shook her head violently, the dark frizzed hair flying. "Alfred would. If he thought the backing was for me and not for him . . ."

Her lovely, unlined face twisted; her eyes darkened. She was speechlessly pleading with Mici to keep her secret and she wasn't acting; the pleading was intense and real. At last Mici understood. It wasn't the play and her co-starring role that Delissa Grace was worried about. She hadn't been paying Julia to keep the secret from the public, but from Alfred. She loved Alfred. It wasn't the show she was afraid to lose, she couldn't lose that, but she might lose the man.

"How did you make the payments? In cash?"

"Of course."

"So that between you and Alfred . . ." Mici began and then remembered someone else. "Billy Zip! Billy says that he was giving Julia whatever money he could spare. Between the three of you, she wasn't so hard up after all. Obviously she didn't spend the money on herself. So where was it going?"

Delissa Grace shrugged. "She drank it up."

Not if she was drinking beer, Mici thought. Drugs? There'd been no traces in the autopsy—the papers would have made headlines out of that, and the police would be tracing the drug connection. "Gambling?" she asked.

"Who knows?"

Mici recalled the days in Chicago when Julia had been comparatively affluent. She'd thrown her money around but she hadn't gambled. At the local Variety Club there'd been all kinds of slot machines rigged to give favorable odds to the performers who frequented the place but, as far as Mici knew, Julia had never put so much as a quarter into one of them. Still, people change. "Was there anyone else Julia could have been hitting for money?" She asked simply because she didn't know what else to ask.

"Oscar Brumleve maybe, her lawyer. He's pretty strapped himself, I hear, but he would have helped her somehow. It's amazing what people were willing to do for Julia. They loved her and forgave her no matter what. I don't know what she had."

Mici got up.

"You're not going to the police, are you? It's not going to help them to know about the play, I mean about the backing for the play."

Mici hesitated; she hadn't thought that far ahead.

"If they examine my bank account, of course, they'll discover the withdrawals and want an explanation, but why should they examine my bank account?"

"You had a strong motive for killing Julia Schuyler."

"No, I didn't. Her hold on me would last only till the show opened. It wouldn't have mattered after that. Alfred is sure to be a hit. If he finds out about the backing then, well, he'll have his pride and self-confidence and he'll forgive me."

"Well . . ."

"Please. We're going into rehearsal next week. Next week. It's taken months of preparation, of delays and disappointments to get to this point. You've been a performer yourself, Miss Anhalt, you know what's involved. If you could just wait a little while . . ."

Maybe the blackmail wouldn't have worked on Delissa Grace once the show opened, Mici thought, but then Julia could have increased the pressure on Alfred. Was Delissa Grace smart enough to have foreseen that? Had she asked her "friend" to have it taken care of?

Mici made up her mind. "I won't go to the police unless I have to. I'm not working for them. I'm working for Julia. I owe her."

Donald Swell surprised Mici. He'd discarded his FBI suit and looked very relaxed in a summer-weight navy blazer and cream slacks. He also turned down the customary drink before leaving, explaining that he'd made reservations at a restaurant out on the Island and that they ought to get started.

"I figured it would do us both good to get out of town for a few hours."

It was nice, Mici thought as they drove along, windows down to let in the cool night breezes, the conversation skipping lightly through the list—opera, theater, sports, both active and spectator—to discover mutual interest. She relaxed and began to enjoy herself.

The restaurant was a revelation, not merely for itself but that it should be Donald's choice. It was on the outskirts of the town of Roslyn, a white frame house much like Mici's home, with plenty of ground around it. They parked under fine old trees and went around to the back to a garden with perhaps a dozen tables lit by flickering candlelight. Swell ordered drinks and then the consultation about dinner began; no menu was ever presented but Donald did not appear to require one. He knew the house specialties and in fact seemed knowledgeable about fine cuisine. Mici had liked Donald but with reservations, the main one being not that he lacked refinement but that he was proud of it, so she was impressed by this new aspect. When the meal was ready, they went indoors to a small room accommodating only three tables so that there would be little distraction from the proper appreciation of the food set before them. It was superb. In fact, Mici willingly admitted that she was not qualified to fully appreciate its excellence.

It was midnight by the time they were back at Mici's door. Again Swell surprised her; he declined the invitation to come in for a nightcap. Oh, there was the customary goodnight kiss, and very nice, too—friendly but with enough intensity to suggest more was available if she were so inclined. What he was telling her was that he was secure enough to play by her rules. She liked that. Interesting man, Mici decided as she stepped inside her apartment, brash but with a certain style. She was looking forward to the next encounter.

She always left a light burning in the living room visible from the street so that the apartment would appear occupied—an ordinary protection against burglary. Passing through with barely a glance, Mici now turned that light off and entered the bedroom which was dark. Here she now turned on the bedside lamp and the air conditioner, then closed the door to keep the cold air in. Pulling off her dress, she started for the closet to hang it up. For some reason, she stopped to listen. There was nothing to hear but the hum of the machine working extra hard to lower the temperature. Otherwise the room was silent. Unusually so, Mici thought. In fact, the whole building, even the street, seemed unnaturally quiet. Well, a lot of people were away at this time of year, she reasoned, but could not shake her sense of unease. Holding her dress in her hands, Mici stood clad in bra and panties in the middle

103

of her bedroom, her skin prickling as though someone watched.

Women who lived alone sometimes became neurotic. They put all kinds of locks on their doors; they kept their shades drawn, they imagined someone watching their comings and goings, even that their phone was being tapped. But Mici liked living alone. She drew strength from it. Her apartment was sleek, functional, and modern—the image of herself she wanted to present to the world. It was unthinkable that she could be afraid here, unthinkable that she should feel threatened.

But she did. Her heartbeat accelerated; her breath came in short, shallow gasps. Ridiculous! There couldn't be anybody in the apartment. The door had been locked until she handed Donald the key and he unlocked it. Striding purposefully to the closet, she flung it open. Empty of course. Laughing at herself, she hung up her dress. Nevertheless, before entering the bathroom she turned on the light. There wasn't anybody there either. Yet the feeling persisted. She took her nightgown off the hook on the back of the door, but instead of putting it on she stared at the closed door to the living room.

Obviously she wasn't going to get any sleep till she went out there and had a thorough look around. If there had been a burglar, say in the kitchen, he'd had plenty of time to get out by now. She hoped he'd taken advantage of it. She was sure he had; still, she hesitated. What she needed was some kind of weapon. What? There were no fire tongs or heavy-based statuettes handy. Her eyes swept the room and rested on the small chintz-covered dressing table. There were scissors in the drawer. Nail scissors, small but sharp.

At the last moment before opening the door and stepping into the living room, Mici remembered to turn out the bedroom light. God! The light would have made her a perfect target. She inched the door open and peered out. As she did so, she had a mental image of herself, scissors clenched in her hand, cowering. She was disgusted. Flinging the door wide open, she turned on the overhead lights and marched boldly forward. There was nobody there. She took a quick look into the kitchen. No one. She checked the front door and it was locked as she had left it. What in heaven's name was the matter with her? She turned every light off again, marched back to her bedroom, closed the door as before, and got ready for bed.

She hadn't been in bed long before she sensed that her bedroom door was opening. Not again, she said to herself, not again. She stiffened under the covers. She heard a step, definitely, no imagination. Before she could decide whether she should open her eyes and throw back the covers and make a run for it, or keep them shut and pretend to be asleep and let him take whatever he'd come for and go away, he was on top of her. In a single move he had one hand over her mouth, the other in her hair holding her head back against the pillow, and he was straddling her. She opened her eyes and looked into his. In the faint light from the street she could make out a ski mask.

"Don't fight." The mask muffled his voice. "Make it easy on yourself." He gave her hair a sharp, warning yank before letting it go so he could reach down to raise her nightgown. He did not take the hand away from her mouth.

Easy! Mici thought. *No way I'm going to make this easy for you, mister!*

Keeping her strong dancer's legs together, she tried to kick upward like a fish swimming. She squirmed under him; she heaved. No good. In fact, it was adding to his excitement and that she didn't need. She thought of grabbing his hair, but the knitted helmet prevented that. There was nothing she could get hold of, no part of him she could bite or scratch or gouge. She gasped for air. Her sobs of fear and anger were thrust back down into her throat by the hand over her mouth. But she wouldn't give in. Arms flailing wildly in the attempt to push him off, an elbow struck the edge of the bedside table. The pain shot up through her arm setting off a tingle of nerves. The scissors. She hadn't put the scissors back in the drawer. They were there on the bedside table. Her groping fingers found them and closed on them. For a moment Mici stopped struggling and

105

lay still, frightened at what she was about to do. She had never purposely injured anyone. If she attacked this man it had to be done forcefully. She had to wound him seriously or it would be useless, worse than useless, for unless he was badly hurt he'd take the weapon away from her. He might even turn it against her.

Drawing as much breath as she could with him on top of her and her mouth and nostrils partially blocked, Mici raised her arm over the middle of his back, held it poised for a moment, then plunged the scissors down full force. She was surprised at how easily they entered the flesh, surprised and even a little relieved.

Then he screamed. It was the worst scream that Mici had ever heard. After the scream, he went limp, lay still on top of her. Had she killed him? Oh, God, not with those little scissors?

"Pull the goddamned thing out," he muttered. "Pull it out." She was so relieved that he was alive that she did as he ordered.

They remained as they were; he resting, she not daring to move. Suddenly he shifted, rolled off her, and was on his feet running across the room and out the door. Before her muscles could relax, she heard the front door slam shut.

It was a long time before Mici was able to swing her legs over the side of the bed and sit up, and longer before she turned on the light. The scissors were still in her hand and she examined them as one might an object completely unfamiliar. The closed points were stained with blood about an inch up. She'd had the feeling of plunging them deeper than that. Thank God she hadn't! A drop or two of blood had dripped on the carpet as he ran and the bedclothes were rumpled; otherwise there appeared to be no trace of what had happened, or nearly happened. Then Mici looked down at herself. There was a white, scummy stain down the front of her nightgown.

She wanted to throw up.

The first thing she did when she could control her nausea was to pad out to the front door, turn the bolt, and put the chain back on. After that she went into the kitchen. There was a fire escape outside. The top half of the window was kept partially open to accommodate a ventilating fan. There was enough space between the fan and the window frame for a hand to reach in and raise the lower half. She pushed the top of the window up and locked the catch. She would never leave it down again.

Then, though she hadn't been raped, Mici Anhalt did what a great many rape victims instinctively do. She took off the soiled garment she was wearing, threw it into the laundry hamper, got under the hottest shower she could tolerate, and just stood there till her skin felt raw. After that she put on a clean gown, changed the bedclothes, and finally, exhausted, lay down between the clean sheets.

Not till then did she let herself cry. She wept quietly into the pillow till she finally fell asleep.

10

Mici awoke at first light. For a few moments she lay warm and groggy as though she'd taken a couple of sleeping pills that hadn't quite worn off. Then, with a jolt, she remembered. Waves of nausea washed over her anew. She kept very, very still till they passed. Her instinct was to put the whole thing out of her mind, forget it ever happened. That, she knew, was a typical reaction of women who had gone through a similar experience.

Mici Anhalt was neither a virgin nor promiscuous. She had what she considered a healthy enjoyment of sex, but she did not lightly enter into a sexual relationship; there had to be an emotional commitment on both sides. She was, therefore, shocked at the way the incident had traumatized her. After all, nothing had actually happened; she had neither been sexually molested nor physically injured. Yet she felt degraded. It was only six but she couldn't stay in bed. She got up, took another shower, and changed the bed linen a second time. She fixed herself coffee and forced herself to eat at least a bowl of cereal in the hot, stuffy kitchen sitting at the table in front of the closed window. All the while as she tried to follow her usual routine, Mici Anhalt knew that she had to go to the police.

She searched for excuses not to go. To start with, she couldn't provide any kind of description of the man who had attacked her. She had only a fleeting glimpse of him as he ran from the room and had been too agitated to note height or general build. The knitted helmet had had a slit in it for his eyes only so that she hadn't been able to tell the color of his hair or the shape of his nose, or even recognize his voice. Yet she must report the incident. The other tenants had a right to know that an intruder had gained admittance and how it had been done. She might not be able to give a description, but she had inflicted an injury and the nature of that injury might serve to identify him at some future time when he attacked someone else. There was even the possibility that he had gone to some hospital emergency room for treatment. In that case there would be a record, and he could be traced right now. For the sake of other future victims, she had to go to the police.

She dressed slowly, but at last was ready. Calling the office offered a further brief postponement. The switchboard wasn't open yet so she dialed Adam's direct line, and he answered as she had known he would. She told him only that she'd surprised a man in her apartment but that she'd been able to drive him off.

"You're all right? He didn't harm you? You're sure you're all right?"

"I gave worse than I got." She managed a chuckle and it made her feel better. "I'm going over to the precinct to report it."

"You didn't report it last night?"

"No." She didn't elaborate. "I'll probably be late for work."

108

Dowd sensed she was holding something back, but he would not force a confidence. "Take your time. Take the day off. It'll do you good, Mici."

"No, thanks, Adam. I'd just as soon come in."

"Whatever you want." His concern was a palpable vibration over the line. "If there's anything I can do . . . You want me to come over to the station house with you?"

She was touched and grateful. "No, no thanks, Adam. There's nothing to it. I'll be fine."

But it wasn't easy. It wasn't easy sitting on the other side of the desk being the victim. Mici had not before fully appreciated a woman's reluctance to report this particular type of crime. And it would have been a lot worse if she'd actually been raped. At least she was spared the medical examination and the recounting of each intimate detail. Even so, the procedure took up most of the morning, and when she was through Mici felt spent, as though she were recuperating from an illness. Adam had suggested she take the day off and she decided to take him up on it. She went back home. Before going upstairs, she got the mail out of her box. Nothing important—a couple of bills, a couple of ads, and a plain white envelope without name or address, just her apartment number. Obviously it had been hand-delivered. Holding it, Mici had the same kind of presentiment, the same sense of menace she'd felt the night before when she entered her apartment. Her hands trembled as she opened the envelope and pulled out a single sheet of paper.

"Mind your own business or you won't get rid of me next time."

Mici stared at the block letters crudely printed with a felt-tipped pen. *Mind your own business*. What did that refer to? The Schuyler case? Had to be. But who besides Donald knew she was taking an interest? Well, of course, Alfred Cassel and his Delissa. And Billy Zip. But that hadn't been either Alfred or Billy in her bed last night. So who? And why? She didn't know anything. Unless . . . wait a minute. Suppose Delissa's "friend" had ordered it?

109

But why rape? Or attempted rape?

Whoever it was knew that that particular kind of assault would affect her deeply, that she would feel used and humiliated. But by leaving the note and connecting it to the Schuyler case he had depersonalized the attack. She could now regard it as she might a shot that had missed or any other attempt to frighten her. That she could deal with.

Mici came up out of the subway at Forty-fourth on the corner near the St. James Theatre. She was struck anew at how seedy and run-down the theatrical district looked by daylight. On this overcast afternoon it seemed dingier and sadder than ever. When she was starting her career as a dancer, Mici had answered several calls at the St. James. It had been all glamour then, day and night. There had been a sense of suppressed excitement in walking along those very special side streets among the silent theatres. To be privileged to enter a grimy alley, open the stage door, and go inside if only for a tryout had been thrilling. It hadn't mattered that the theatre was dark and cold, that when you walked down to the apron to give your name you had to squint into the glare of an unshaded pilot light. Now there were porno houses interspersed with the legitimate theatres, amusement arcades, quick food shoppes, cheap bars; once elegant hotels had either been torn down or become SRO, Single Room Occupancy dwellings. Actors looking for work still walked the streets, but they mingled with addicts, pushers, male and female prostitutes. Mici decided she was glad she was out of the business.

Had Julia Schuyler seen the dirt and decay? Mici wondered. She could have lived anywhere else more decently and comfortably, yet this had been her choice. Because it was close to her memories or close to her hopes? Julia had had hopes. She had spoken of them to Mici on the night of her murder. She had spoken of offers, of a comeback. Mici had discounted them as the usual actor's talk. Had it been more?

Climbing the crumbling steps of the brownstone in

which Julia Schuyler had died, Mici rang the bell of the only other person who knew about her interest in the case. The answering buzzer released the lock and she entered. Bettedene Barber was leaning out over the railing of the third-floor hallway.

"Who wants me?"

Mici waited till she'd reached the landing and was face to face with the girl. "My name is Mici Anhalt. I was here a couple of days ago to see Detective Swell."

"Oh, sure, I remember."

"I thought, if you don't mind and if you can spare the time, that we might talk."

"What about?"

Mici looked around the dingy hall, then toward the door the blonde teenager had left ajar. "Could we go inside?"

The girl shrugged. "Okay."

There was no sun in the apartment, but the curtains were pulled back from sparkling clean windows and let in plenty of light. There were bright, flowered chintz covers on what was obviously a set of dilapitated furniture; tables were skirted and flounced, pillows abounded. Everything that could be covered and camouflaged was.

"You've done a fine decorating job, Miss Barber."

The thin, sallow face lit up. Seeing her without makeup, wearing jeans and a sloppy shirt, blonde hair tied up in a ponytail, Mici was struck at the girl's youth. She couldn't be more than sixteen at the outside.

"I like to sew."

"You're certainly good at it."

"I make all my own clothes. Oh, not what I'm wearing now, my good stuff. I go to all these wholesale outlets where they have remnants. You can get some real nice material for very little money." She pointed with pride to a table in front of the window on which was spread some cream-colored silk which she'd been cutting to pattern. "That's a shirt I'm making for Dominic. He's my old man."

"Lovely."

"Think he'll like it?"

"How could he help it? Tell me, Miss Barber, how long have you been in New York?"

The eager light in her face died. "Why do you want to know?"

Mici instantly realized she'd made a mistake. She shrugged it off. "No reason. Just making conversation."

"You some kind of social worker or something? I'm eighteen years old. I can show you my birth certificate."

"No, no." Mici held up her hand. "I'm not a social worker.

The girl was only partially reassured. "What makes you think I come from out of town?"

"You don't talk like a New Yorker. Your voice is softer, kind of southern. Nice."

"Thank you." She colored shyly. "I've been here for two years. I thought I'd gotten rid of the accent."

Mici didn't believe that she was more than sixteen, so that would have made her fourteen when she started hustling. "Do you like it? New York, I mean."

"It's all right. One place is pretty much like another, don't you think? I mean, I don't get to see much of New York, you know? I don't go to the fancy places you read about in the papers. I don't go to the shows; they're just down the street, but I don't get to see them. But who cares? I probably wouldn't like them. I see all the movies I want, and I've got this terrific color TV." She pointed to the big, blank screen in a corner. "Dom's real good to me."

"I'm glad."

"He cares about me. He really does. There's never a day goes by that he doesn't check to see how I'm making out. He spends as much time with me as he can."

"That's good."

"Yes. I'm lucky. There's some girls . . . I could tell you stories . . . ." She stopped, wary again. "What do you want anyway?"

Mici took a breath. Why not level? If she wanted this

112

girl to be straight with her, shouldn't she set the example? "Julia Schuyler was an old friend. I visited with her Friday night. She got drunk and passed out, and I left her like that. I feel really bad about it."

The hooker nodded. "I can see that. I can see how it would bug you." She frowned. "You want some coffee?" she asked abruptly.

"Yes." Mici responded quickly and positively. "A cup of coffee would go great." A barrier had been breached.

"It'll only take a couple of minutes to perk. I don't go for the instant."

"Neither do I."

"How about some toast? Cinnamon toast?"

"I haven't had cinnamon toast in years. It would be a treat."

They smiled at each other.

"I'm a good cook, if I say it myself," the girl confided. "When Dom stays over—that's not often because he's so busy. He has . . . so much to do—I fix him a real fine breakfast, homemade pancakes from scratch. He loves them. Come on into the kitchen and sit with me while I fix our snack."

The girl was some housekeeper, Mici thought, as she sat at the table near the window while the ruffled curtains billowed in gusts that foretold a heavy storm. She hadn't properly taken it in when she was here before, but she saw now that, as in the living room, everything had been lovingly camouflaged with paint, paper, or fabric—except the stove; there was nothing that could be done with that relic. "Miss Barber, it's about my friend's murder that I'm here. We all keep to ourselves in New York. We respect our neighbor's privacy because we want him to respect ours. But when somebody's killed, then we have a duty to tell what we know. I'm appealing to you, Miss Barber . . ."

"I don't know who you're talking to when you call me that."

"Barbi . . ."

"Bettedene's my given name. Bette for my aunt and Dene is a family name. Nobody hardly calls me Bettedene any more."

"Bettedene. It's pretty and it suits you. Will you call me Mici?"

"Yes, Mici, and I wish I could help you, but I didn't know Miss Schuyler. I told Detective Swell. We met sometimes on the stairs, going in and out the front door. We'd say hello, nice day, lousy day, and that was it. She wasn't snooty or anything, but, like you said, we respected each other's privacy."

"And her husband?"

"Mr. Cassel?" Her thin, heart-shaped face broke into a real smile. "He was something else! He held the door for me every time and stood aside so I got to go through ahead of him. Once he bowed and kissed my hand. Made me feel like a princess."

"How did he and Miss Schuyler get along?"

"They had plenty of fights. I mean, they were always yelling at each other. You could hear them all over the building, but they weren't the only ones. The woman upstairs with the four kids? When her old man gets a couple of belts in him—watch out!" Bettedene clucked and shook her head.

"Do you think that Alfred Cassel ever beat his wife? Did you ever see any sign that he had beaten her?"

"No, ma'am . . . Mici, I never did."

"When I visited her Friday, she had bruises all over her arms and a cut on her cheek."

"That was after Mr. Cassel had moved out. I thought you meant before."

"I did. But he was still coming to see her occasionally."

"If he didn't beat her while he was living with her, why should he do it after?"

The question had already come up and the answer, of course, was that he was driven to it by Julia's stubborn refusal to give him a divorce. No use going into that with the girl. "About Friday night, Bettedene, did you hear anything—an argument, sounds of a fight— coming from Miss Schuyler's apartment?"

"It was raining and I had the windows shut. I couldn't hear anything. I told Detective Swell."

"Were you alone? I'm not prying, Bettedene," Mici

114

hastened to assure her. "I just thought that maybe . . . if you had a friend here he might have heard . . ."

"I was alone."

"Maybe going in and out of the building you noticed somebody, some man who could have been visiting Julia Schuyler?"

"It was raining. I don't work outdoors in the rain."

Mici flushed. "How about other nights?"

"What other nights?"

Was she being purposely dense? "The other nights she got beaten up. There had to be other nights, Bettedene."

Without the layers of makeup the girl's small brown eyes were undistinguished, but they were completely steady as she fixed them on Mici. "I'm busy nights. That's when I earn my living. I don't have time to snoop."

She was blunt enough now, Mici thought; why had she been almost coy earlier? "Did you see Alfred Cassel in the building and then notice Miss Schuyler with bruises afterwards?"

"No."

"You're answering without thinking, Bettedene."

"I don't have to think, I know. You say Mr. Cassel's been around and I have no reason to doubt you, but I haven't seen him, not once since he moved out."

Might as well drop it, Mici thought, the girl wasn't going to believe anything against Cassel. Her loyalty was as stubborn and unquestioning as a little girl's. What had gone wrong for Bettedene Barber? she wondered. She knew that there were hundreds like her nestled in hutches in the seamy fifteen-block stretch along Eighth Avenue paralleling Times Square. They were recruited in the small towns of middle America, put on buses and shipped like parcels to the big city to be claimed by strangers who turned them into virtual slaves. The stories varied only in detail, with lack of love as perceived by the girl always at the core.

"Coffee and toast's ready, if you still want it." The wispy, blonde teenager sulked beside the stove.

"Of course, I do. No hard feelings, Bettedene?"

"I can't tell you what I don't know."

"I had to ask."

"I guess." Partly mollified, the girl set out the food.

Mici took a bite of the toast. "Delicious." After a satisfying swallow of the coffee, she pronounced it, "Perfect, best I ever had."

Beaming at the praise, Bettedene sat down opposite and they shared the snack in companionable silence.

"I really enjoyed that," Mici said, wiping her mouth and setting the napkin down beside her plate. "Thanks for everything, Bettedene." She hesitated, feeling that somehow she had left some question unasked, some area unexplored. "I agree with you that Alfred Cassel wouldn't have beaten his wife. But she did accuse him of it. Why should she do that?"

"You don't know?"

"No. She was getting a fair amount of money every month, but she claimed she was broke. Could she have been gambling? Could some bookie have had her beaten up?"

Bettedene just shook her head.

Mici didn't believe that herself. A bookie would have had it done once, just once would have been enough. Then who? she asked herself. It came with a jolt that all the while she'd been agonizing over why Julia had accused Alfred she'd never asked herself who else it might be. If Cassel hadn't beaten his wife, who had? The killer, of course. Fine. He'd evidently been at it for some time before graduating to murder. Who could it be?

"You honestly mean you don't know?" Bettedene Barber was amazed. "She was covering for her boyfriend."

"Her boyfriend?" Mici repeated stupidly.

"Sure. That explains what she did with her money, doesn't it?"

"You're telling me that Julia Schuyler was keeping a man?"

"No, that's what you're telling me." The girl was almost patronizing. "If a woman really loves a man, she wants to do everything she can for him, give him

116

everything he needs and wants. If it's not enough, what she can do—why, he lets her know it, and if she refuses to understand he has no choice but to beat her up. I've been through it. I know. I had a hard time learning. At first, Dom and me, we were together all the time. It was wonderful, a dream come true. But it couldn't last. He explained to me that we couldn't live without money. When I found out about the other girls I was hysterical. I cried and carried on. He explained to me that much as he loved me, it wouldn't be fair for them to be working and bringing in all the money and for me not to do my share. It took some pretty hard knocks before I got the message. It wasn't that Dom enjoyed beating me, just that I was so dumb, real dumb."

"Are you telling me that Julia Schuyler . . ."

"That she went out to turn tricks? No, of course not. Not her. But she was keeping a man and he was beating her, regular."

"Did you ever see him with her? Going in or out of her place?"

"Didn't need to. I saw her the mornings after he'd been with her. A lot of mornings."

Her absolute certainty compelled belief. Thinking back to Julia's behavior that Friday night, Mici had to admit that there had been a certain . . . smugness about her. All the while she was railing against Cassel, she seemed to be hugging a secret to herself. Bemoaning her pain, she'd seemed at the same time to relish it. Mici had noted that and assumed that the actress was anticipating her revenge. Now she wondered if Julia hadn't derived a masochistic pleasure from her lover's violence. Maybe the beatings heightened the sexual satisfaction. Yet for Julia to permit herself to be abused in that way, Julia Schuyler who had once been so proud, who could have had any man . . . Mici sighed.

"It doesn't hurt all that much when you love the man," the hooker explained. "At least you know he cares."

Mici licked her lips nervously. It was too late for Julia, but this girl, this child, could still be helped. "Have you ever thought of going back home, Bettedene?"

117

"You mean to Richmond? Why should I? Dom doesn't beat me any more. That's over. He's very good to me, I told you."

"But someday, when you get older . . ." Mici couldn't finish.

"I know what you mean. I've thought about it. But that's a long way off. I don't drink or shoot up so I'll keep my looks for a long time." Then, with a smile of real pleasure, she spread out her arms to include the antiquated kitchen and the squalid rooms she'd swaddled in fabric. "I could never have anything as nice as this back home."

11

Julia with a lover? Why not? Nothing new in that. Julia had never stayed alone for long. It was Bettedene Barber's paralleling Julia's situation with hers that shocked Mici. But there are many ways a man can exploit a woman without putting her out on the street. At such a low point of her life, Julia would have been easy prey for such a man. It could have been his idea for Julia to contact Mici and ask for benefits. Naturally, he couldn't let her name him as the assailant. The ploy had a double edge: possible monetary gain and the squeeze on Cassel to get him to increase his allowance to Julia.

The murder was certainly a crime of passion, Mici thought. But who was Julia's lover? How could he be found?

Was he someone Julia had known a long time, or someone she'd met recently? More likely the latter and, if so, the meeting could have been casual, perhaps in a bar—Julia was very friendly when she'd had a few. What was needed was a team to canvass the bars in the area. It was a police job, but by the time she got hold of Donald and he went to his lieutenant—forget it. From what she'd heard about John LaRock, the lieut was not likely to throw a task force on the street in response to the theory of a teenage hooker.

So . . . Mici glanced at her watch. Nearly four. She'd been with Bettedene longer than she'd realized, but it was still early for most bars. However, the kind of place Julia would have been frequenting lately opened early in the morning. Down the street, on the corner, was O'Malley's, as good a place to start as any. Placing both hands at the back of her neck, Mici lifted her red-gold hair high and held it there to let the air cool her; then she let it drop and with a toss of her head walked into the dark, dank saloon.

She spent the rest of the afternoon and well into the evening going from one rancid bar to the next, up and down the side streets, along Eighth Avenue: the Red Rose, the Shamrock, the Pub, P.J. McGrath's, P.J. Callaghan's, or just plain P.J.'s. Some were strictly gin mills with paper banners glued across the front window proclaiming the house double-shot special, sawdust on the floor, and the row of regulars on their stools, others had pretensions to style and were decorated in chrome and tinted glass reminiscent of the thirties, but they had the same row of rummies. Mici had no compunction about going into these bars alone; she knew that no one would bother her—these sad men had no interest in women or in anything else but booze. As for the bartenders, at that hour they weren't busy; they welcomed a diversion.

"I'm working on the Schuyler case," Mici would announce and flash her ID.

They'd all heard about the case and no one challenged her right to ask questions. No one really looked at her credentials. New Yorkers were gullible. You could stand on a street corner shaking a can and passersby would drop in contributions without ever asking what it was for.

Though Julia hadn't been around for a while, she was known in several of the bars. She'd made no secret

119

of her identity; not for Julia Schuyler the "I want to be alone" or "I'm entitled to my privacy" routine. Julia let them all know who she was, or had been, and what she intended to be again. They listened till they'd heard all her stories and weren't impressed any more, till she got boring, till she was accepted as part of the scene. Then nobody noticed and nobody remembered Julia picking anybody up or getting picked up.

"She wasn't on the make. She just came in to forget her troubles like they all do."

That was the summation of Joe, the bartender-owner of Joe's Place, which appeared to have been her principal hangout. It was the general opinion and Mici accepted it. Wherever Julia had met her new lover it wasn't in any of these joints, she decided. Though she hadn't really expected to find the man, she had hoped for some clue to his identity and she was disappointed. Yet she had learned something from the past hours' investigation, and that was that the new man in Julia's life had not been a casual pickup. Julia had not been out looking for sex but for sympathy. What type of man could have offered her that? An actor. Julia Schuyler had been married twice, both times to actors. Her romances had been with actors working in her shows, but now that she was out of work why shouldn't she be involved with an actor who was also out of work? The question was how to find him. Go to Actors' Equity again? AFTRA, the Screen Actors' Guild, and check out their rosters of the unemployed? Those unions had more members out of work than working.

Would Billy Zip know? Mici wasn't sure. The stage manager had obviously believed Julia's message that her husband was beating her. He had delivered the message with conviction. However, he might know about a new man in the actress's life without being aware of the depth or quality of the relationship. Mici called the studio and was told that Billy had left for the day. She called his home and got a recorded announcement. She did not leave a message.

It was nearly dark when Mici came out of the phone booth. The lights would be coming on all over the city, but here in the Tenderloin the lights consisted of a kaleidoscope of theater marquees, neon signs, and bright hotel canopies.

A slow smile illumined her face as she watched the magic being turned on. What did actors want more than anything else in the world? To act. What did the deepening dusk mean to an actor? It meant getting ready to come down here, to walk along one of these dirty alleys and enter a stage door, to sit in a bare dressing room, squint into the glare of naked bulbs around an often blurred mirror, and put on makeup. Julia Schuyler had been down and nearly out, but she still had connections in the business. She couldn't get a job herself, but she could have helped her lover get one. By simply picking up a telephone, she could at least have assured him a sympathetic interview or audition with practically anybody casting anything in New York or Hollywood. Mici's smile reached her pale, crystal-clear eyes that mirrored the lights around her. All she had to do was make the rounds of the theatrical offices. It would be like the old days.

She'd tell Adam she needed a rest. She was pretty much turned off by the job anyway, and a few days away from it would do her good. What she did with them was her own business.

In the more than ten years since Mici Anhalt had been a dancer sitting in these same offices, the scene hadn't changed. The faces were the same. At least, they wore the same anxious expression, the false cheeriness, the eagerness to please in spite of rebuff after rebuff. Some had talent, others not—all were treated with contempt, actors being a glut on the market. It was no wonder that when one of them made it he paid back the humiliation with arrogance and outlandish demands. The only thing different now was that Mici was no longer a job applicant and so she got in, where before she would have sat outside with the others.

Every agent, director, and producer was eager to talk. Each wanted to know everything that Mici knew, which was the tip-off that he didn't know anything

121

himself. In the end, each was forced to admit, reluctantly, that Julia Schuyler had not contacted him in her own behalf or anybody else's.

Dead end.

Not quite. She'd forgotten Billy Zip, probably because she didn't have much hope that he'd be forthcoming. Billy would not divulge anything that might be detrimental to Julia. On the other hand, he would surely want to see her murder avenged.

Since "Storm of Life" was televised daily, it was simply a matter of catching Billy after the show went off the air. Seconds after the red warning light over the door of the studio went out, the door opened and the actors started filing toward their dressing rooms; the crew was next, then last, as usual, the stage manager. William Zipprodt came out of studio 2A, shirt-sleeves rolled to the elbow, sweating, carrying a stack of scripts, and looking generally harried behind a pair of clear, horn-rimmed glasses. Mici had to step right into his path to get him to notice her.

"You?" He was surprised, then confused. "What are you doing here?"

"I want to talk to you. Can we go somewhere? It's important."

"I don't know. . . . This is a bad time. I'm sorry, but as soon as everybody's changed we're due upstairs to rehearse tomorrow's episode."

"I just want a few minutes, Billy," she pleaded and didn't move out of his way.

"All right. Come on."

The rehearsal room was like all rehearsal rooms, bare, utilitarian, but for the actors who used it it was the most glamorous of environments—the workshop, the place of creation. Though she was no longer a part of this particular world, Mici felt a twinge of the old, familiar exhilaration. There was the usual large table with a number of folding chairs set up around it where the actors would gather for the first reading. On the floor, purposely bare so that a chalk outline of the setting could be drawn, Mici noted that there were several outlines laid down in vari-colored masking

122

tapes indicating that several shows used the room as permanent rehearsal quarters. The building had once been a stable which had been converted in the early days of television when studio space had been nearly impossible to find. As a result, this room was relatively modern and cleaner than most other such facilities.

Billy Zip dumped his scripts on the table and began to lay out a copy at each place as though he were setting the table for dinner. That done, he went to a stack of folding chairs in one corner and began to set them within the area of the green floor tape; they would represent the various pieces of furniture in the set.

Mici waited for him to finish and give her his attention. He must have done this a thousand times by now, she thought, yet he was being inordinately finicky.

"Who do you think killed Julia?" she asked.

The chair he had been unfolding clattered in his hands. "I thought . . . Alfred." He swallowed, put the chair in place. "Who else?"

"You told the police about Alfred?"

"I had to."

"Yes, so did I."

They both sighed.

"He hasn't been arrested," Mici observed.

"I assume it's a matter of time."

"He has an alibi."

"I know all about his alibi and I don't think much of it," the stage manager snapped. "I don't think much of Delissa Grace's alibi either. I wonder which one is covering for the other?" Now that he'd set the scene and had no further activity to cover his nervousness, William Zipprodt fished into his pocket for cigarettes. "If you want to know what I think, I think they were in it together—to get Julia off their backs."

Mici was silent.

Billy Zip lit up and took a deep drag. "Julia could have had Alfred arrested; you were the one who told us that. With Alfred in jail there'd be no show, or at least no show as far as Delissa Grace was concerned. She was only in it because he wanted her."

123

"That's not quite true."

Billy Zip blew out a puff of smoke and squinted at her with his sad eyes. "She's strictly no-talent."

For a moment, Mici wondered whether Billy knew about Delissa's friend, the backer of the show. She decided that he didn't, that he was jealous on Julia's behalf. "You think they cold-bloodedly planned it together?"

He turned away.

"Billy dear . . ." Mici followed him and put a hand on his shoulder. "I know you loved Julia and you mourn her and you want to see her avenged. But it won't help to have the wrong man blamed."

"If it's not Alfred, then who?"

Now she could ask the question she had come to ask. "Did Julia have a lover?"

The response was a slow rise of color in the stage manager's sallow, haggard face. "How should I know?"

"You were as close to Julia as anyone could be."

"But I never pried. If she wanted to confide in me, I was there, but I didn't pry or snoop."

"She never mentioned another man?"

"No."

"You didn't suspect there might be another man?"

He hesitated a fraction of a second. "No."

For now that was enough. Mici tried another approach. "Did she tell you what she did with her money? The money you gave her and Alfred gave her and Delissa and God knows who else?"

"What are you talking about?"

"You did tell me that you helped her out from time to time."

"Right. I did."

"You weren't the only one. Alfred was paying her rent and something besides. Delissa was making a contribution."

"How do you know?" Billy Zip croaked.

"They told me and since it strengthens their motives for murder, I believe them."

"Where did the money go?" he cried.

"I was hoping you could tell me."

He shook his head.

"She wasn't exactly living high and she wasn't drinking that much. Was she gambling?"

"I never knew her to gamble."

"Then she was giving it to a man."

The door of the rehearsal room opened, and the actor Mici recognized as the leading man of "Storm of Life" entered, going directly to the table where he took his accustomed place and immersed himself in his copy of the next day's drama. Though she was sure that he wasn't paying any attention to them, Mici drew closer to Billy and lowered her voice. "Isn't it possible that it was this other man who was beating her? Not Alfred?"

The stage manager was in a daze. She put a hand on his arm and shook him gently. "Billy, isn't it possible?"

"I don't know." His whole face quivered, his eyes narrowed as though he had just been hit. "I went over one night to work on the book and I found her sitting on the sofa, half drunk, whimpering, her face a bloody mess. My first instinct was to call a doctor, but she wouldn't let me. She screamed at me that she didn't want a doctor. She screamed at me to mind my own business or to get out. Well, what could I do? I cleaned her up the best I could, made sure that there weren't any bones broken but . . . oh my God! You have no idea the state she was in. Anyway, after I was through I tried to call the police, but she wouldn't let me do that either. It finally filtered through to me that this wasn't any ordinary mugging, that someone she knew had done it. I nearly went crazy then. If I could have got my hands on the man, I think I would have killed him. I pleaded with her, I begged her to tell me who it was. No use. I demanded. I threatened. Nothing had any effect. For once in my life I was not going to give in to Julia. For once I was going to have my way. I picked up the phone and dialed 911. This was when she named Alfred."

He was silent for a few moments. "That was almost as big a shock as walking in and finding her like that. I wouldn't have believed it except that she was threatening to sue him for nonsupport. I went to see Alfred about it. It was my idea that he should visit her. He was reluctant; I urged him. And this was the result."

Mici gave him a couple of moments to compose himself. "Alfred might have lost his temper, gone completely out of control—I suppose anything is possible—but Alfred would never, never have got Julia drunk."

"No." William Zipprodt bowed his head. "She lied to me."

"Maybe she was afraid to tell you the truth." Mici didn't believe that. Billy Zip had loved Julia and loyally accepted her marriage to another man, to Cassel, because he believed Cassel was her equal. But how would he have felt about a new lover? One so brutish? Julia had been fond of Billy in her way. Certainly he'd been useful to her over the years. She wouldn't have wanted to lose him. Maybe she had sensed his reluctance to accept the charge against Cassel and had sent him to Mici as a way of reenforcing the accusation. "This man, whoever he was, was in complete control."

The door of the rehearsal room opened again; more actors entered and took their places around the table. There wasn't much time left.

"Did she ever send anybody to you for a job on the show?"

"You mean—him? She wouldn't do that."

"Why not?"

"She wouldn't ask me to give anybody a job unless he had real talent. Julia might have sunk low, but whatever else she did she wouldn't prostitute her professional integrity. Never."

"How do you know he didn't have talent?"

A man Mici had not seen on the show came in. He had an air of authority. "Say, Zip?" he called. "See your friend later and let's get the show on the road, okay?"

From the way Billy jumped, it had to be the director. Mici held his arm for one moment more. "How do you know he didn't have any talent?"

"Because then she would have told everybody about him; she would have touted him to the skies. But she must have been ashamed of him. She lied to me because she was ashamed."

So, Mici thought, an actor but one without special talent. Run-of-the-mill at best. If he was her lover, however, what more natural than that he should ask her to recommend him to her friends? But she refused. He was stunned. They argued. He beat her. But kill her? That was going a bit far. Besides, she was no use to him dead. Mici had already considered the possibility that the murder was not premeditated but committed in the heat of passion, yet the image now taking shape was of a cool and calculating man. He used women. He would not be likely to lose control. Besides, if making love to Julia failed, if beating her didn't get him what he wanted, he had another weapon in his arsenal. He could simply stay away from her. If her addiction to him was strong enough, she would do anything to get him back. She would renounce integrity, accept any humiliation. Mici believed that was what had happened.

She had covered all the agents and directors in New York. Would Julia have used her Hollywood connections for her lover? She could check Julia's old studio—which was it? Or her lawyer. Of course. Oscar Brumleve was a theatrical institution. He would be a more valuable ally to an aspiring actor than any casting director or producer. Brumleve knew everybody, and any favor he asked would not be lightly ignored.

Oscar Brumleve was legend, and so was his apartment at the top of the John Malcolm Schuyler Theatre. The theatre had been dark for several momths, but it had a tenant now. As she passed the lobby, Mici noted that there was no one waiting at the box office—an ominous indication that the run was going to be short. She continued past the marquee to a short flight of steps and pressed the bell beside the door. An answering buzz released the lock and she stepped into a small, dingy vestibule where an antiquated elevator stood open.

There were two buttons—Up and Down. She pressed the Up. The car shuddered and groaned its way to the top, then halted. The door opened directly into the famous lawyer's office-apartment.

Entering Oscar Brumleve's domain was like stepping back into the days of past theatrical glories. The hallway was long and broad, a gallery in fact, lined on both sides with photographs and portraits of famous clients and settings, playbills, and theatrical mementoes. Unfortunately, the light coming from a skylight in the center was harsh. It revealed the worn spots in the Turkish floor runner, the dents and rust on the suit of armor, and showed that the Jacobean armchairs and the rose tree with its blooms long since turned brown were merely stage props. Everywhere there was the dust of neglect.

"Miss Anhalt?"

A dark-haired young man, pale as though he seldom saw the outdoors, appeared at the end of the corridor. He indicated a pair of double doors. "You can go right in but be brief as possible. He tires easily."

The first thing she saw was not the lawyer but the portrait of his most famous client, John Malcolm Schuyler, for whom Brumleve had built the theatre. It was over the fireplace, the focal point of the room. It showed the actor as Macbeth, hand stretched out, fingers clawing toward the ghostly, non-existent dagger. For a moment Mici stood where she was, transfixed by the painted eyes. She had to shake herself free. She looked around. The room was large, the walls paneled in wood as intricately carved as the chamber of the Knights of the Bath at Windsor Castle. Tall, old-fashioned, glass-doored bookcases were filled with dusty tomes, manuscripts, files, all in haphazard stacks. Twin beams of light passing through a pair of stained-glass windows colored the gloom and created the effect of stage lighting, softening the general shabbiness which in the hallway had been so sadly obvious.

"Well, don't just stand there. Come over here. Come over here where I can get a look at you."

She jumped at the voice. "It's very good of you to see

me, Mr. Brumleve," Mici said as she approached the shrunken figure at the desk to the right of the fireplace.

"No, young lady, it's good of you to come. I don't get many visitors nowadays."

Oscar Brumleve was a celebrity. Mici had seen countless pictures of him with countless other celebrities; there were even pictures of him outside in the hall, but if she had met him anywhere else she wouldn't have recognized him. He was a wasted man. He had had, she recalled, an abundant head of hair, but it was thinned now to a few pitiful white tufts. The flesh of his face had been consumed, and the skull showed through prophetically. His eyes were sunk deep in their sockets, but they burned brightly. She had not heard that Brumleve was sick; in fact, she realized that she had not heard about him at all for a very long time and that probably was the reason.

A shaft of light picked up the row of golden statuettes lined up along the front of the desk—awards. She recognized some: the Oscars, of course; the Tonys; a Drama Critics Award; the Valentino, a statuette from the film festival in Bari, Italy. The light bounced from the tarnished metal, streaking the burgundy velvet drapes behind Brumleve's chair. Was there a window back there? Mici frowned because she couldn't quite get the layout of the building clear in her mind.

"You were a dancer, I see."

She started. "How did you know?"

"I recognize a dancer's legs when I see them, particularly if they're as good as yours," Brumleve chuckled. "But you don't dance any more. You haven't in some time."

"I still take classes."

"Not the same. Too bad."

"I wasn't a very good dancer."

"Oh, you were good enough, I'm sure. With your looks you were more than good enough. What happened?"

Mici shrugged. "I didn't care enough. Getting my name up there in lights just didn't seem that important."

Oscar Brumleve nodded. "In that case, you did well to get out." He consulted a paper in front of him. "So now you're in Criminal Justice. Quite a switch."

She didn't feel that required comment.

But he did. "Crime Victims Compensation Board. You do good work down there, but don't you find it depressing?"

"Sometimes," she admitted.

The sunken eyes gleamed in the colored light. "But you like it better than dancing."

"It's real."

"Ah." He nodded. "Well, now, what can I do to help you? Which one of your claims am I involved in, eh?" He chortled as though that were a farfetched idea.

Mici had given a great deal of thought to her approach. The mere presentation of credentials would not impress Brumleve; he would know that she had no official standing and that he was under no obligation to tell her anything. She had decided to be honest.

"The Julia Schuyler case."

"You're not working on that. That's police business."

"I have a personal interest. I knew Julia."

"A great many people knew Julia."

"I was with her on Friday night not long before she was killed."

He merely narrowed his eyes slightly. "Have you informed the police?"

"Yes."

"Then you've done all you can and should do. You're a professional. I suggest you let the police do their job as you'd want to be allowed to do yours."

It was exactly the reaction she'd expected. "I would if I thought they were conducting an unbiased investigation, but all they're trying to do is pin the crime on Alfred Cassel."

"That's a serious allegation."

"I make it seriously."

"And it matters to you—what happens to Alfred Cassel?"

"Yes, sir. Partly because it's my fault that he's under

130

suspicion, but mainly because I believe that he's innocent. Don't you?"

"I'd like to." The lawyer was thoughtful. "I considered Alfred Cassel decent and honorable. I thought Julia was lucky to get him. Now I'm not so sure. I realize he's been through a trying period and the provocation must have been great. Still, my loyalty has to be to the daughter of my old friend." His eyes went to the towering portrait. "Everything points to Alfred. If it weren't for that alibi, which in my opinion is flimsy, he'd already be in custody."

"So you refuse to help him?"

"He hasn't been arrested." Brumleve raised a skeletal hand, then let it fall limply to the top of the desk. "If he were arrested and charged, I'm not sure he'd want me to represent him. We had a falling-out a short while back."

"Would you help if you could?"

Brumleve considered. "How?"

"By answering some questions."

The thin lips stretched into a taut line that passed for a smile, cracking the flesh around the mouth in the unaccustomed movement. "My dear young lady, the police have been here; they have asked every imaginable question, and I have answered fully and unequivocally."

"I have other questions."

"Indeed? Questions the police didn't think to ask?" He didn't bother to hide either his amusement or disbelief.

"Well, actually only one."

She had piqued his interest. He might not take her seriously, but he was curious. It was enough, Mici thought, and she waited patiently while he studied her anew. She became aware that she was perspiring heavily. Was she that anxious? No, the room was that hot. There was no air conditioning. She realized that the sick old man did not feel the heat, that he required it.

"What's the question?"

131

"Did Julia send a man to you, an actor, and ask you to help him get a job?"

This time she had to wait even longer, but she knew it was no use adding anything. He would either answer or he would not.

He uttered a long, drawn-out sigh. "Yes."

"Who was he?"

"One question, you said."

She suppressed a surge of excitement. "It's a two-parter."

"Ah . . . you're a clever girl, very clever. I don't know how you found out about . . . Did Julia tell you? No, of course not, if she had you wouldn't have needed to come to me. Well, what does it matter? She's gone. It's over for her."

"Just his name, Mr. Brumleve."

He didn't hear her; he was away among his memories. "Poor Julia, poor Julia. Everything she touched went bad."

"If you'll just give me his name I won't trouble you . . ."

"Handsome devil, ingratiating, charming when he wanted to be. Of course, he was using her. What could I do? No use telling her, she knew it; she wasn't that much of a fool."

"What did you do? Did you find him a job?"

Brumleve looked at Mici and shifted from the past to the present. "Didn't know what to do with him. Face like a choir boy along with plenty of sex appeal, devastating combination, but froze up in front of an audience. I wanted to oblige Julia but didn't know what to do with him. Finally got Steinberg-Farber to take him on, use him in their commercials. Only thing he was good for."

"You haven't told me his name, Mr. Brumleve."

"No, and I'm not going to, young lady. I thought . . . I was so sure that Alfred . . . but if there's a doubt . . . I will tell the police. I'll tell them. It's their business." A spasm of pain traveled like a current through his emaciated frame. Sweat broke out all over his gray face and trickled in the deeply grooved lines like fresh rain in dry gutters. With a shaking hand he reached toward the electric bell set in a square, flat box at the desk's corner and pressed. His face a gargoyle mask, the spittle running from a corner of his mouth down to his chin, he collapsed across the desk.

Mici ran to the door, but as she did it opened and the young male secretary came hurrying in with the equipment for a hypodermic injection. With every indication of expertise, he slipped Brumleve's left arm out of his jacket, rolled up the shirt-sleeve, prepared the area, and made the injection.

Mici watched and waited and was relieved to see the lawyer revive.

"You'll have to leave now, miss," the secretary-nurse told her.

"Yes, yes, of course." Mici didn't know what the lawyer's illness was, but he was fighting it and fighting it valiantly. She feared it might be a losing battle. "Just his name, Mr. Brumleve."

His pain-filled eyes met hers and seemed to share her thought. "Kord . . . ," he murmured. "Janos Kord."

12

"Say! That's good work. You're a real pro. I'm impressed." Donald Swell beamed at Mici.

"You don't mind?"

"Why should I mind? You did a great job."

"Well, I thought . . . other times . . . my past experience has been that police officers resent what they call interference."

"That's because they're insecure. I'm not."

Mici's elation at having discovered the identity of Julia's lover was still high. However, she had promised Oscar Brumleve to go to the police and she did agree

133

that it was time for them to take over. So she'd called Donald and Donald had immediately suggested dinner. "Even cops have to eat," he'd pointed out. Now they sat opposite each other in a booth in the back room of a small, pleasant, neighborhood bar and grill near the precinct. Having expected to be chewed out, Mici was both relieved and gratified to be complimented instead.

"You never cease to amaze me, Donald."

He bent slightly, reached under the table, and rested a hand on her knee. "I'll continue to amaze you, if you'll let me."

"I spoke too soon." Laughing, she removed his hand. "What are you going to do?"

He sighed heavily. "Go the route, I guess—send flowers, perfume, call two or three times a day, order a singing telegram, maybe."

She grinned. "You know what I'm talking about."

"Oh, that." Swell shrugged. "The usual. Check out this guy Kord. Find out where he was and what he was doing Friday P.M. and Saturday A.M. around the time we think the murder may have been committed, and . . . like that. Then we'll see."

"Okay."

"I'm not downgrading your accomplishment in tracking this Janos Kord, doll," the detective continued, "but we don't have anything on him yet. Assuming Julia Schuyler had the hots for him, that she was giving him all her money and that in return he was beating the . . . hell . . . out of her, that still doesn't make him a murderer. In fact, it seems to me that it was in his interest to keep her alive."

"You'd think so," Mici agreed. "Obviously what he wanted from Julia was a boost to his career, and she gave it to him by sending him to Brumleve who in turn passed him on to Steinberg-Farber. I understand they put him into a couple of their commercials and that they liked him. Nowadays, that can be a route to the top. So then maybe he figured he didn't need Julia any more."

"Wouldn't killing her be a little drastic? Why not just dump her?"

134

"Julia wouldn't have been easy to dump."

Swell grunted. "So far it's all conjecture, sweetie pie. Now be honest, isn't it? We can't even prove the relationship."

"I wouldn't say that."

"If he chooses to deny it, how are we going to nail him on it?"

"Well, for one thing, the very fact that Julia sent him to Brumleve . . . All right, all right. Somebody in the building had to have seen him with her, going in and out of her place, if not on the night of the murder, other nights," Mici insisted. "You could get a picture of Kord from the advertising agency and show it around."

"I'll do that."

"And what about those two officers in the squad car, what are their names? Emmenecher and Pace. Maybe they'd recognize the picture."

"Don't count on them. They've taken too much flak on this thing already. What they haven't remembered by now is forgotten for good."

Their steaks were served and they ate in silence.

"The weapon never turned up?" Mici asked when they were finishing.

"Nope. Never will either, if you ask me."

"There were no additional clues?"

"No clues period. Zilch. This Kord, if he was having an affair with the lady, was sure discreet. He didn't even keep a razor at her place."

"The autopsy shows that besides being beaten shortly before her death, Julia had had sexual intercourse."

"It doesn't show with whom."

"Kord, who else? Julia had a lot of men in her life, but, like the song, she was always true—to one at a time."

"I don't doubt you."

They continued eating. After the plates were cleared, Mici tried again. "How about fingerprints?"

"The lab came up with a couple of unidentified dabs. Assuming they turn out to be Kord's, there's no way to prove they were made on the night of the murder." Swell reached over and put his hand over hers. "You've

135

done your thing, Red; relax and let me do mine."

She nodded.

He patted her hand, then signaled the waiter for the check. "Listen, kid, I've got to run. You stay, take your time, have dessert, whatever." He pushed some crumpled bills at the waiter. "Give the lady anything she wants." He hesitated, considered, made up his mind. "I get off at midnight. How about I drop over to your place?"

"What happened to the flowers and the perfume?"

"This is business. I'm coming to report."

"Oh. Just to report?"

He looked straight down and into her eyes. His tongue flicked lightly out at the corner of his lips and disappeared again. "That'll be up to you, babe."

The phone was ringing.

Mici came to with a start. It took her a couple of minutes to orient herself: she was at home on the livingroom couch. It was dark outside; the lamps were lit. Conclusion: she'd fallen asleep waiting for Donald.

The phone went on ringing.

Yawning, making automatic note of the time—11:40—getting up and going into the bedroom to answer were all part of one continuous reflex action.

"Hello?"

"Miss Anhalt? Just a moment, please, Mr. Brumleve calling."

She reached under the shade and turned on the light at her bedside.

"Miss Anhalt? Sorry to disturb you at this hour." The lawyer sounded strong and very alert.

"Perfectly all right."

"I was wondering if you'd taken action on that matter we discussed?"

Mici considered before answering. The time, the very fact of his calling, indicated it was not an idle question. The ambiguity with which he put it suggested he was in a public place. She was mystified. "I took your advice and contacted the police but . . . unofficially."

136

She waited for a comment and, getting none, continued. "I passed the information to a friend, a detective on the Schuyler case. He'll look into it and let us know what he finds out."

The lawyer sighed. "I'm afraid it's too late. Alfred Cassel has been arrested. I'm down here at the precinct now."

"Oh, God! But his alibi . . ."

"They appear to have broken it."

"How?"

"I can't go into it right now."

"I'm so sorry."

"Don't be. Before you came to see me, I believed that Alfred was guilty. Now I not only believe that he's innocent, but I have a basis on which to defend him. What I must know is how far your friend has progressed with his inquiries."

"When was Alfred arrested?"

"A couple of hours ago. I got his call at nine-thirty."

"Well, then, I doubt that my friend could have gotten very far. We had dinner together. He left me at a little before eight."

"Do you think he might have passed the information on? To a superior?"

"I'll find out."

"That would be helpful."

Mici clenched and unclenched her free hand. "Is there anything else I can do?"

"For the moment, no. If something should occur, I'll call."

"Please do that." She let the receiver clatter back onto the cradle. For a few moments Mici just stood where she was, arms folded across her chest, feeling the pounding of her heart, the warmth in her cheeks, giving in to her anger. Her next move was to return to the living room and flip on the television. There would be a news broadcast at midnight. She sat down and waited for it. At about five minutes of the hour, the phone in the bedroom rang again. She ignored it; she didn't even look in its direction, but she counted ten rings before it finally stopped. At midnight precisely it rang again, but the news was on and she watched and listened to that.

When the phone rang the next time, she got up and answered.

"Hey! This is the third time I've called. Where were you? In the shower?"

It was Swell, of course. "No," she answered curtly.

He was puzzled by her tone but chose to ignore it. "Listen, babe, I'm really sorry but I'm going to have to break our date. Business. Something came up. *Capish?*"

"No, I don't."

"Sure you do." He laughed. "I don't punch a time clock. Something comes up, I stick with it and see it through."

"Like what? What came up? Did you make an arrest?" She heard him suck in his breath.

"How did you know? Was it on the news? Already?"

"No, it was not on the news."

"Then how did you know?"

"His lawyer called me. Alfred Cassel's lawyer, Oscar Brumleve, called me. You've heard me speak of him? He called and wanted to know if I'd informed the police about Janos Kord. I told him yes. I told him I had a good friend working on it. I felt like a fool."

"I'm sorry, babe."

"And don't call me babe or kid or sweetie pie. I hate it. You could have told me an arrest was imminent. But no! Great work, you said. You're a real terrific investigator, you said. You let me go on and on and all the time you knew. . . ."

"I didn't. I swear I didn't know."

"You were the one who made the arrest; it was your duty; you explained that to me."

"Yeah, sure, all right. It was me, but it wasn't on my own initiative. And I wasn't given advance notice, either. Oh, I knew LaRock had a team working to break Cassel's alibi, but I had no idea how close they were. I didn't find out till I got back from dinner. Then I was just told to tag along with the lieut and we went to the Algonquin. We waited in the lobby, and when an

138

inspector showed up I knew we weren't there for just another interrogation. Sure, I made the collar, but it won't be my picture you'll see in tomorrow's papers."

His bitterness convinced her. "How did they break Cassel's alibi?"

"I can't tell you that, babe . . . sorry, Mici."

She could make a guess. Alfred Cassel and Delissa Grace had been guests at a big movie premiere Friday night and at a party at the Tavern-on-the-Green afterwards. The movie ended at eleven-thirty and everyone headed straight from the theatre uptown to the restaurant. There was only one way that Cassel could have squeezed in a visit to Julia and arrived at the function along with everyone else—to which fact there were countless witnesses.

"He left before the end of the picture, right?"

"Right," Swell replied.

But how had they proved it? Mici wondered. Delissa knew, of course, but she wouldn't tell. "You found the driver who picked Cassel up in front of Julia's place and drove him to the restaurant."

"Not me."

One of LaRock's team, of course. That was what was griping Donald; he had wanted to be the one to break the case. She sympathized. "How could the driver make a positive ID nearly a week later?"

"As soon as he pulled up in front of the Tavern, the driver could tell it was a big celebrity affair and he was naturally curious about his passenger, figured he was a celebrity, too. So he looked him over real close," Swell explained.

As simple as that, Mici thought, feeling a twinge of the detective's frustration. "What does Alfred say?"

"What can he say? He has to admit he was there, but he claims he left Julia alive and kicking."

"Does he say anything about the scream the two officers heard?"

Swell paused a beat. "He says she was drinking beer and she wasn't too coherent. So he tried to take the can away from her and she screamed like a banshee."

Not exactly the death scream described in the newspapers, but a possible explanation, Mici thought, having been in Julia Schuyler's presence when someone was trying to separate her from a drink. "What reason does he give for going to see her?"

"To talk to her, to get her to stop spreading ugly rumors about him. Like that."

He couldn't have picked a worse time, Mici thought. Unless the police could now find someone else who had visited Julia later on . . . But they really had no reason to try.

"What have you done about Janos Kord?" she asked.

"Kord?"

"You haven't done anything at all, have you? You never intended to."

"Now hold it. That's not fair. I didn't have the time. The lieut grabbed me as soon as I walked in the door."

"So what are you going to do?"

"Have a heart, Red . . . Mici? Do you know what's involved in an arrest like Cassel's? Do you know how many hours I'm going to be tied up with the arraignment alone? It could run from twelve to sixteen hours, till tomorrow night, for God's sake!"

"I mean after that."

He groaned. "Listen, I might as well tell you straight. Both the brass and the DA are satisfied they've got the perpetrator. That's it. Case closed. Okay?"

"You mean you're not going to tell them there was another man? You're just going to forget about it?"

"It's not up to me. The case is closed, and I'll be assigned to something else. I'm sorry. I'm as disappointed as you are, believe me. Believe me. I have no choice. I do what I'm told."

"You could tell LaRock."

"It wouldn't do any good. Anyhow, your friend's got a lawyer. Let his lawyer talk to the lieut."

"You just said it wouldn't do any good."

"So then let him hire a private eye."

"That takes money."

Swell sighed lugubriously. "I'll do it. I'll do it. As soon as I've got some free time after I catch up on some sleep, I'll check out your man. Okay, kid?"

"Forget it."

"Ah, come on . . ."

"Forget it. I'll do it myself."

There was a long pause. "Maybe that would be best."

"What?"

Mici was stunned. She had thrown out the challenge impulsively, expecting that he would argue her out of it and end up agreeing to get on the case himself and promptly.

"It would be best," Swell reiterated. "After all, you can go anywhere you want, talk to anybody you want. It's your civil right."

"It is?" She was surprised he'd admit it.

"Sure."

"All right then, I will." She tossed her hair back. "I'll do it myself."

"Fine. And let me know how you make out." He was chuckling as he hung up.

The next morning Mici had a headache, dry mouth, rubbery legs, and all the signs of a hangover with none of the causatory pleasures to remember. Though the shower helped, she couldn't get down more than a cup of coffee for breakfast. She was due back at work, but she toyed with the idea of calling in sick. She'd never done that before and the fact that she was even considering it dismayed her. She had a good job, a job that basically she liked, and she ought to be glad to be getting back to it. She dumped some cereal into a bowl, poured milk over it, and sat down determined to eat.

The phone rang.

"Mici?"

"Oh, Adam, good morning."

"How are you feeling?"

She'd almost forgotten the reason that he was asking—the attack of the night before last. If she wanted to beg off work one more day, this was her chance. "Fine. I'm just fine, thanks."

"Good. Police come up with anything?"

"Ah . . ." She had to keep reminding herself that he was talking about the attempted rape. "No. I doubt

141

that they will. I didn't give them much to go on."

"You never know. Anyhow, I'm glad you're feeling better. You are coming in this morning?"

"Oh, sure." She made herself sound bright and eager. "What's up?"

"I'll tell you when you get here. Make it as early as you can."

Adam had a new case for her! Mici was sure of it, and she felt a surge of energy, a glow of satisfaction. Nothing like being good at your job and having it acknowledged. She could eat now. Afterwards she dressed quickly and when she checked herself in the mirror decided that she looked better than she had in days, her blue eyes were wide and bright, her red-blonde hair shining. She tossed her head in satisfaction and was humming softly as she closed the apartment door behind her.

She made it to the office by eight-twenty and stopped downstairs to pick up the coffee and jelly doughnuts that had become the traditional early snack when she and Dowd had a meeting. She marched straight into his office and set the paper bag down on a corner of his desk.

"We haven't done this in a long time," she beamed and started to set out the food, napkins, and plastic spoons as though laying out a picnic. Then she sat down in her usual chair. "So?"

Dowd looked tired. There were dark circles under his eyes, and his homely, pockmarked face was drawn. The man had troubles at home. His wife was an alcoholic. God only knew what kind of night he'd had.

The supervisor didn't touch his snack. He kept looking at Mici. "Clay Marin wants you off his case."

Her mouth dropped open.

Then Dowd delivered the second stunner. "He wants Lischner."

A tumult of events and their possible interpretations tumbled through her head. It must go back to the day she'd missed her appointment with Clay Marin and Wally had taken over for her. Wally had probably fed

Marin's indignation and sense of rejection, though why he should covet Marin as a client was beyond her—unless it was to denigrate her. Wally was an able investigator in his own right; he shouldn't need to put anybody down. As for Marin, he was an extremely difficult client, but she thought she'd done a good job with him and for him. Evidently she hadn't.

"If that's what Mr. Marin wants. Did he say why?"

Neither one was eating.

"He says you've been taking kickbacks from his doctors."

It was so completely unexpected, so baldly false that she couldn't speak.

"Specifically, he claims that you won't put through a request for surgery at the Retina Foundation."

That at least she could deal with. "That's not true. I told Mr. Marin that I would put the request through, but that I would have to append to it Dr. Harden's report advising against the operation."

"Did you put it through?" Dowd asked.

"Not yet. I've been meaning to." At the supervisor's heavy sigh, she hurried on. "It's okay, Adam. Both forms are still in my desk drawer completely filled out, dated, and ready to go."

"No, they're not."

"You looked?"

He nodded. "I had to."

She let that go for the moment to address the more crucial aspect. "They have to be there. Maybe you didn't look in the right place." His expression told her the search had been thorough. "Who could have taken them? And why? Why would anyone . . ." She stopped, closed her eyes for just a moment, and then answered her own question. "Mr. Marin asked me to suppress Dr. Harden's report stating that surgery would be useless, and I refused."

Dowd said nothing.

"Adam, the man has gone through three psychiatrists. He changes doctors like dirty socks."

"He claims that was your doing. He claims he was perfectly satisfied with each one of his physicians, but

143

you moved him because the doctors balked at paying you off."

She passed a hand over her eyes. "I'd like to laugh but I can't." She took her hand away and looked directly at the supervisor. "You don't believe this, Adam, do you?"

"The charge has to be investigated."

"Yes, all right, I understand that. What I'm asking is whether you yourself, personally, believe that I did these things?" She had recovered from her initial shock and confusion and was beginning to fight back. Her eyes blazed as she waited for the man who had taught and befriended her to give his answer.

"No, I don't."

She slumped back into the chair.

"But I can't ignore the charge."

"I don't want you to. Do you think I want to have this kind of suspicion hanging over me? All we have to do is contact the various physicians who treated Marin and . . ."

"Ask them if they paid kickbacks? They'd hardly admit it."

"Well, what am I supposed to do? How can I prove my innocence? I can't believe this is happening to me. I can't. I've done good work here. I have, haven't I?" Again she demanded an answer.

"Yes, you have."

"Yet on the unsupported word of an embittered man . . . Clay Marin hates everybody, resents everybody. He's lost his sight and is on the verge of losing his wife. He's trying to revenge himself on me because I refused to suppress Dr. Harden's report. Can't you see that?"

"Mr. Cornelius doesn't want even the suggestion of impropriety to tarnish the reputation of this office and the program we are administering."

"Clay Marin asked me to suppress a medical report." Mici spaced the words as though Dowd were hard-of-hearing.

"It's your word against his. We'll check with Dr. Harden, of course, and if he did make a negative report on Marin . . . that will certainly help."

144

"Wonderful."

"In any case, Mr. Cornelius has decided to send Clay Marin to the Retina Foundation. If the doctors there concur that surgery is not indicated, that will be another point for you."

"It should be a point for Dr. Harden," Mici said bitterly. "Never mind, I understand. Either way, Clay Marin wins. It's okay; he's the one who's sick." She got up, recapped her coffee container, put the untouched doughnut back into the brown bag, and reached for Dowd's portion. "Might as well throw this out."

He watched her with growing distress. "I don't think you understand the situation yet."

"Oh?"

"While Mr. Marin's allegations are being investigated . . ." He paused. The color rose in his face. "You're suspended."

There was a roaring in her ears. She felt as though the structure of her days had come crashing down around her, leaving her without purpose, without function.

"What about my current cases?"

"They'll be taken care of."

"You mean parceled out among the staff."

"That's it."

"How about Karl Spychalski? At least let me see him through?"

"The Spychalski case is closed. His claim has been disallowed."

She gasped. "Why?"

"You know why. The fire was of suspicious origin to begin with. It has now definitely been labeled arson. The Geramita brothers are out so that leaves—Spychalski."

"I know all that but . . ."

"He's the logical suspect and as long as he can't or won't offer an alibi . . ." Dowd shrugged. "There's nothing we can do for him."

Suspended! In plain language: dumped, not wanted, out of a job. Mici Anhalt left 270 Broadway in a daze

145

and headed for the City Hall park, oblivious of the throngs just going to work or of the traffic as she crossed against the light. Suspended pending investigation! Thanks a lot. Thanks for nothing. If the denials of the doctors allegedly involved were not sufficient, how in the world could she be cleared? The best she could hope for was a grudging "Not proven." That would mean that from here on she would be tainted, mistrusted, given the least sensitive assignments. In essence, she was finished at the Compensation Board. She might as well quit now while it could be done with a semblance of dignity.

The morning sun was already hot on this seventh day of the heat wave as she looked for a place to sit in the shade, but the shady spots were already taken.

Why was she so crazy about the job anyway? There was no future in it. It was a dead-end job. You were an investigator and you stayed an investigator till you were sixty-five or seventy or whatever the retirement age would be when you got to it. The only thing you could hope for in the way of advancement was to become the supervisor, and that meant sitting at a desk and handing out assignments. "Depressing," Oscar Brumleve had characterized it and he was right. Frustrating, too. So why hang on? She could probably get a job with one of the big insurance companies—less headaches and more money. Trouble was, Mici wasn't interested. She was too old to go back to dancing and too out of shape. Classes three nights a week were not enough to keep you in professional condition. Brumleve had said that, too. If she were thrown out of this job, what could she do with her life? At thirty-four, had she already missed the boat?

Mici could have understood an emotional outburst from Clay Marin. If he'd accused her to her face of taking kickbacks, if he'd raved and ranted, she might even have sympathized. But the cold, deliberate, behind-her-back scheming was what appalled her and made her feel so helpless. Of course, it would have been simple enough for Marin to steal the reports in her desk. Her office wasn't locked. All he had to do was

146

announce that he had an appointment, and he would have been left to wait in there for as long as it suited him. Yet somehow Mici didn't think it would have occurred to the blind man to go through her desk. . . .

She stopped short in the middle of the path.

How could the blind man have gone through her desk? How could he have known which documents to take?

If not Marin, then who? The answer was obvious: the man Marin had requested to take over his case—Wally Lischner. Why? Why should Wally do this to her? Surely not because of that one awkward date? Granted it had been worse than awkward—embarrassing for her, humiliating for him. But she thought he'd gotten over it. Evidently he hadn't. Evidently his friendliness had been pretense. Abruptly, Mici turned around and headed back toward Broadway. She was going back to the office. She was going to march straight up to Wally Lischner and accuse him to his face of setting her up.

"Watch out where you're going!"

A nice-looking young man dressed in a neat business suit had slammed into Mici's left shoulder, nearly spinning her around.

"Bitch," he muttered under his breath as he passed.

"Why don't *you* watch?" she was on the verge of calling after him, but the hate she'd glimpsed on his face kept her silent. His entire body was knotted with tension, she thought, as she watched him stride along the crowded, sunlit path. With so much hostility from a stranger, what could she expect from Wally Lischner? Naturally he'd deny her accusation. It would be her word against his, and at the moment her word wasn't worth much. What she had to do was get proof that it was Wally who had destroyed the application to the Retina Foundation and then put Clay Marin up to bringing the charge against her. She didn't know how she was going to accomplish it, but she did know that however satisfying it would be to confront Wally now, Mici would be tipping him off that she'd caught on. Keeping that knowledge from him was the only advantage she had.

* * *

Mici Anhalt was something of a fatalist but in the best sense of the word, a believer that time solves many apparently insoluble problems, or at least shows the way to solutions. The problem regarding Wally Lischner was one with which she hoped time would take a hand. Meanwhile, that feeling of emptiness that had come over her when Adam first informed her that she was suspended washed over her again. She felt lost and disoriented, without direction. But she reminded herself that she was also free of all obligations and could do whatever she wanted. For example, she could go and talk to Karl Spychalski and make one more try at getting an alibi out of him.

Then there was Donald. She could hand him a surprise by picking up his challenge. A slight twitch began at the corners of her mouth as she imagined the detective's reaction if she actually did approach Julia's lover. The manner of the approach suddenly occurred to her, and the twitch became a faint smile. It was a natural and what was more could only be handled by a civilian. She grinned broadly.

Why not? Mici tossed her hair back over her shoulders and spotting a food cart bought herself a hot dog, smeared it with mustard, and ate voraciously.

13

The actor emerged from the wings and walked out on the bare stage and down to the apron, peering into the dark house. He was tall, elegantly slim, with wavy blond hair and blue eyes. His lips were full, the lower one glinting sensuously. He squinted against the glare of the pilot light as he tried to locate the person or persons he was addressing. He couldn't and was forced to sacrifice intimacy and announce in a loud voice, "I am Janos Kord. I live at 333 West . . ."

"Thank you, Mr. Kord, we have all your particulars. If you'll just turn to act 2, scene 2 in your script, we'd like you to read the part of Phillip, please."

Eagerly Kord turned his head toward the voice coming from the left rear of the auditorium, at the same time thumbing the manuscript in his hand to find the indicated place. "Phillip. Yes . . . uh, ma'am."

"I'm Miss Anhalt, and you'll get better light if you step upstage, Mr. Kord," Mici called out with professional courtesy and coolness. "Mr. Zipprodt will cue you in. Please begin."

Oscar Brumleve had arranged everything—lent them the theatre, provided the script, one from the pile that every theatrical lawyer, producer, director accumulated. She'd got hold of Billy Zip and he'd agreed to act as stage manager for the audition. Billy had also arranged for other actors to participate to land authenticity. It was the only aspect of the scheme Mici felt guilty about—raising false hopes in these others.

Billy gave the cue, but Kord didn't pick it up.

"Well, Mr. Kord?" Mici called out with an edge of impatience. "Shall we get started?"

"I'm sorry . . . the light . . . there's so much glare."

"Do you have glasses? Well, use them, Mr. Kord. It's no disgrace to need reading glasses. Use them and let's get on with it, please."

Reluctantly the actor produced the glasses and put them on. They certainly didn't enhance his good looks, Mici thought, and smiled in the darkness.

"What is it now, Mr. Kord?"

"I'm waiting for my cue."

Mici sighed aloud. "Cue him in again, Billy, please."

The reading began. Though Mici was not interested and barely listened, she heard enough to know that it was going badly. Not only had Kord got off on the wrong foot, he was a bad actor. In the middle of a sentence she stopped him, abruptly and unkindly.

"Thank you, Mr. Kord. We'll call you."

His jaw went slack; he stood where he was. It took him a couple of seconds to respond. "But . . . I haven't finished."

"We've heard enough."

"But . . ." He was embarrassed at the poor figure he was cutting and angry at the treatment.

"We're looking for a certain quality, Mr. Kord," Mici told him, and she didn't need to add that he didn't have it. "If you don't mind, there are others waiting."

At that he gave a sardonic bow in her direction. Then he walked off the stage and another actor came on.

To the new man and to the others who followed, Mici listened with real courtesy. She complimented each one and tried to make him feel good about the reading without leading him to expect a job that didn't exist.

"How'd it go?" Billy Zip asked when it was all over and the last applicant had been heard.

Mici nodded. "The way we wanted, I think. Thanks for your help."

"Any time."

The purpose of the audition had been to lay the groundwork for a personal interview. She intended to wait a couple of days and then call Kord. He delighted her by calling her first, and he didn't wait. He called that very night.

"I want to apologize for my ineptness this afternoon," he began, charm oozing over the telephone.

Mici was cool. "How did you get my number?"

"There aren't that many Anhalts in the book; fewer females. I called each one till I got you." He waited for some comment, some recognition of his determination, at least. When it was evident there would be none, Janos Kord tried harder. "I'm notoriously bad at sight reading. . . ."

"A great many fine actors are notoriously bad readers, Mr. Kord. I'm aware of that. As I told you at the theatre, we are looking for a certain quality . . ."

"Please, I had the wrong glasses with me. I could hardly see the page. Nothing but confusion could have come through to you. Let me do it again. I could come
150

to your office, or to your home. I could come tonight if you're not busy."

"That would hardly be fair to the others."

"Give me a chance, Miss Anhalt. You won't be sorry, I promise you. Look, I'll read one speech, and if you stop me I won't say a word, I won't argue. I'll leave and I won't bother you again."

"Well . . ."

"That's a promise, Miss Anhalt, on my word of honor."

"All right."

"I'll be there in twenty minutes."

She expected Kord to make it ahead of time and arrive effusive and eager to please. Actually, he was five minutes late and didn't apologize. He did hesitate on the threshold when she opened the door, his blue eyes several shades darker than hers looking her over with appreciation. Then with one of his little bows, very respectful this time, he handed her a bunch of sweetheart roses.

"For interrupting your evening."

"I was just going to wash my hair."

"You have beautiful hair." He was moderating his tactics. "Excuse me for staring, Miss Anhalt, but you saw me at the audition; I didn't see you. I didn't expect you to be either so young or so beautiful." He was gauging her emotional climate.

"Did you bring your glasses?" she asked. "The right glasses?"

It didn't discourage him at all. "I don't need glasses to see you."

"You'll need them for the reading. That is why you came, Mr. Kord, isn't it?"

He made her another bow. "And I do appreciate the opportunity, Miss Anhalt."

"Is Kord your real name?" Mici asked abruptly.

"No, Korda," he replied. "I didn't want to appear to be trading on a famous reputation."

"Typically Magyar."

"It takes one to know one."

If he thought that their common ancestry established a bond between them, he was wrong. Mici was wary of Hungarian men, considered them utterly charming and completely selfish and ruthless—with the exceptions of her father and grandfather, of course.

"As you know, we're looking for an unknown to play the lead in our production. It will be low budget and we can't afford an established star. But we feel the material is strong enough to create a new star. However, we still require an actor with a strong theatrical background. You don't have many credits, Mr. Kord."

Instead of defending himself, instead of producing a string of meaningless and even false credits, Janos Kord counterattacked.

"Then why did you audition me?"

Mici smiled. "I saw a print of a commercial you made for Steinberg-Farber. It suggested possibilities. Also, you were recommended by Oscar Brumleve."

"Ah . . ."

"To whom you were in turn recommended by Julia Schuyler. I thought it an interesting sequence."

"Ah, yes, poor Julia. I'll never forget her."

"You were friends?"

"Good friends, yes. We'd worked together."

"What was the show?"

"*Sweet Bird of Youth.*"

A natural, Mici thought. Julia had always had empathy for a Williams heroine and though too young for this particular role she had tasted the disillusion that the part called for and would have projected the age with a minimum of makeup. As for Kord, his talents might just have stretched to the portrayal of the young lover. "When was this?"

"About four years ago. In summer stock."

"She was married to Cassel at the time, wasn't she?"

"Yes. He directed the show."

And outclassed Kord in every way, Mici thought. "What else? What other show did you do with Miss Schuyler?"

"Just that one, just *Sweet Bird.*"

"On a tour of the summer theatres?"

"Just that one week."

"Oh? She didn't carry her leading man with her?"

"Not then. It wasn't in her contract. Later . . . she tried to get me for the part, but I wasn't available."

I'll bet: Mici commented silently. "You must have had further contact with Miss Schuyler for her to send you to Oscar Brumleve." Questions which in another situation might have made him suspicious were natural in the guise of a job interview, and he was eager to answer them.

"We ran into each other on the street. She was looking dejected, lost. Turned out she'd been up for an interview. I was surprised; I didn't think a star of her caliber had to submit to that kind of thing."

"If the part is good enough and the star wants it badly enough . . ." Mici shrugged. "Carol Channing wasn't too proud to audition for *Dolly*, and Angela Lansbury for *Mame*. There are plenty of others and most of them are willing to admit it."

Kord nodded. "Julia didn't say so, but I could see that the interview hadn't gone well. We were standing in front of Sardi's so I invited her in for a drink to cheer her up."

Because he saw a chance to latch on to her.

"She had a hell of a lot more than one. It was embarrassing because I didn't have enough on me to pay the tab." Kord's sensuous lips twisted into a self-deprecating smile. "They know me at Sardi's, of course, and took my check."

They knew Julia and took his check because he was with her. Mici had no doubt that Kord made the check good and so established himself in the famous theatrical hangout.

"I took her home." He looked into Mici's eyes indicating that he had something to confide, then lowered his voice. "I was really horrified to see where she was living. It was no better than a tenement."

"Is that so?"

"I was appalled that Cassel would abandon her in a place like that."

Mici said nothing.

153

"I didn't like to leave her alone . . . in that condition but . . . there was nothing I could do for her."

He must have been frustrated, Mici thought. Obviously he'd misjudged Julia's capacity and had let her get too drunk. Mici assumed he'd learned just how much would get her to exactly what condition, and had been more careful on subsequent occasions.

"I called the next day to find out if she was all right," Kord went on. "She was very vague about everything, including me." Again that self-deprecating smile intended to engage sympathy, which, surprisingly, it did. "I must say I was annoyed. I'd spent a lot of money on the lady and not even to be remembered . . ." He shrugged.

Mici nodded sympathetically. She sensed that he was skirting the edges of the truth and wondered just how close he'd dare to go.

"A couple of weeks later I heard a show was casting and the director used to be a friend of Julia Schuyler's. I thought, what the hell, she owed me at least an introduction to him. So, as I didn't want to make any pitch over the telephone, I went over there. She couldn't have been nicer. Remembered everything, apologized for crying on my shoulder, and invited me to dinner."

"Did she give you the introduction?"

"Oh, sure, no problem. She was eager to help."

"But you didn't get the part."

"Actually, there was nothing in the show for me."

"I see. How about the Cassel show? Did she recommend you for that?"

"Well, they had split up so I didn't like to ask."

"And in any case, you knew Alfred Cassel. You could have gone to him on your own."

"Well, there wasn't anything in that for me, either."

"Too bad. Still, it may turn out to be your good fortune. We'll see, eh?" Mici dangled the bait. Then she withdrew it. "You must have been deeply shocked to learn of Miss Schuyler's murder. To lose such a friend, a friend so willing to help . . ."

"Julia was always generous to actors."

"Do you think that Cassel was actually beating her?" Mici asked abruptly.

"Beating her?" He was startled. Perhaps he'd expected her to ask if he thought Cassel had killed her?

"Yes. You must have noticed the bruises. If you were seeing her recently . . . In view of all the recommendations, including the latest to Brumleve, I assumed you'd been seeing her often."

"Yes, we saw each other, but of course I didn't feel I should mention . . ."

"You surely couldn't ignore her condition." Mici pretended to be shocked.

"Well, no, but . . ."

"Surely you offered your help. As a friend."

"I tried, but she was a very private person. She didn't want to talk about it."

"Too bad you didn't try a little harder."

"Don't think I haven't told myself that a thousand times. Don't think it hasn't cost me sleepless nights."

Mici let out a long, slow sigh. "I just can't understand a woman letting herself be mistreated like that."

"Some derive pleasure from it."

"Julia Schuyler?"

He shrugged.

"I'd call it sexual perversion."

Janos Kord smiled. "There's a lot of that around."

She felt that she had brought him as far as she could on this tack. Time to try another. "When was the last time you saw Julia Schuyler alive?"

A mistake. She knew it instantly. Fear leaped into Kord's blue eyes, followed by suspicion. She tried to make amends. "I'm sorry. It's none of my business. I had no right to ask. I'm sure you've told the police everything that's pertinent, and I'm sure they don't want you discussing it with anyone else."

"As a matter of fact . . ."

"No, no, please. Say no more. I was very indiscreet. Let's get back to business. Do you have a picture?"

"Of course." He handed her the standard eight-by-ten glossy, pulling it out of a manila envelope.

"How about your other credits?"

He rattled off a lot of inflated data: off-Broadway, off-off Broadway, independent films, stock, all tough to check—as she'd expected. He talked commercials and TV appearances. Part of the flim-flam. Mici let him go on till he ran down.

"Certainly, Miss Schuyler must have thought highly of your talents." Mici sweetened the disparagement implied with a smile. She reached for one of the pile of manuscripts she'd set out on the coffee table for the occasion.

Very conscious of the script in her hands, Kord murmured shyly, "I hope you'll think so, too."

She met his gaze, let him beam all the sensuality he could at her, then very deliberately turned him off. "That remains to be seen."

Janos Kord wasn't that easy to turn off. He got up, walked over to her and sat down beside her on the couch, his shoulder lightly brushing her shoulder, his thigh not quite touching hers. "I'm ready any time," he said, reaching as though to place his hand on her knee but taking the manuscript from her lap instead.

"Will you cue me in, Miss Anhalt?"

Mici didn't realize till then that she'd been holding her breath.

14

Mici decided to go and see Bettedene Barber once more. After all, it was the young hooker who had suggested that Julia Schuyler had a lover. And it was she who had set Mici on the trail of Janos Kord. She'd insisted that she'd never seen him, never had so much as a glimpse of him. Mici had no idea why the girl was so determined to deny ever having set eyes on the man she claimed had been beating Julia, and she hadn't pressed the matter then. But now she had to. She hoped that she had built up the teenager's trust in her.

She rang the doorbell of 3A and the voice that called out was the same as before, light and youthful.

"Door's open. Come on in."

Mici was completely unprepared for what she saw.

"Bettedene! My God, what happened to you?"

Her face was a misshapen assortment of bruises. One eye was ringed black and blue and nearly swollen shut. Both lips were cut. Her jaw was lopsided. Yet Bettedene Barber sat at her kitchen window calmly sewing a white organdy ruffle to the edge of a baby-blue quilted bedspread.

"Are you all right?" Dumb question, Mici thought. "I mean, nothing's broken? Have you seen a doctor?"

"I'm okay. I don't need a doctor."

Mici wanted to go to her and put an arm around the scrawny shoulders and cry. But something in the girl's manner held her off.

"What happened?"

"He found out. Dominic. My pimp. I guess he was bound to find out sooner or later."

Heretofore she'd referred to him as "my old man." Mici found this dropping of pretense as sad as Bettedene's mauled face.

"I knew he'd beat me if he ever found out, but I didn't figure he'd mark me where it would show. But I should have figured that in a case like this that would be exactly what he would do."

"I don't understand. What did Dominic find out?"

"About my boyfriend. I got me a real boyfriend. He wants to marry me. I've been seeing him up here on my own time, except I don't have any time that's my own," Bettedene qualified.

"But that's wonderful!"

"Not so wonderful. He won't want me now. Allan, that's my friend, he's real straight, got a regular job, lives in Queens. When he sees me like this—he'll know what I am."

"He doesn't know?"

"We never talked about it, but I suppose he had a pretty good idea. Thing is, he could pretend he didn't know. Now . . ." She shrugged.

"He might surprise you," Mici told her. "He might be ready to face the situation and just be waiting for you to let him."

Bettedene shook her head. "It's too late. I've broken it off. I called him and told him not to come around, that I don't want to see him any more." She continued to sew the pristine white ruffle to the blue quilt.

"You're prejudging him," Mici persisted. "If he cares for you, really cares, Allan won't abandon you. He'll protect you. Why don't you give him a chance?"

Now Bettedene stopped sewing and the tears rolled down her thin, battered face. "Dom said that the next time . . . the next time he'd do a job a plastic surgeon couldn't fix." She burst into sobs.

"Oh, my dear . . ." Mici went to her. She put her arms around the heaving shoulders and felt the sharp bones underneath and stood awhile just holding the trembling girl. When she seemed calm again, Mici made a suggestion. "You could go to the police."

"Are you crazy?" Bettedene shook free. "Dom would kill me."

Mici saw real terror in the young girl's eyes. "There's a shelter just five blocks from here for girls . . ."

"That's the first place Dom would look."

"Let him look. What can he do?"

"Nothing while I'm in there, but I can't stay in there forever and when I come out . . . Forget it, Mici. Forget it. You mean well. You're a real fine lady, but you just don't understand." She picked up her sewing. "What did you want? Why did you come?" As Mici hesitated, Bettedene did the reassuring. "Listen, don't worry about it. It's all part of the game."

"You could go back home. Bettedene, why can't you just go back home?"

"You came about the murder, right? I guess you don't think that Mr. Cassel did it."

Mici sighed. "No, I don't."

"Neither do I. I never thought they'd arrest him. If

158

I'd spoken up, maybe they wouldn't have. I'm real sorry."

This was what she had come for, yet now that the girl was apparently willing, Mici balked. "If it's going to make trouble for you, Bettedene . . ."

"Cat's out of the bag now," she shrugged. "I had Allan here the Friday night and I didn't want Dom to know. Well, now he knows. So anyhow, Allan was here till about one-thirty. When he was ready to leave I went out on the landing to make sure the coast was clear, to make sure Dom didn't have anybody lurking in the halls. Dom sends people to check up, make sure we're not holding out . . . like that. Well, just as I was about to give Allan the high sign, I heard Miss Schuyler's door open and this man just kind of . . . sidled out."

"Could you describe him?"

"I didn't pay any particular attention. As long as it wasn't anybody from Dom, I didn't care. You know?"

Mici groaned. "Try, Bettedene. Please, try."

"Well . . ." She scowled in concentration. "He was blond and tall."

"Did you see his face? Did he happen to look up?"

"Yeah, he did, for a second. I guess he was as anxious to make sure nobody was around as I was."

"Well?"

"He was good-looking. Real good-looking."

Mici stifled her impatience. "You already said he was tall. How about his build? Light? Heavy?"

"I'd say just right. I'm sorry. I really had other things on my mind."

"Sure." Mici refused to give up. "Had you ever seen him coming out of Miss Schuyler's apartment before?" Bettedene shook her head. So, Mici thought, she'd have to try for a direct identification. She took out the eight-by-ten glossy Janos Kord had given her and held it out. "Could this be the man?"

The girl took her time. "Real handsome, isn't he?"

"Is he the man you saw the night of the murder?"

"Could be. Yeah, I guess so."

"Are you sure?"

Bettedene's tongue licked her cut lips. "I guess so."

159

Not very satisfactory, Mici thought. "Did you hear any sounds from inside the apartment while the door was open? Did Julia call out to say good-bye, anything like that?"

"You're trying to find out if she was still alive when he left? Gee, I didn't hear a thing. Like I told you . . ."

"I know, I know. Let's go back to the man for a minute. Let's try to reconstruct his appearance. How was he dressed?"

The only thing that moved in Bettedene's poor smashed face were her eyes blinking open and shut, open and shut like a sleeping doll mauled by a bad-tempered child. "A suit, I suppose," she shrugged. "Nothing flashy or flaky, anyway. Nothing that caught my attention."

"How about a raincoat? It had been raining all night."

"I don't recollect a raincoat. I didn't take notice. I had other things on my mind."

"Well, was he carrying an umbrella? Was he carrying anything? A package of any kind," Mici urged. "A newspaper?"

Slowly the girl shook her head. "I don't think so. I just don't see him with anything in his hands."

It would have to do. Mici took the photograph back. It had not been the proper—certainly not the legal—way to get identification. She should have had a number of photographs and offered them all so that the witness could make a selection. She hadn't had them handy. Anyhow, it didn't matter, it would take a lot more than placing him at the scene to nail Janos Kord for murder. Assuming he were brought to trial and Bettedene agreed to testify, she was less than a reputable witness.

"I don't know if he killed her." Bettedene indicated the shoulder bag in which Mici had stowed Kord's picture. "But he was her lover. Take my word. And he was the one beating up on her. I'll lay you any odds you want."

Mici agreed, but as Bettedene had seen the actor

160

only once, even that couldn't be proved. "I appreciate your trying to help. I wish that . . ." Suddenly she had an idea. "Why don't you come and stay with me for a while?"

The girl was startled. Her face lit up; she even managed a shy, lopsided smile though it must have hurt. "You wouldn't want me."

"Yes, I would. Really. What do you say?"

"That's nice, but . . ." She thought a while, then reluctantly shook her head. "It wouldn't work. Not after the first couple of days."

Mici had spoken impulsively and now, already, was beginning to regret it. What Bettedene said was true. She was used to living alone, suiting herself, maintaining her own schedule. A roommate would inevitably disrupt that.

"And where would I go afterwards?" Bettedene asked quietly.

Mici flushed, shamed that she couldn't press the invitation. "Why don't you call Allan? Why don't you give him a chance?"

"You are dumb!" Suddenly the girl screeched; suddenly she lost control. "You are so, so dumb! Don't you get it? So far Dom doesn't know who the man is. He doesn't know Allan's name. I don't want him ever to find out. If Allan sees me like this, he'll go looking for Dom and he's no match for him. He'll get beat up like me—maybe worse."

"I'm sorry." Mici laid her hand over Bettedene's. "I didn't think. I'm sorry."

Bettedene shook it off. "Don't be sorry. Just try to wise up a little."

Mici bit her lip. "You could get out of town, you and Allan together."

"I just told you . . ."

"Yes, all right. Just you then. Alone. I'll lend you money."

"What happens when it runs out?"

"You get a job."

"Yeah. I don't know how to do anything."

"Sure, you do. There are all kinds of jobs for whic[h] you could qualify. There's waitress work and sale[s] work and . . ."

"Domestic work." The cut lips curled with disdain.

"Just to start, Bettedene."

"I could have had that kind of work back home. [I] didn't want it then; I don't want it now. You're wastin[g] your time trying to save me. I don't want to be saved[.] Bug off, Miss Anhalt, will you?" The girl picked up he[r] sewing. "Just bug off."

Mici dragged along Forty-fifth Street. The heat wa[s] just about unsupportable, but that was not what de[-] pleted her energies and made her feel so dejected. I[t] seemed that there was no way to prove Janos Kord'[s] involvement with Julia Schuyler, much less pin th[e] murder on him. Assuming Bettedene Barber's shak[y] identification stood up, which was highly unlikely, i[t] still placed Kord at the scene over two hours after th[e] presumed time of death.

So what was she going to do about Janos Kord? The[n] answer was—nothing. In time he'd get tired of waitin[g] to hear from her about the nonexistent play and call[.] Then she'd simply tell him the production was off. I[t] had run into snags and was indefinitely postponed[.] He'd heard that song before, why should he question it[?] In due course, Cassel would come to trial and she'd be[e] called as a prosecution witness. The DA would dub her "hostile," which would actually serve to give added importance to her reluctant account of Julia's charge that Cassel was the one who was beating her. Brumleve[r] or, if his health did not permit, whoever he engaged to handle the defense would point out the fallacy, but nevertheless the jury would regard that as an accusa- tion from the grave. The defense would argue hearsay and whatever else, but Cassel would be convicted and it would be largely due to her evidence.

Reaching the subway entrance, Mici went under- ground. It was even hotter. Sweat ran in rivulets all over her body, but at least she was out of the sun. She put a token into the slot and proceeded down the stairs[.]

to the uptown platform. Gusts of hot air caused by arriving and departing trains were like gusts from a giant fan.

Well, she thought, maybe Alfred was guilty after all. Maybe Julia hadn't lied. Maybe Janos Kord's relationship with Julia had been platonic.

Not in this world! Mici formed the words silently with her lips. As her train rattled and roared out of the tunnel and pulled up along the platform, she shouted out loud: "Not in this world!"

Nobody heard; nobody even noticed she was yelling.

A kid with a scraggy beard beat her to the only seat. Mici hung onto the strap above his head and thought about Kord sitting beside her on the sofa, script in hand, reading the lines on the page but investing them with a meaning that was wholly personal and directed at her. The man was incapable of any kind of relationship with a woman that didn't involve sex, particularly if that woman might be of use to him. Mici had no doubt that he had been Julia's lover and that he had beaten her and, worse, had been supplying her with liquor. He wouldn't have cared that she was an alcoholic; all Kord would have cared about was what he could get out of her. He hadn't needed to put a knife in her, Mici thought; supplying the booze was another form of murder.

Alfred Cassel said that he had left Julia alive around eleven-twenty and that she had been drinking beer. Kord had come in afterwards, bringing the scotch. Probably he had been trying to wheedle something out of her, more money, another introduction, whatever. She had refused; he had beaten her. This time she had resisted. He had stabbed her.

So what had he done with the knife?

In trying to recreate the moment, to put herself into Kord's skin and react as he might have reacted. Mici was only vaguely aware of her surroundings. She got off at her stop by pure habit and climbed the stairs to the street. She didn't feel the renewed assault of the blazing sun or the windblown grit that stung her eyes.

Okay, she thought, Julia's lying at his feet. He has

the knife in his hand and he realizes it has his finger-prints on it. He could wash it and put it back in a drawer. That would take too long; he's too nervous; he wants to get out. Okay. So he takes the knife with him, intending to get rid of it at the first opportunity. Does he just walk out with it in his hand? Hardly. He has to put it in something—a newspaper or a brown bag, if he can find a newspaper or a brown bag.

Mici scowled. Bettedene had said he wasn't carrying anything. She had seemed certain. It was the only thing she'd been certain about.

So, he puts the knife in his pocket: Mici continued her reconstruction. Raincoat pockets would be deep enough to hide even a large carving knife. Assuming that there'd been even one drop of blood left on that knife, there should be traces in the pocket.

A prickling of goose bumps brought Mici back to reality. She had been strolling; now she hurried. She couldn't wait to get home and call Donald. She hoped he wouldn't make a production out of the search, but of course he would. Donald Swell wouldn't do one blessed thing without being sure he was covered in all direc-tions. He wouldn't enter Kord's place without a war-rant, and Mici knew that no judge was likely to grant one on the evidence. What evidence?

The evidence she intended to find.

So instead of calling the detective when she got home, Mici called Kord's number. It was answered by a recorded announcement informing her that the actor wasn't at home and wouldn't return till eight. Very helpful. The next problem was to gain access. She could present her credentials to the super or claim she was a friend or even a relative from out of town—a cousin. She had a feeling the super might have heard the cousin bit before and decided to try it. She considered carrying a small suitcase to reinforce it but decided it wouldn't be necessary. She was right. All the super needed was one leering, longing look, and then he let her into the apartment.

It wasn't much of a place. Evidently Kord didn't

require luxurious surroundings for his conquests, or more likely, his rendezvous took place at the lady's pad. Mici couldn't have cared less. All she was interested in was his clothes closet and that was something else! The man had the best of everything: fine suits stored in individual bags, fine shoes polished and in wooden shoe trees. There were no overcoats—probably stored for the summer—but the raincoat was there. Mici brought it out, hanger and all, and laid it on the bed. She put a hand inside the right pocket. Deep, very deep. She turned it inside out. She peered at it. Nothing that looked like blood, no stain of any kind. Okay, the left. She turned that out. Nothing. No spots, no dust, no lint. God! Had he already sent it out to be cleaned?

It didn't look like it, but how could one be sure? Maybe he had another raincoat? She went back to the closet. No. Maybe he hadn't put the knife in the pocket. Maybe he'd held it inside against his chest. Or stuck it up one sleeve? Quickly, she took the coat off the hanger, turned it inside out, including the sleeves, and went over every inch of the lining.

"Hi, cousin."

She jumped, but before she could turn he had his arms around her waist, hugging her close, head buried in her hair and nuzzling her neck. She was too busy thinking of what she would say to do more than squirm a little; then it occurred to her that squirming was not the optimum reaction. She should cooperate; encouragement gained time.

Finally, of course, he was not content with mere nuzzling. He raised his head and turned her around so that they were face to face.

"Why, Miss Anhalt!" he exclaimed in mock dismay. "The super told me my cousin was here."

"I happened to be passing and I decided, on impulse, to stop by."

"Of course, of course. My dear Miss Anhalt, how charming."

He was smirking at her, smugly licking his chops over the conquest just achieved and the one yet to

165

come. Wondering perhaps how much of the preliminaries she would require, he glanced down at the bed and saw the coat spread out.

Too late Mici realized she should have tried to lead him to the other room. Too late.

"What've you got—some kind of raincoat fetish?"

15

Before Mici could answer, and she wasn't very quick because she didn't have an answer ready, Janos Kord noticed that the coat was turned inside out.

"What the hell is going on?"

She still couldn't come up with anything plausible. "Why don't we go into the living room?"

She made a move. He blocked her. "No, you don't. We'll stay right here till you explain, cousin." Taking a look around, Kord now noticed the door of his closet was open. "Why were you going through my things? What are you looking for? What the hell do you want?"

Mici sighed. At least he knew that she hadn't come to jump into bed with him, she thought. "Let's just say I didn't find it and let it go at that."

Once more she tried to get past him and again he stopped her, this time by grasping her right wrist. He pulled her to him in a movement that could have been passionate but had so much force that the pain brought tears to Mici's eyes. His face was near, so near that it filled the entire range of her vision, a close-up on a giant screen into which she felt herself being absorbed.

He shook her. "I want to know what's going on. I don't want to hurt you, cousin." He was still grasping her by the wrist, but now he raised his other hand, and it was all Mici could do to keep from shrinking in anticipation of the blow. Instead of striking, he laid the hand on her

166

heek, caressing her, and laughed because he knew
what she'd expected. "I don't want to hurt you," he
repeated, breathing faster. "I would prefer to make
love to you. Much prefer it."

She understood that the two would go together, that he
was both threatening her with the pain and promising
her its pleasure. Janos was arousing himself. And
Mici, who up to now had not doubted her control of
the situation, shivered and was dismayed to find herself responding.

No, she told herself, no. She felt the warming in
her loins. No! Yet she made no move to pull away,
staring instead into Kord's deep blue eyes, losing
herself in them. She felt her whole being melt, dis-
solve into his, and she wanted him . . . wanted
him. . . . He bent her arm back till she moaned but
still did not resist. It was pain and delight as he
put his leg between her legs and pushed her back
towards the bed. She felt degraded and exalted. She
marveled at her own sensations and, in that last sane
moment of disbelief of what was happening, she
rebelled.

"No!"

With a sudden movement that took Kord off guard
because he had thought her compliant, she wrenched
her arm out of his grasp and, wriggling free, ran to the
far side of the room.

"I'm not Julia Schuyler!"

He gaped at her. Thwarted when he thought that he
had conquered, Kord's eyes narrowed. "What's that
supposed to mean?"

Mici Anhalt was a strong, healthy, young woman,
her body fit and agile and kept so by her regular ballet
classes. Janos Kord was not much taller or heavier
than she, but in a test of strength she knew that she
could not match him. She might fight, kick, bite, and
scream, but in the end he would prevail. What she was
afraid of, still afraid of, was that in the struggle she
might let him win. Gritting her teeth, she bit back the
last vestiges of the sweet sickness she had briefly
tasted, swallowing it like bile. She understood Julia

167

better now. She pitied her, not as someone superior but as a sister.

"What about Julia?" Kord demanded.

She had to get out of there and fast, and the only way was to hit him with the truth.

"Will you let me get my handbag?" She pointed to it on the bed.

With a mock smile of deference, raising his hands as though he were at the point of a gun, Kord took a step back. Quickly Mici got the bag and pulled out her wallet to show him her ID.

"Crime Victims Compensation Board," he read. "You're not a producer?"

"No."

"There's no show? The audition, the theatre, the other actors . . ."

"A setup."

That was all Janos Kord cared about. He turned pale, stared at her transfixed. After moments that seemed to her interminable, his color began to return. She was almost relieved. His lips barely parted to release a slow hiss of air. His tongue darted out and in. He hissed again.

"You bitch," he murmured. "You lying, cheating bitch." He took one step toward her and before she knew what was happening raised his hand and slapped her.

The blow was full force and sent her reeling across the room and against the wall. There was no pleasure in this, none at all and thank God, Mick thought, looking around for something with which to fight back. There was nothing. She'd have to talk her way out.

"Don't you want to know why I went to so much trouble?"

"Oh, yes. And you're going to tell me. Make no mistake."

"I'm not alone in this, you know."

"At the moment you are. All alone with me."

"Oscar Brumleve set it up. It was his idea. He knows that you were Julia's lover and that she was giving you money. He'll show that you had as much motive for killing her as Cassel."

"If she was giving me money, why would I kill her?"

"Passion. You quarreled. You lost control. You don't have very much control, do you, Janos?"

He glared, then laughed. "And you have too much, cousin. A pity. It's all academic, in any case. Cassel was there on that night. I wasn't."

"Oh yes, you were . . . cousin," Mici mimicked. "You were seen leaving Julia's apartment well after Cassel was back at his party and among his friends. Don't bother to deny it. There's a witness."

He stared at her as though he thought that if he looked hard enough he'd be able to tell whether she was bluffing or not. "You can call on all the angels in heaven or devils in hell as witnesses, but I did not kill Julia. She was alive when I left."

"You were the one beating her, not Cassel."

He shrugged.

"Why?"

"She liked it. It turned her on. You understand that, don't you?"

Mici flushed.

"Julia wanted to be dominated. Most women do. In Julia's case, the need was extra strong because of her father. Her father ignored her through her childhood and afterwards. What she was looking for was a father figure and lover combined. For a while Cassel seemed to fill the bill. He was older; he had a touch of John Malcolm's style and talent, but then he walked out on her. Subconsciously, she believed that there was something wrong with her that both men she'd loved had rejected her. She turned to me. I was her punishment. She needed me."

"And why did you need her?"

"She was royalty, theatrical royalty, and I owned her. I could make her do anything I wanted. Not at first, oh, no. The first time I struck her she threw me out. I had asked her to give me a recommendation to a director friend of hers and she refused. She didn't think

169

I was good enough. In fact, she told me I had no talent, that I was a lousy actor. She laughed. That was when I hit her. I didn't mean to. Actually, I was shocked at having done it. I thought we were finished; I never expected to see her again. I didn't even make any attempt to see her or call her. . . ." He trailed off into silence for a few moments. Then he resumed. "*She* called *me* the very next day, said she'd set up the appointment I wanted for three that afternoon. She said it wasn't up to her to make a judgment on whether I was right for the part when she didn't know what the part was. That was up to the director. She suggested I stop over afterwards and let her know how I'd made out. I arrived with roses and a bottle. We drank, we made love, we argued—I don't remember about what, but she seemed to be trying to provoke me. I held my temper as long as I could; then it came to me that she needed an emotional catharsis and that she actually wanted me to strike her again."

And you obliged, Mici thought, and the pattern of the relationship was set. "What triggered it Friday night? Did you beat her out of habit or did you have a reason? An excuse, at least?"

"I hadn't even planned to see Julia on Friday night. I had another appointment, a business dinner. She called me at the restaurant."

"I take it the business was with a lady."

"The producer of the commercial you saw, or said you saw. A genuine producer," he taunted. "The phone was brought to the table and Julia's voice squawked across half the room. It was embarrassing. I took the lady home, but . . . the mood had been broken. The evening was spoiled. So I went to see Julia."

"To punish her," Mici concluded. "Only this time she wasn't in the mood for physical violence. She defended herself. She had a knife. You wrested it from her. There was a struggle and you killed her." She was offering him an out—self-defense.

He ignored it. "No, it wasn't like that. She knew that I'd be coming, that I'd be furious, and she was looking forward to the scene. In fact, she'd set the stage for it. I

170

walked in to find her sitting at the kitchen table scribbling on her dumb book and gnawing on a chicken leg. She had a smug smile on her face because she knew she'd ruined my evening. I knocked the chicken leg right out of her hand but not the smile off her face. Her adrenalin was flowing. She taunted me and screeched at me. The more I slapped her around, the bigger her high. I didn't know what to do to get through to her, to really hurt her. I wanted to make her feel pain. Finally, some instinct made me snatch at those pages she'd been working on, but she sensed what I was about and grabbed them first. We struggled; we fought over those dumb pages. She screamed she'd found a publisher, that they'd taken an option on the book. Well, of course, I didn't believe it. 'Who the hell would pay money for the story of a has-been?' I yelled back. We pulled some more and inevitably the paper tore and we were left standing there with the shreds in our hands and looking at each other. 'The book is about my father, not me,' she said and started to cry. I mean, she cried . . ." He paused as though analyzing it himself. "She cried like a heartbroken child, gave herself up to complete despair. I couldn't figure it. I mean, what the hell, it was only a few pages."

"Then what?" Mici asked.

He shrugged. "Then we went to bed."

Mici sighed. "What time did you leave?"

Kord started to answer, then caught himself. "If you have a witness, you already know."

She had to give him that. "Let me ask you this. If you were so angry at Julia, why did you bring the scotch?"

"What scotch? We couldn't afford that kind of booze. And I didn't bring anything that night."

"Are you sure?"

"Yes, I'm sure. Now you owe me some answers. Why do you care? What are you getting out of all this?"

"I'm working for Oscar Brumleve. I've been temporarily laid off my regular job and I need the money."

She was talking his language. "What did you expect to find here? Why were you going through my clothes?"

"I thought there might be bloodstains."

"On my raincoat? I wasn't wearing it. It wasn't raining."

"Yes, it was."

"It hadn't started when I picked up my date at five-thirty, and it had stopped when I went over to Julia's."

It was true the rain hadn't started till about six. As to when it had stopped, she'd been in Connecticut, but she'd check with the weather bureau. "She could have marked you during your fight."

"How?"

"Scratched you or cut you or bitten you."

"Would you like me to take my clothes off?"

"If you don't mind."

He smirked in surprise; then with deliberate slowness, watching her all the while, he complied. Janos Kord was proud of his body and he had a right to be. He was lean, well muscled, with good skin tone.

And there wasn't a mark on him.

What Mici had been looking for was not so much Julia Schuyler's marks on Janos Kord but her own.

He was clean. There was no sign of a wound between his shoulder blades. He was not the man who had attacked her after her date with Donald Swell.

As for the actor, if he'd expected Mici to succumb at the sight of him naked, he was disappointed. It was his back she'd wanted to see and, having made sure that the scars of her scissors were not on him, Mici quickly slipped out the door. Kord let her go. His moment had passed; further pursuit was useless.

Out in the street Mici hailed a cab; she was in no shape to ride the subway. Not till she was home with the apartment door safely shut behind her did the tension snap. Then suddenly her knees wobbled, hot and cold flashes alternated, and she shook all over. A shower and then a cold beer would set her right. But before any of that, before she would even kick off her shoes, she had to call Oscar Brumleve and tell him the good news. Janos Kord had admitted being with Julia well after Cassel was supposed to have murdered her. Cassel was in the clear.

Again she awoke in the dark to the ringing of the telephone. She remembered having a couple of beers and lying down, fully dressed, for a short rest before fixing dinner. She must have fallen asleep. The phone on her bedside table clamored insistently. She fumbled for the receiver.

"Hello?" she murmured in a sleep-hoarse voice.

"You took your time. Did you just walk in?"

"Donald? Is that you, Donald?"

"I want to talk to you. Don't go to bed. I'm coming right over."

The numbers of the digital clock glowed in the dark: 12:51. "Why? What's up? Donald? Donald . . ." He'd hung up. Mici started to laugh. *Don't go to bed.* Kord wouldn't have said that. She turned on the light.

Swell made good time getting there. "What the hell do you think you're doing?" was his greeting as he swept through the door and past her into the living room.

She was too tired to do anything but laugh weakly.

"It's not funny," Swell glared.

"Okay." She shrugged. "I made coffee and sandwiches for us, but I guess you're not interested."

"Well . . . I didn't have any dinner."

"Neither did I. Come on."

She led the way into the kitchen where she sat him at the table while she set out the food and poured the coffee.

"I'm really very disappointed in you, kid." Swell adopted an aggrieved tone. "I trusted you and you let me down. I thought we had a deal."

"What deal? I don't know what you're talking about."

"Come on, babe." He threw both arms out in a dramatic gesture of frustration. "I'm talking about all this investigating you've been doing. Oh, it was okay about the kid hooker; I'd already covered her. But this actor . . . this Kord . . ."

"Wait a minute. Just hold the line. I told you about him and you weren't interested."

"I said I didn't have the time."

"Okay, you didn't have the time. You told me I could go ahead and talk to him. You told me I was a private citizen and I could go anywhere, talk to anybody, ask any questions I wanted. It was my civil right. You as good as urged me to conduct my own investigation."

"Okay, yes, that's right, but . . ."

"You didn't expect me to come up with anything."

"If you did, I expected you to come to me with it."

"Why should I? I'm not working for you."

"Are you working for Brumleve?"

"Of course not, but considering the evidence I turned up to clear his client I could hardly not tell him, could I?"

"You should have told me first."

"So you could get the credit?"

"To hell with the credit. Don't you understand? You've made the whole squad look like shit. I mean, we had to release Cassel. We've got nothing on Kord. We're left holding the bag and it's empty."

"Sorry about that."

"I thought we were friends."

"So did I." Mici stared at him, her blue eyes growing lighter. "I was wrong."

"No, you weren't."

"You're using me. Or trying to."

"No!" Though his denial was instantaneous, his high color belied it. "I told you the case was officially closed. I told you that anything further that I did would have to be on my own time and that I didn't have any time."

"You told me to go ahead on my own."

"I said I couldn't stop you."

"You wanted me to do your legwork for you."

"No."

"Yes. Oh, yes. You were so understanding all along the line. You didn't mind my horning in on your territory. Secure; you said you were secure. You figured that I was your private pipeline to Julia Schuyler and Alfred Cassel and all their crowd. You figured that if I did come up with any kind of information and passed it on to you, you'd break the case." Mici shook her head dolefully. "Oh, Donald."

"I'm sorry, kid. Things haven't been breaking for me in the last few years. I figured this was a chance to make a big bust."

"I should have known that no pro lets an amateur mess around without a reason. You have a nice line, Donald. I really went for it."

"Ah, now, listen, it wasn't all a line. I like you. I really do. You're a real fine lady."

Mici blinked. "Gee, thanks." She smiled ruefully. "You know what? I don't blame you. I just wish you'd told me. If you'd told me straight out what you were after, I would have cooperated."

"You would?"

"Sure. All I'm after is for the real killer to be caught."

The detective's eyes lit up; he sagged with relief. "You're all right, kid. You're all right." He reached for her hand. "So where do we go from here?"

"You don't expect me to go on doing your legwork?"

"Don't put it like that."

"You've got some nerve."

"You've done great work. You're a born investigator."

"Just a minute. Hey, hold it. I had a lead. I followed it to its logical end. Kord is clean. He was Julia's lover, all right. He did beat her. He did visit her the night of the murder and they had intercourse. But he didn't kill her. She was alive when he left."

"You believe that?"

"He could as easily have said she was already dead when he got there. That way nothing would have changed. Cassel would still be in jail, and the police wouldn't be *forced* to look for a new suspect."

"So he's not so smart. He didn't think of it."

"When Kord arrived, she was working on her book and eating a chicken leg. As far as I know, neither of those facts were mentioned in any of the stories about her death. All you have to do is check the autopsy report and find out what the stomach contents . . ."

Swell took a breath. "Chicken. She died maybe an hour after eating chicken."

"That puts the time of death at about two-thirty or three Saturday morning."

"How do you get that?"

"Bettedene Barber saw Kord leaving Julia's place at about one-thirty."

"He could have come back."

"What for? They had a fight; they made it up; that was it for the night. The big question now is what happened to the manuscript."

"What manuscript?"

Mici waggled a finger at him. "Exactly. What manuscript? You didn't find anything that looked like a book manuscript when you searched the place, did you?"

"No."

"But Julia was working on a book about her father. Kord says she'd actually found a publisher."

"Kord again."

"Not just him, Billy Zip, too. He was helping her, transcribing her notes and so on. Check it out with him. The point is that Julia was working on the book when Kord visited her Friday night. They had a fight, and the pages got torn up. He didn't take them. By the time the body was found, they were gone. What happened to them? What happened to the rest of the manuscript?"

"If you ask me it's all part of Kord's alibi. Julia could have eaten the chicken a lot earlier. He saw the leftovers and said that she was eating when he came. Then he threw in the bit about the book just to add to the confusion."

"Kord is out." Mici was emphatic. "You remember the night you took me to dinner out on the island? When you brought me home there was someone in here, waiting."

"How do you mean—waiting?"

"He stayed hidden till I got into bed and put out the light. Then he tried to rape me."

"God! Why didn't you tell me?"

"Nothing happened. I had a small pair of nail scissors handy. I used them."

"All right!" Swell regarded her with admiration. "All right!" he repeated. "Just the same, you should have called me."

176

"I reported it to the precinct. It was dark and he was wearing a ski mask, so I couldn't give them more than an impression of height and bulk. It never would have occurred to me that there was any connection with Julia's murder . . ."

"What connection?"

"When I got back I found a note in my mailbox. It had been hand-delivered. It warned me to lay off."

Swell pushed his chair back and crossed his legs. "You marked him up pretty good with those scissors?"

"I did."

"How sure are you that Kord isn't scarred?"

"Positive."

Swell didn't ask how she knew.

"If I'd used my head, I would have known right away that Kord couldn't be the killer." Swell's eyebrows shot up. "At the time of the attack we didn't even know each other."

"Correction. You didn't know him." Swell frowned. "Of course, you weren't that active on the Schuyler case at the time. What did the note actually say?"

"It said: Mind your own business."

"I think you better look closer to home."

Mici nodded. She was already doing just that.

"And if you get any ideas, you let me know. Don't try to go after this guy on your own," Swell admonished. "Let me take care of it. Promise?"

"Sure."

"I mean it, babe. I owe you."

"No, you don't. Forget it."

"Listen, I want to get this guy for you. I want to do it. So you just let me know anything that occurs to you."

"That's nice and I appreciate it, Donald. I really do."

"That's my girl. Now about Kord, if he's telling the truth and Julia really did have a publisher, why hasn't the publisher been cashing in on the publicity?"

"That shouldn't be hard to find out."

Swell grinned. "That's the spirit."

"Me?" Mici gasped. She poked a finger into her own breast. "You expect me to canvass the publishers? No way."

"Ah, doll, I thought you felt a responsibility to your friend."

"I've discharged that responsibility. Julia did not die because I left her door on the latch. Alfred Cassel is not standing trial because I reported Julia's accusation against him. This real fine lady is out of it."

"But . . ."

"You do it, Detective Swell. Do it yourself. It's your job, not mine."

"Ah, babe . . ." He took her hand; he looked into her eyes.

"Save it. Save it for your girlfriend. Oh, that's right, you told me you have no regular girlfriend. You never did tell me why."

He let go her hand. He swallowed a couple of times. He looked away. "Ah . . ." He cleared his throat. "My wife won't let me."

"You're married?" Mici smiled weakly. "Oh, boy. Oh, Donald. You sure did a number on me. You sure did."

16

Could it have been Karl Spychalski who had tried to rape her?

As she walked down the street of identical, two-family row houses just east of the burned-out property, Mici Anhalt worried the question as she had been doing since it first occurred to her. Was it Spychalski who had waited in the darkness of her apartment till she came home, till she got into bed, then hurled himself on her? She could feel again the weight of the stranger's body, his groping hand, his fetid breath mingling with hers, and she shuddered, her skin prickling with revulsion. She had been working on two cases at the time—the ironworker's and Clay Marin's. Con-

178

trary to general opinion, the blind do not find it easier than the sighted to maneuver in the dark. They can only find their way in familiar surroundings, having studied and memorized the topography and the obstacles. Clay Marin had never been in Mici's apartment; he would have stumbled, knocked over furniture, and announced his presence long before he ever made it to the bedroom door. It had to be Spychalski.

Having reached the last house on the block, Mici climbed to the second-floor porch entrance and rang the bell marked Havelka. The Spychalskis were staying with Rose's aunt and uncle.

Spychalski himself came to the door. He had aged years in the few days since Mici had last seen him. His craggy face was eroded by grief; his cheeks were sunken; the skin hung loose around his jowls; his eyebrows had turned white. Worst of all, his strong, broad shoulders were stooped in defeat. Mici had never expected this man to give up.

Spychalski did not hide his displeasure at her visit and he would have liked to have kept her from entering, but Mici swept past him before he had a chance to collect himself and deny her admittance. He shut the door and followed her inside but stayed close, ready to let her out as soon as possible.

"I don't know why you're here, Miss Anhalt. My claim has been disallowed. I told you that I am not interested in pursuing the matter."

Even his voice was apathetic.

The voice of her assailant that night, though muffled by the ski mask, had been laced with lust and hate. Mici tried to put the man in front of her now into the mental image of the shadowy figure. There was, of course, only one way she could be sure.

She replied formally, "You need not accept the local board's finding as final, Mr. Spychalski. You have the right to appeal. In which case, your claim will be reviewed by the full board of governors."

A low gurgle turned Mici's attention to the corner of the room where a woman sat beside the window in the only comfortable chair. Rose Spychalski, turning the

179

pages of what appeared to be an old family album, was completely oblivious of Mici Anhalt's presence. Her face was a patchwork of skin grafts of varying shades of lividity. Bandages covered her arms and legs and probably swathed a good portion of her body. She should have remained at the burn center, but Spychalski had insisted on bringing her home and on her further treatment as an outpatient. She gurgled again, and it was hard to tell whether she was expressing mirth or sorrow. Physically, Rose Spychalski appeared to be healing, but mentally she was close to being in a stupor.

Putting her suspicions of the man aside for the moment, Mici concerned herself with the stricken woman. "I'm sure that if you appeal to the full board the decision will be reversed," she told Spychalski. "I'll do everything in my power to help."

"We don't want charity."

"Mr. Spychalski, I believe that your claim is valid and that you should pursue it. Besides, if the negative decision of the local office is reversed by the full board, that in itself will be a strong presumption of innocence. The insurance company might well decide on that basis to pay your claim."

For a moment the hard eyes glinted with hope. Then it was gone. "No."

"But why?" Mici pleaded. "You don't have to do anything. I'll do it all."

"No."

How could he turn it down? Mici was at a loss. Everything had gone wrong for this man in the past couple of years, starting with the loss of his job and culminating in the fire that had destroyed his home, killed his daughters, and apparently—Mici gazed at Rose Spychalski nodding placidly over the pages of the album—destroyed the sanity of his wife. Yet he was still physically strong and mentally tough. He'd have to be for what lay ahead, she thought. She took a slower, more comprehensive look around the cramped living room with its cut-velvet "suite," fringed lamps

180

under plastic covers, porcelain figurines protected by glass domes, and the inevitable battery of faded photographs on the mantel. The Spychalskis were sharing the upper half of the two-family house. Out of regard for Rose's condition, Mici had no doubt that they had been given the master bedroom while the Havelkas made do in what were certainly smaller, cramped quarters.

"You have to be realistic," she told Spychalski. "You'll have to move out to a place of your own soon, and your wife will require medical treatment for a very long time. Psychiatric treatment, too."

"I've got a job."

"Oh? I'm very happy to hear it, but . . . construction jobs don't last forever, as we both know. If the decision on your claim is reversed, at least your wife's medical expenses will be taken care of for as long as necessary."

"There'll be other jobs."

Mici just looked at him.

"If a man is willing, he can find work."

He knew, he must know, what she was after, and still he refused to offer an alibi. Mici thought she understood why he wouldn't tell his whereabouts at the time of the fire. He'd been with another woman. Whether it had been a one-time thing or an ongoing relationship; she thought the ironworker was afraid that the shock would finally destroy his wife. Mici had come to promise him confidentiality, but she could hardly do that in Rose Spychalski's presence. Though she didn't think that Rose was aware of anything going on around her, she had no right to take the risk.

"I have some papers here that I would like to go over with you. Is there some place we could . . ." Her eyes pleaded for a few moments alone.

"I am not interested, Miss Anhalt. I told you before, and I haven't changed my mind and I never will."

It couldn't be plainer. She got up. "It's your decision, sir."

She started for the door, but a cry stopped her. It came from the corner where Rose Spychalski sat, a harsh gasp deep down in her throat. She seemed to be trying to speak. Mici and Spychalski hurried to her with one accord, but all she could produce was a series of inarticulate choking sounds.

Her scarred, patchwork face was contorted; she began to heave convulsively. But she was not having a fit, Mici realized as she watched helplessly. Rose Spychalski was sobbing. Her eyes were dry, but she was crying.

Gently, her husband took the album from her nerveless hands and, finding no convenient place to set it, handed it to Mici. Then he lifted the pain-wracked body and, murmuring softly as he might to a child, carried her into the next room.

He kicked the door shut behind him, but Mici could still hear the retching sobs and Spychalski's rough voice in its surprising gentleness.

Had she intimated too much in Rose's presence? Mici wondered. Was it possible the wife knew what her husband had been up to at the time of the fire? And was she torn now between the need to pretend she didn't know and the need to admit that she did so he could exonerate himself from the suspicion of arson?

That was a problem to be resolved between them, Mici decided. The sobs inside the bedroom were subsiding. There was nothing more she could do here, no point in waiting for Spychalski to come out. About to set the album on a table, some instinct made her open it and look inside. She had assumed it to be the Havelka family album with perhaps a few pictures of Rose as a child, of Rose's parents, but as she turned the pages Mici saw only pictures of Rose and Karl.

She sat down in the chair beside the window and started at the beginning.

There were courting pictures, wedding pictures, pictures of what had apparently been the first home, the first baby, the second, the new house, the new car, the girls growing up. It was only half filled. It was the Spychalski family album and the blank pages would remain blank forever. But how had it gotten here to the Havelka home? Rescued from the fire by Rose Spychalski who had not been able to save her own children? There were no traces on the cover or on any of the pages of charring or smoke damage. The book was worn by handling but otherwise in good condition.

The answer was taking shape. It was ugly and infinitely sad. Mici was still sitting by the window, still holding the book, when Spychalski returned.

He had not expected her to be there.

"How is she?" Mici asked.

"Resting. I gave her a tranquilizer. I have made my decision, Miss Anhalt. I thank you for your trouble and your concern, but there is nothing for us to discuss."

She stayed where she was, the open album still on her lap. "I understood that nothing was saved from the fire."

"Nothing was."

She closed the album and put her hand on its cover. "How did this get here?"

He stared at it. He swallowed. His face was granite gray, bleak but determined. It took him a very long time but he found an explanation. "I brought it over . . . before the fire . . . to show relatives. We had relatives coming to visit . . . from Omaha."

"Why not show them the album in your own home?"

"We could not afford to entertain them. They were to come here, so I brought the album here."

"Why didn't you take it back? After your relatives had seen it, why didn't you take it back home again? Your relatives were from—Omaha, did you say?"

"I forgot. Yes, Omaha."

Sadly, Mici watched as he tried to evade the net. "When? When were they here?"

"Ah . . . they didn't come, after all. We had the fire. So naturally it was not a good time for them to come to visit."

"I see." She sighed. "So you brought the album over before your relatives even arrived and left it here. Then there was the fire."

"That's right. Yes. It was preserved by chance. Pure chance. We are fortunate," he said bitterly. "We are fortunate to have this much left of our lives."

"*You* brought it here?"

"Yes."

"Providentially."

"Yes."

No, Mici thought, *not providentially; on purpose.* The album had been brought over here before the fire by the person who had set the fire. To preserve it. Spychalski did not seem like a person who would be so sentimental, but his wife did. Mici thought about the woman sleeping in the next room, ravaged by burns, by the loss of everything she'd held dear in her life, but worst of all ravaged by guilt. Her man had been out of work for over two years. They'd been in dire straits. They would have lost their home anyway when they could no longer meet the mortgage payments. The insurance company could have saved them and even made it possible to build a new home eventually. Probably the earlier garage fire set by the Geramita boys had suggested the plan. She must have reasoned that they would be blamed and that they would get off as they had before when they had actually been responsible. To speculate on what she would have done if the boys hadn't been exonerated was fruitless; that part of the plan had gone as anticipated. The rest had been disaster. Rose Spychalski had chosen a time for the fire when her husband should have been at his hiring hall, the two girls safely at school for a drama-club meeting, and she herself away from the house in the course of her regular routine. She hadn't known till she was a distance from the burning building, till she heard their shrieks from the upstairs bedroom, that the girls had come home early—and that they were trapped. She ran back, but she couldn't save them.

Mici had no idea how Karl Spychalski had found out that his wife had set the fire, but she was certain that he knew. Had Rose babbled in her sleep? Or under the influence of the painkilling drugs? Was that why Spychalski had insisted on getting her home before anyone else made sense of her ravings? At least Mici now understood why he refused to produce an alibi for himself. He never would. As long as suspicion remained directed at him, his wife was safe.

Mici raised her eyes. Of course he wanted the case closed. Naturally he didn't want a review. He didn't want anybody, particularly Mici with her good intentions, meddling. He had broken into her apartment intending to frighten her off, but she had stabbed him with the scissors before he could deliver his message. So then he'd left the note in her mailbox not realizing that there was another case to which it could refer.

Spychalski took a step toward her. His sagging shoulders had squared; his slack jaw was so tight it set the pulse at his temple throbbing; his bloodshot eyes burned fiercely.

Mici got out of the chair and took a step sideways. If she screamed, who would hear?

Not the woman in the bedroom who was locked into a fantasy world. Downstairs? She had no idea whether there was anyone downstairs. In any case, Spychalski could easily stifle her screams with one big hand. She looked around quickly. The ornaments were glass and porcelain which would break and cut superficially. While her eyes darted wildly, he took another step toward her and extended his hands. They could circle her neck and crush it, she thought. She flinched but held her ground.

"It was just chance that the album was preserved." Karl Spychalski's strong hands trembled, they were reaching out not for her throat but to take the book. "It was just chance that I brought it over here," he repeated and his voice broke. He was not threatening. He was pleading, begging for her silence.

Mici hesitated. Spychalski's claim had already been disallowed by the compensation board. The insurance company was not likely to pay off on his policy. So what purpose would be served by charging Rose Spychalski with arson and involuntary manslaughter? She had set the fire that had killed her children. It was their dying screams that she listened to in her near catatonic state, their screams that were shutting out all other voices, all other sounds. Could there be a worse hell for Rose Spychalski? Or for the husband who shared it with her?

Mici put the heavy book into Spychalski's hands.

"Lock it up," she advised. "Or better yet, destroy it."

Mici hadn't needed to look for a possible scar on Spychalski's back. The clue to the man who had assaulted her was in the nature of the attack. Violence obviously was not in the ironworker's character; that was clear in his reaction to her discovery. There was only one other candidate left, and she didn't feel like confronting him on her own. She had to call Donald once more.

"Oh, say, babe . . . I mean Mici. Nice to hear from you. Got over your mad, huh?"

She marveled at his resilience and was at the same time amused. "You wanted to make a deal."

He was instantly on the alert, eager and at the same time wary. "What kind of deal?"

"Oh, well, if you've changed your mind . . ."

"No, no. Keep your shirt on. What's up?"

"First, did you find out who Julia's publisher is?"

"Sure, no sweat, but they don't have the manuscript. Seems all she showed them was a few chapters and an outline. They were interested, but they told her she had to jazz it up, make it more sensational. So she took the thing home with her to work on it. Now, of course, they're eager to get their hands on it."

"They have no idea who might have it?"

"None. They called Brumleve, thinking that since he's the executor of the estate he might know. But he'd never even heard of its existence."

"Well, I've got an idea."

"Where do you think it is?"

"First I want you to do something for me."

"What?"

"Come on, Donald, for once in your life make a commitment on trust."

"It's not that I don't trust you, kid . . ."

"You do realize that whoever has the manuscript is the killer?"

"Probably."

"No probably. There'll be proof."

"How do you mean, there'll be proof?"

"It had stopped raining, you see. I hadn't realized that till Kord mentioned it. Then I called the weather bureau and was told that in mid-Manhattan the rain had stopped completely just before midnight."

"So?"

"So the killer wasn't wearing a raincoat."

"Are you enjoying yourself?" he asked with exasperation.

Mici laughed: then she sighed. "Not really. Billy Zip was helping Julia with the book, but he considered it therapy for her. I don't think he ever expected that she would find a publisher."

"So? He should have been glad for her. He was her buddy, right?" Swell asked.

"He loved her," Mici replied simply.

17

Activity in the news building was at its height; the last live show of the day, the eleven o'clock report, had yet to go on the air. By contrast, the main building next door was just about shut down and most office and production personnel had long since gone home. Billy Zip, however, had not. He was working on a special, and Mici knew that he would be in the studio till every detail had been checked and double-checked. From the street the brightly lit reception area appeared deserted, but as soon as Mici walked in, guards materialized as though out of nowhere to challenge her. She showed her ID and was allowed to pass through to the elevators.

She rode up to the inevitable and irritating accompaniment of canned music. On the third floor she stepped out into a wide, dimly lit corridor. The doors hissing shut behind her cut off the canned music. Suddenly she missed it. The difference in atmosphere between the offices downstairs and the studios up here was palpable. She found the silence oppressive. Her steps echoed hollowly as she walked along the shadowy hallways cluttered with flats, props, cables, dismantled spotlights, all kind of theatrical paraphernalia. A faint light showed behind the glass insets of the swinging door to studio B. Mici put a hand against the push panel, then hesitated. She was supposed to meet Donald but she had come early—not to put one over on him, not even because she thought she could handle the interrogation better than he, though she believed she could. Actually, Mici Anhalt would have preferred to have no part in the coming confrontation. Billy was an old friend. What had happened between him and Julia had been inevitable, programmed into their relationship from their very first meeting. Mici had arrived before the detective to make the ordeal a little easier for Billy. She considered William Zipprodt as much a victim as Julia Schuyler.

Squaring her shoulders, tossing her loose hair back, Mici gave the door a firm shove and entered the studio.

There was nobody there. The light that she had seen through the glass came from a weak dome fixture. In contrast to the standard stage worklight, this was less garish and hurtful to the eyes. It was also less eerie, producing none of those harsh and mysterious shadows, instead turning the empty studio into nothing more than a prosaic warehouse of unused equipment. The mini sets—the camera requires only that portion of a scene which its lens will encompass and not the complete setting required for the stage—were arranged in the usual pattern on the perimeter with the cameras in the center of the floor, from which position they could swing back and forth, dolly in and out, as the action required. To the left, at the far end of the studio and almost completely hidden by a stack of unused flats, Mici could just glimpse the glass front of

188

the control room. While the show was on the air or being taped, the control room would be dark, lit only by the glow from the bank of monitors inside. Now there should be some light. Mici frowned because she could discern none.

"Hello!" she called. "Billy? Hello!"

There was no answer. Naturally, there wouldn't be; the control room, like the studio, was soundproof, and unless the audio switch was open he couldn't hear her. He couldn't see her either because those flats were in the way. Carefully picking a path between snaking cables, dodging spotlights and cameras, and ducking under booms, Mici reached the center of the floor and stood in what she thought was a narrow sight line to the booth. Now he should be able to see her if he looked. She waited, but nothing happened. Obviously he was too immersed in his work. There was nothing to do but go around to the control room itself. Left or right? She chose left simply because the way seemed a bit clearer. She had just taken the first few steps when the ceiling light went out and she was hit full face by a baby spot that dazzled and momentarily blinded her.

"Billy?" She stopped where she was, blinking. "Billy?" She squinted, then, shielding her eyes, tried to see past the glare. "Turn that thing off, will you, Billy? I have to talk to you." She assumed that now the audio was on.

There was no answer from the control room.

"Let's not play games, Billy. This is important. Either come out here or let me come in there. Okay?"

Still no answer. If he was testing his lighting, then he must surely look up and see her.

"It's about Julia's book, Billy. The publisher wants to go ahead with it, but he doesn't have the manuscript. If you can produce it and show that you were helping Julia with it, you can probably make a very profitable deal. It would mean a lot of money and, what's more, recognition. You deserve it, Billy. After all these years, you really do."

No sound from the control room, none at all. Did he have the audio on? Was he listening? She had no idea.

All she knew was that the glare of that spotlight made her feel like an insect under a microscope. Head down, eyes on the floor, Mici shuffled out of its reach. But she had barely savored the relief when it went out and another spotlight came on, pinpointing her again.

"Ah, Billy!" she cried, convinced that he did hear her as plainly as he saw her. "What is this cat-and-mouse bit? You and I go too far back for this kind of thing. We're friends. Either let me in there or you come on out here."

Silence. She took another couple of steps forward, testing, and sure enough the light illuminating the area she'd been standing in went out and a new spot brilliantly lit the area into which she'd moved.

"Okay, Billy. I'll give it to you from here, since that's the way you seem to want it. The publisher is anxious to go ahead with Julia's book. If you can produce the original manuscript and notes, they're prepared to draw up a new contract with you as author." She waited a beat. She hadn't actually spoken to the publisher, but it was a reasonable assumption. "Of course, you don't have to deal with them at all. You can take the material elsewhere. If you have it."

Still no reply, but now Mici thought she detected a low hum which meant an open mike. She intensified her appeal. "I know you didn't approve of Julia's writing the book, but there will undoubtedly be a rash of books about her now, so why not give your version of her life? You've got the inside track, particularly if you can produce her manuscript. You can, can't you, Billy?"

By now she was growing accustomed to the spotlight. It was like being on stage. The audience was out there; you could sense their presence, but you gave a better performance if you tried to forget about them.

"I know that you loved Julia and I know you put up with a lot from her. I know you were deeply dejected when she married Cassel, but you also liked Alfred and respected him and so you could accept the marriage. When they broke up you must have hoped, you must have expected that Julia would finally turn to you.

"But she didn't turn to you. Instead, she took a new

lover, a man completely unworthy of her and who treated her shamefully. You were deeply hurt, but she needed you as never before and you remained loyal. Still, it must have been terrible for you, knowing how Janos Kord used Julia and abused her, sucked her dry and degraded her. You tried to help her, to hold her together, to save her pride. You used the book to that purpose. You told me yourself that you didn't have much hope for it, that you were doing it with little expectation that it would amount to anything. Night after night, when you were through here at the studio, you'd go over to her place and pick up her scrawled pages and try to make sense out of them. You pored over them, edited them, typed them."

She paused. Up to now, Mici had been on firm ground, but she was moving into the realm of conjecture, using her instinct. She believed that she could put herself into the skin of these two people because she'd known them and felt affection for them.

"Then one day Julia went out and actually sold the book. But she didn't tell you. How did you find out? Maybe you happened to find the contract among the papers you took home with you. She wasn't exactly orderly, was she? Anyhow, you discovered that you weren't mentioned in it; no credit was given for your part of the work and certainly no financial consideration, though I'm sure that didn't matter to you. You were deeply hurt. It was the final humiliation, the bottom line to the years of loyalty you'd lavished on Julia Schuyler. You knew that her friends had always looked down on you, considered you Julia's *gofer;* now it seemed that that was her opinion of you, too."

Mici was coming to the climax. She believed that she had reached Billy Zip's reason and touched his emotion and that very soon he would admit the truth.

"I know that you never meant to hurt Julia. I know that, after all these years of loving her and serving her, you couldn't deliberately hurt her. I think you were upset and angry and determined to get the recognition you deserved. You went over there and told her you couldn't continue with the book unless you got credit.

191

You threatened to walk out on her. She told you to go ahead; she didn't need you; she could write the book herself. You quarreled. Somehow, she got hold of a knife. She'd been drinking and she didn't know what she was doing. She came at you with the knife. In trying to turn it away from yourself, you turned it on her. It was an accident. Any jury will see that."

The hum of the open mike was clearly audible; now it intensified and became a shrill feedback.

Mici winced till it subsided. "Where is the manuscript, Billy? Julia had it on Friday night. Janos Kord saw it when he was there after midnight. Now it's gone. You have to produce it or your story won't hold up. The manuscript is your defense. You do see that, don't you, Billy?"

A new dread seized her. Suppose while she was talking he'd slipped away to destroy the evidence. "Billy?" she called out. "Billy!" She took several steps forward till once again she was out of the spotlight, in darkness. She waited for another light to blink on and pick her up, but none did.

"Billy! Billy, listen to me. You have got to produce that manuscript. Billy, answer me."

The answer was an explosion. Throwing her arms up around her head, Mici cringed, expecting a rain of plaster and God knew what kind of debris to shower down on her. It took seconds that seemed like minutes to realize that the blast was pure sound—music, if you could call the ear-shattering, magnified discordance music. It was fed from the control room through speakers all around the studio so that it seemed to surround her and at the same time to be directly focused at her.

"Turn it off!" she shrieked.

She couldn't hope to stop it.

Well, at least he was still there, she thought, and he'd given up trying to blind her with those damned spots. So she was finally able to make her way around to the side and up the flight of steps to the control-room door. It was open. She stepped inside. Within the confined space the sound was physically painful. Squinting in the gloom she could just make out the stage manager at the control console. How could he bear the noise? She took a couple of steps toward him, and as her eyes adjusted she saw that he was slumped forward across the counter. On the back of his stark white shirt, a black stain was spreading.

"Billy!" She ran to him.

He didn't stir. His head was nestled in the crook of his left arm and his right arm was stretched out to its limit, fingers clawed, groping among the various switches. *Oh God, my God!* Mici thought. Gently, she turned his head to look into eyes that were wide open, unblinking, pupils dilated. No use. There was nothing to be done. She was too late. She had waited too long.

In a sudden fury of frustration and self-blame, Mici reached across the body, found the master switch, and flipped it. Everything went off—light and sound, inside and out. Then, turning blindly, banging her shins against a filing cabinet, knocking down what sounded like a stack of metal film cans, she blundered out of there. In the corridor she managed to take the wrong turn and went down fire stairs that led directly to the street. Once out, she couldn't get back in again and had to run around to the main entrance. She nearly crashed into Donald coming from the opposite direction.

He grabbed her and held her. "Hey, hey. What's the matter? Where are you going?"

"He's dead. He's dead. Billy. Poor Billy. All the time I was out there talking to him, or thought I was talking to him . . . poor Billy Zip—Zipprodt. William Zipprodt," she amended in an attempt to show respect. "Come on." She grabbed the detective by the hand and literally dragged him into the building. As before, guards appeared, startled by Mici's obvious distress, but Swell showed his badge and waved them off. The two of them barely broke stride on the way to the elevators.

On the third floor, Mici took him to the double door of studio B. "Here, I went in here. I thought the audio was open so I was talking to him, but when he didn't answer . . ." Realizing that the place was pitch-dark and Donald didn't know what she was talking about, she took his hand again and led him to the control

193

room by way of the corridor, still dark as she had left it. Feeling her way along the counter, she found the master switch and threw it. The monitors, the studio spots, the sound, everything came on.

Donald jumped.

Mici turned the sound off, then stepped to one side so that he could see the body.

"I was out there," she pointed through the glass, "and he was in here. Every time I moved, one spotlight went out and another came on, following me. Like this." She manipulated various switches, a trial-and-error process but close enough to give the detective the idea. "On and off. On and off. I thought he was baiting me, but he was calling for help." She pointed to the stage manager's outstretched hand. "He was dying. He couldn't reach the audio . . . see. It was just beyond him so he used the lights to attract my attention. I didn't understand. I didn't understand."

"Okay now, kid, take it easy."

"He was calling for help."

"Now, babe, you couldn't know that. There was no way you could have known." He patted her shoulder with gruff sympathy. "Listen, how the hell do we get some regular light on in here?"

She pointed to the ordinary light switch just inside the door. After Swell put it on, things seemed more normal, as normal as they could be with a dead man sitting between them. The detective turned his attention to the body, feeling first for the carotid artery, and for one wild moment Mici thought she might have been mistaken, that Billy Zip might still be alive. Then Donald took his hand away.

"How long do you estimate you were out there?"

"Maybe ten minutes. I don't know. It's hard to say."

He scowled. "Why the hell couldn't you have waited for me?"

She glanced at the electric clock on the wall and noted that he had come early, too. "Were you intending to wait for me?" she challenged. "Oh, let's not squabble, Donald. I feel bad enough. The man was dying in here and I stood out there giving a monologue."

194

Swell sighed. "First things first. I've got to report . . ." He glanced at the row of telephones along the back wall and decided against using one of them. "There must be a booth outside. Come on."

She was glad to get out and quite content to sit in the chair Donald indicated in the hall. She wasn't at all aware of the fact that he had placed her where he could keep an eye on her while he made his call. As she had no basis for comparison, she didn't realize that it was unusually lengthy.

"The lieutenant's coming over himself," he informed her when he came out of the booth. "He wants to talk to you."

"Okay."

"So you just sit there while I go back and see if I can locate the manuscript."

"You're wasting your time. Why do you think poor Billy was killed?"

"For the manuscript?"

"What else?"

"According to you, he was the killer."

"I made a mistake. I was wrong about Billy. And belive me, I regret it. I was wrong from the beginning. I see that now."

"Fine."

"Somebody doesn't want that book published and we've got to find out why."

"Okay, you think about it and let me know." Swell started for the control room.

"Do I have to? Wait, I mean."

"You're kidding. You're a witness, for God's sake!"

"I've already told you everything."

"By your own admission, you were alone with the victim for a full ten minutes."

"I was in the studio; he was in the control room. The areas are separate and soundproof. I couldn't see or hear what was going on where he was."

Swell shook his head.

"You can't seriously believe that I . . . Why? What motive could I have? You can't believe it!"

"I guess not."

"You guess not?" she sputtered. "All right, all right. Where's the knife then? You did notice, I suppose, that the murder weapon is missing again? So what did I do with it? How did I get rid of it?"

"Dumped it in the street somewhere. You were out in the street when I ran into you," he reminded her.

"I took the wrong turn down the corridor and I was out on the fire stairs before I realized it, and then I had no choice but to continue on down to the street. I was trying to get back in and notify the guards and call you."

He shrugged.

She clutched her forehead in mock despair. "I can't believe this is happening to me. Would I have made a date to meet you here if I intended to commit murder? I mean, I ask you, does it make sense?"

"Okay, okay. So why don't you just sit here quietly and relax until Lieutenant LaRock arrives and you can tell him the whole thing."

She sighed aggrievedly.

"I'm sorry, kid, that's the way it's got to be."

He lit a cigarette; he paced; he did not go into the control room. Whether Donald agreed with Mici that the manuscript was gone and that Zipprodt had been killed for it, or whether he was afraid to let her out of his sight, he was obviously relieved when the door at the far end of the corridor opened and the first pair of uniformed officers arrived. After a whispered consultation accompanied by significant glances in her direction, the detective finally entered the control room, taking one of the men with him and leaving the other behind with Mici.

To keep an eye on her, she thought, and sat back in the plastic chair to wait.

It distressed her that she'd been so wrong about poor Billy. Her initial error had been in jumping to the conclusion that the murder of Julia Schuyler was a crime of passion. The scene, Julia's past and current history, her emotionalism, all had indicated it. But it was not so, and that error had inevitably led to the

196

next—that the crime was unpremeditated. As for Billy—Mici had never really thought him guilty; she had talked herself into it. She'd misread the clues. No, she corrected herself; she'd let the clues mislead her and in doing so ignored the essential core of the stage manager's character—loyalty. She'd discounted William Zipprodt's years of devotion to Julia Schuyler. So Julia didn't acknowledge his help with the book. Billy wouldn't have cared. He had done and was prepared to do a great deal more for the woman he'd idolized. And Julia knew it. She used him because he allowed himself to be used. But she'd loved him, too.

The crime appeared sloppy and haphazard. It might have been preceded by a quarrel, but it was not a crime of passion. Its motive was neither love nor hatred, but fear. The fear of something in that manuscript. Janos Kord didn't take it; there would have been no point in his mentioning it if he had. Obviously Billy hadn't taken it or he wouldn't be dead.

But if the killer already had the manuscript, why was Billy a threat?

Because he knew what was in it.

Mici sighed. What had Billy said to her that first day in her office? He'd said that it was pitiful to see Julia trying to sell her degradation. He'd said that nobody would care unless she could find an angle for her story. Obviously she had found an angle and Billy knew what it was.

So then why hadn't he been killed right away? Why had the murderer waited so long?

Because the murderer hadn't known that Billy was working on the book with Julia. He'd only recently found out. Mici's heart pounded; her pulse raced. She jumped to her feet and started down the corridor.

"Miss! Miss!" The cop sprinted after her. "I'm sorry, miss, but you're supposed to wait."

She raised her eyebrows at him. "I'm going to the ladies' room."

"Oh. Well, sure." He was young, chubby, and earnest. Evidently Donald had cautioned him severely, for though he stood aside politely to let her pass he kept his eye on Mici till she actually entered the rest room.

She was sure he'd be right there beside the door till she came out. A quick examination of the premises revealed there was no convenient rear exit, no window with a fire escape, in fact, there was no window at all. So now what? It looked as though she had no choice but to wait for the lieutenant and make her case to him.

"The first turn to your left, sir, then left again, and it's the first door to your right, sir."

That was her young guard giving someone directions to the control room.

"Would it be too much trouble, Officer, for you to lead the way?"

"Ah . . ."

The sarcasm of the request was the badge of the authority of the speaker, Mici thought, listening from inside, and the poor rookie was torn between one duty and another.

"Yes, sir, right this way, sir."

The poor guy probably figured he'd be back before she could get out of the john, and he would have been right if she'd gone to the john. Mici grinned, waited till the footsteps faded, then, inching the door open, peered outside. All clear. Avoiding the elevator, she took the stairs and made it down to the main lobby. The guards were all standing around where they could be seen as well as see, but they were watching the parade of police and weren't interested in her. At the reception desk, she helped herself to a page from a memo pad and scribbled a message. Folding it, she handed it to the nearest guard.

"Give this to Detective Swell when he comes down."

It was always a good idea to have a backup.

18

With one or two exceptions, New York—famed for its
night life—had become an early town. By ten thirty,
eleven for musicals, the legitimate theatres would be
empty, their marquees dark, and glamorous Broadway left to the late movie and porno palaces, the
shabby bars and girlie joints, and the night prowlers.
Mici told the driver to hurry; she had to get to the
theatre before the final curtain.

The cab arrived just as the audience was pouring
out. Good enough. Mici paid and crossed the sidewalk
to mix with the crowd, only she was going the wrong
way—in. If anyone should challenge her, she would say
she'd forgotten her gloves at her seat, but nobody
bothered her as she made her way against the tide into
the John Malcolm Schuyler Theatre. She knew that
the lawyer would not refuse to see her, but she preferred some element of surprise. She reasoned that the
man who had built this theatre and loved it so much
that he had an apartment above it would surely have
provided private access backstage for himself. That
was how she intended to reach him; it shouldn't be
hard. Once inside the house, it was simply a matter of
whether the connecting door between front and back
was at the right or left of the stage. A stream of visitors
going back provided the answer. Mici joined them and
passed over from the world of watchers to that of
pretenders. She found herself on the prompt side—that
side from which the stage manager ran the show,
where the fly rail and electrician's boards were located.
Slipping through the narrow space between the elec-
trical boards, she found what she'd confidently expected

to find—a door. Stepping through it, she was in Osca[r]
Brumleve's vestibule with the elevator waiting.

Probably the decrepit car creaked and groaned n[o]
more than it had on her initial visit, but tonight t[o]
Mici's sensitive ears it seemed to shake the entir[e]
building. It seemed impossible that the man up ther[e]
and whoever might be with him didn't know tha[t]
someone was coming. When the car shuddered to a sto[p]
and she got out, it was a relief to find the long galler[y]
empty and silent.

Bathed in the rose glow of simulated torches a[t]
intervals along the wall, the shabby theatrical mementoes seemed almost real—the portraits painted b[y]
masters, the papier-mâché masks, rubber daggers, he-
raldic flags took on substance and grandeur. The orien-
tal runner glowed with color and even felt softe[r]
underfoot. It was a stage set waiting for the curtain t[o]
rise. Mici crossed quickly and quietly up center an[d]
tapped lightly on the door of the lawyer's library-
office.

There was no response. She knocked again, waited,
then entered.

A green, glass-globed lamp cast a pool of light over
the massive desk at one end of the room, glinting off
the row of golden statuettes lined up along the front
edge. But Brumleve was not at his desk. He was on her
right, a hunched figure sitting sideways to a small
window and looking down, completely engrossed. Mici
frowned. The light coming from the window was too
bright to be reflected from the street, and anyhow the
window was cut into what she judged to be an inner
wall. Of course! It overlooked the stage—a kind of
Judas hole. Hadn't David Belasco had one in his quarters? And Daniel Frohman? She'd noted the drawn
curtains on her earlier visit; now she knew what was
behind them.

"Mr. Brumleve?"

The show was over, but the man looking down
remained completely absorbed.

As before, the room was hot and stuffy, without air

200

conditioning, all the windows closed, the one over the stage was not a working window. Sick as he was, Brumleve must find the atmosphere comfortable, but she was already starting to sweat.

"Mr. Brumleve?" She raised her voice.

At last he looked over his shoulder. "Who's that?"

"Mici Anhalt, Mr. Brumleve."

For a moment he scowled; then the scowl cleared. "Oh, yes, I remember you. The girl with the good legs. You used to be a dancer. Yes." He motioned her closer. "Too bad you didn't come a little sooner; you could have watched the play with me. It's quite an experience to see it from up here above the flies. Like watching puppets." He raised his arms, hands arched, fingers tapping the air as though he were manipulating the strings. "I watch every performance, matinees included. That's the only way to keep a company on its toes; I let them know they're being watched."

But it wasn't his play! Mici thought. He hadn't produced it, only rented out the theatre.

"The crew, too—props, juice, grips, you've got to keep an eye on them all. They can get sloppy, put in for overtime to which they're not entitled. Constantly alert, you have to be constantly alert." His voice was thin and querulous.

"I'm sure that's true."

"It certainly is." He was testy as though she were arguing. "Ah there. They've finished striking the set," he announced with satisfaction. "Yes, all right, good time, good time," he murmured, having consulted his watch. "The house should be empty by now. Yes." Again he nodded approvingly, and Mici taking a step forward could look over his shoulder as the curtain was raised on an empty auditorium, the stage lights went out, and the worklight, its single bulb protected by a wire cage, was set on the apron of the bare stage. At the same time, the light coming through the Judas window diminished.

As though that was a signal, Oscar Brumleve rose and started across the room. Mici was shocked at how

201

much he'd regressed in just the few days since she'd first met him. He'd been thin, pitifully thin, but now he was a cadaver. He couldn't seem to straighten up, and he tottered as he moved from his post beside the inner window so that instinctively she moved to offer support. He waved her aside. It took a few moments, but he steadied himself and then walked, slowly but firmly, to his desk where, grasping the arms, he lowered himself carefully into the leather chair.

"What can I do for you, Miss Anhalt?" he asked. The very fact of his presence in the seat of his power, behind that row of golden awards, seemed to act as a restorative. "Anything you want, if I can do it, I will. Just ask. You did me and my client a great favor. We've never properly thanked you."

"There's no need. I'm glad it turned out as it did."

"You're a clever young woman. Both Alfred and I owe you a debt of gratitude. We'd like to repay it."

"There's no debt."

"My dear, you must want something, everybody does. I don't suppose you'd be here otherwise, would you now, my dear? Be honest, eh? Out with it, young lady, out with it." He had become almost unctuous.

"I'm looking for the manuscript."

"What manuscript is that, my dear? I have all kinds."

"Julia Schuyler's book manuscript."

"I didn't know that Julia was writing a book."

Inwardly Mici sighed, partly with relief and partly with regret. "Her editor called you. He thought that, being her executor, you might have it among her effects."

"Oh, yes. Well, that was the first I'd heard that Julia was trying her hand at writing." He dismissed it as beneath notice.

Mici didn't buy it. "I think you've known about that book for some time, Mr. Brumleve. I believe that you were determined it should never be published."

"You're wrong. However, if I had known about the book ..." He shrugged. "If Julia wanted to do an emotional striptease in public, that was her business.

202

That's the fashion nowadays, to bare all. Why should I care?"

If she knew that, she'd know everything, Mici thought. Never mind, a case could be made without knowing his specific objection to the book.

"You tried to talk Julia out of writing it, but she was determined. Maybe you paid her, I don't know, but obviously when she found a publisher whatever you could give her wouldn't have been enough. On Friday night you went over there to make one more effort to get her to give up the project. It was late, well after one-thirty. It had stopped raining. You brought a bottle of scotch to soften her up. Julia was much easier to deal with when she'd had a few."

He didn't comment. Maybe he was waiting to see what kind of case she had. She didn't mind letting him know.

"You rang her bell. You knew she'd still be up because Julia never went to bed till three or four A.M. So she was up, though she was in bad shape, bruised and half drunk but rational. You gave her the bottle and she had herself a couple more belts; only this time, instead of making her amenable, the drink turned her obstinate. You argued, you pleaded, but the book was her chance to get back into the limelight, to be somebody again. Nothing you could say could stack up against that. She wasn't only determined, she was eager and excited about writing the book, and she kept tossing off the drinks till she finally passed out.

"Well, that was your chance. That was your chance to find the manuscript and get out. You looked everywhere. The drawer of the kitchen table was the last place and by then Julia came to."

Mici paused. The heat of the room was terrible. The sweat poured off her, but Brumleve seemed unaffected. He sat perfectly still in his chair, his eyes fixed intently on her.

"She followed you into the kitchen and demanded the manuscript back. You refused, and she tried to wrest it from you. You struggled, but she was very

203

weak, weaker than you, and suddenly she just gave up. She told you you could have it—burn it, flush it down the toilet, do any damn thing you wanted with it. She'd just write it over. That was when you realized you had to kill her."

Still Brumleve neither moved nor spoke, watching Mici with the same intensity of concentration which he'd earlier expended on the stage below his window. For her part, Mici was drawing from him the kind of electric charge an actor derives from a rapt audience—one mesmerizing the other, each a part of the process of creation.

She took a deep breath. "You were both in the kitchen. Earlier, Julia had cut up one of those deli roasted chickens and the knife was on the drain board. You picked it up. You held it for several moments. For several moments you just stood there with the knife in your hands. Julia didn't move either; she didn't try to get away. She didn't lunge and try to take the knife from you. She didn't even scream because she didn't believe that you would actually use it. You'd known her since she was a child. You had been her father's best friend. You built this theatre to honor John Malcolm Schuyler and to perpetuate his memory. How could you injure his only child, his little girl?

"How could you raise that knife high and plunge it into Julia Schuyler's heart?"

Mici could visualize the scene as clearly as though she'd been there. "The knife went in easily, and Julia slid down in a heap at your feet with little more than a sigh of surprise—and disappointment. You panicked. All you wanted at that moment was to get out. You took the knife with you. And, of course, the manuscript."

For one moment Brumleve's eyes left Mici's face and darted to a small picture on the wall, then back again to her. Fast, but not fast enough.

"You should have destroyed it, Mr. Brumleve."

He was silent for a long time. Then, with a deep sigh as though the curtain had been lowered on a particularly affecting scene, Oscar Brumleve stirred, raised

204

his thin hands, and applauded. "Spellbinding, Miss Anhalt. What a performance!"

"What was in that book? What was in it that made you kill Julia?"

The lawyer leaned forward and rested his elbows on the desk. "I assume that you have a reason for coming up here and putting on this show."

"Why?" Mici pressed. "What was she threatening to reveal?"

"What do you want?" he countered. "Money? Fame? Have you decided you want to go back to dancing, after all? Do you want to be in a movie, a Broadway show? Or maybe you're like Julia and you have a friend you want to help. Speak up."

Mici kept to her own script. "When did you find out that Billy Zip was helping Julia with the book? You should have realized that she was in no shape to write it herself, that someone had to be helping her, but you didn't—not till a couple of days ago. Not till the publisher called you in an effort to locate the manuscript. He told you then that he'd checked with her collaborator, Mr. Zipprodt, but that Mr. Zipprodt didn't have it. And now poor Billy is dead, too. Stabbed, like Julia, but in the back. It happened less than an hour ago."

"I'm a sick man, Miss Anhalt, and I'm getting very, very tired. Either tell me what it is you want or go. While you still can."

It was the first hint of a threat, and from a man like Brumleve it was an admission.

"You have no reason to hurt me," Mici said. "I don't know your secret."

"There is no secret. You have no proof of any of these irresponsible allegations."

"The proof does exist though, and it is in your possession. In that safe." Mici indicated the picture toward which the lawyer had surreptitiously glanced a few moments before.

He shrugged. "Very well. I do admit that Julia's manuscript is in there, all three chapters of it which deal with her childhood and are no threat to anyone, believe me. However, my acquisition of it was nothing so dramatic as you've enacted. It was quite prosaically simple. Julia wanted my opinion and offered it to me to read."

"If that's so, why did you tell her publisher you didn't have it?"

"That's my business."

"If Julia gave it to you voluntarily and there's nothing in it that would affect you, then you won't mind my glancing through it, will you? If she gave it to you voluntarily, then there won't be any blood on any of the pages, will there?"

"Blood?"

"From the murder knife. You could hardly carry the knife out in your hand for any passerby to see. You weren't wearing a raincoat because it had stopped raining. The pockets of a regular jacket wouldn't be deep enough. Of course, you could have held it against you under your jacket, but that would have been awkward and perhaps you were a bit squeamish about it. It was so much simpler just to roll it up inside the manuscript between the pages. Surely there must have been some blood on the knife and surely the blood will be on the pages. Julia Schuyler's blood."

He was transfixed, hardly breathing. Then suddenly his mouth fell open and his breath began to come in short, shallow gasps. In that hot, airless room, Oscar Brumleve began to shake as though he had an arctic chill, and at the same time sweat oozed out of his pores as he strained to rise from the chair. Either he'd forgotten Mici's presence or assigned to it a lesser priority, but for the moment he had one concern only, one compulsion—to check the manuscript. Somehow he tottered the few steps from the desk to the picture on the wall, pushed it aside to reveal the safe Mici had surmised was there. So anxious was he to get it open that he misdialed twice before he managed it correctly and the door swung open. Cradling the thin sheaf of papers in both hands like the most fragile of treasures, Brumleve stumbled back to his desk near exhaustion.

Hunching forward, he placed the pages directly under

the student lamp and turned them over one by one, scrutinizing each meticulously before setting it aside and proceeding to the next. From where she stood, Mici couldn't get a really good look, but she didn't need to. About halfway through he stopped, and the sudden drop of his head told her what she needed to know. Now she could approach and see for herself the spattering of brown spots along the inner edge of the topmost page.

Oscar Brumleve stared for a very long time at those damning spots. Then, as though coming out of a quiet reverie, he shifted in his chair and turned his head sideways to look up at Mici. "You shouldn't have come here alone, Miss Anhalt. That was a bad mistake."

"The police are right behind me."

"So you say." A slight, sardonic smile twisted the bloodless lips as he reached across the desk toward the row of statuettes ranged along the edge and picked up the Valentino, a slim figurine with a heavy base.

"They'll be here before you can get rid of my body," Mici warned.

"The door downstairs is locked."

"I came through the theatre."

"I'll turn the power off. They won't be able to use the elevator."

"They'll come up the fire escape."

"That will be my concern, not yours."

He rose and came around the desk towards her, steps remarkably firm, statuette held tightly in a hand that was completely steady, eyes fixed with purpose. Involuntarily Mici took a step back. Sick, old, and weak, Oscar Brumleve nevertheless had killed twice. True, Julia had been even weaker than he, and Billy Zip taken unawares from behind, but desperation could provide all the strength Brumleve would need to murder again. She must not back off; she must not even flinch. Her fear would fuel his confidence.

"Killing me would serve no purpose," she told him as reasonably as she could in the circumstances. To her surprise, he stopped where he was.

"Right again, Miss Anhalt, killing you would gain

207

me little. I am, one way or another, a dying man."

Slowly, hand trembling as before, he put the statuette down. Mici, too, was shaking—with relief.

Shrunken, the ravages of his illness upon him, Brumleve turned his back on Mici Anhalt and shambled across the dark area beyond his desk to the baronial fireplace and the life-sized portrait hung above it. At the flip of a switch, a soft light illumined the famous face and figure of John Malcolm Schuyler.

"He was the greatest actor in the American theatre," Brumleve proclaimed, gazing up at the deep-set, haunted eyes, the contorted yet noble visage. "He had the sensitivity of a Booth, the flamboyance of a Barrymore, the technique of an Olivier. Offstage, as a lover, he was *nonpareil*. Julia meant to destoy him. For a few dollars of cheap profit, she intended to besmirch his memory."

"How?"

"By claiming that John Malcolm Schuyler—married three times, with a list of conquests to equal Don Juan's, the great lover and sex symbol of his time—was impotent. She would contend that I was his lackey and provided women as window dressing to create the aura of irresistible masculinity that turned him into a matinee idol. That together we cheated the public."

Mici gasped. "But she was his daughter!"

"No, she was not."

Oscar Brumleve heaved a sigh. "While no match for John Malcolm and a great deal more discreet, Julia's mother, Angela Vaughn, had her share of escapades—in part a reaction to John Malcolm's vicissitudes. No matter. Julia was the result of one of Angela's affairs. Of course, the child didn't know and she idolized John Malcolm. Her adulation was flattering but also an annoyance, sometimes even an embarrassment. She had a habit of bursting in on him at any moment, and on one particular occasion she chose a very private moment indeed. Provoked, John Malcolm let the truth slip. Once out, there was no taking it back. So, knowing that she was not biologically his, she set out to prove that artistically she was his child. She wanted to show him and to convince the world that she was his—most of all, she needed to prove it to herself. To his credit, John Malcolm did try to help her, to teach her. He did feel that much responsibility for her, but what he possessed could not be taught and, in any case, he was a poor teacher and not the most patient of men. She was a worse pupil, paralyzed when he uttered a word of advice. The harder she tried, the more severe his criticism and finally his ridicule. That was *his* nature. Having failed on the stage, she tried to imitate him in life. He told her she didn't have the talent to carry it off. I don't think Julia ever forgave him for that.

"When he died, with the fear of his disapproval removed, Julia did improve. She gained some success. There was hope that she could finally make it in her own right. But either she wasn't quite good enough or her luck ran out, I don't know. It wasn't in the cards. She hit the skids. Well, you know all that."

Mici nodded. "I still don't understand why she'd want to destroy . . ."

"It was all she had left to sell. Not her own story and her own reputation—her father's. I killed her and that poor . . . toady of hers to preserve it." Brumleve looked up into the handsome face, the haunted face of Schuyler in the role of Macbeth. He stared at it for a long time; then as though under its spell he cried out, "I didn't do it for him! I did it for myself!" Brumleve's ravaged features resembled the painted ones, but the horrors he saw were real.

"Everyone accused Julia of trading on John Malcolm's reputation, but she wasn't the only one. I nurtured my career on his talent. What would I have been without him? Because he was my client, others flocked to me. At one time I had just about every major talent under personal management, and producers had to come to me and accept the terms I dictated. I built this theatre and called it the John Malcolm Schuyler Theatre because I didn't have the nerve to call it the Oscar Brumleve. But it was my monument as much as his. It's been losing money for years. At the end of next month, the bank will foreclose, tear it down, and

209

put—God knows what in its place: an office building, a hamburger joint, a garage. When that happens, all that will be left of me will be my association with John Malcolm."

He cast one last look at the portrait; then, as though wrenching himself free of its domination, Brumleve turned and went back to his desk. With infinite weariness he reached for the Valentino and picked it up. For a moment, Mici was afraid that he meant to go for her after all, now that she knew his secret. But he just stood there, hefting the thing thoughtfully in his hand.

"I killed two people to keep a secret that no longer matters. Who cares? Nowadays, who gives a damn?" With a suddenness that took her unawares and a violence that made her gasp, he reared back and hurled the golden statue at the plate glass of the Judas window overlooking the stage below. The glass shattered, and before she could recover, Oscar Brumleve walked the few short paces and stepped through the jagged opening.

His shriek echoed and reechoed in the empty theatre for what seemed an endless time after his body had splattered on the stage six stories below.

Mici remained frozen long after the echoes had stilled. She moved at last, drawn without consciously being aware, to the opening from which a cool draft now wafted clearing the room's fetid atmosphere. Careful to avoid the sharp-edged shards, she leaned out and looked down from above the fly floor, past the old-fashioned festoons of ropes and sandbag counterweights, past the hanging flats for tomorrow's show, down to the floor of the bare stage. Thank God she was too far up to make out anything more than a sprawled outline.

19

From then on, Mici would always associate a hard downpour with that night's lonely wait in the dead lawyer's aerie. It seemed hours that she sat in the long gallery listening to the rain bombarding the skylight till Donald finally showed up, accompanied by Lieutenant LaRock and Captain Schumacher. It was evident that Detective Swell was in trouble. Both officers held him responsible for everything that had gone wrong because of her: for the murderer's having had ample time to get away while she carried on her one-sided conversation with Billy and for the suicide of a very important witness. That was how they insisted on referring to Oscar Brumleve—a witness. Donald defended her as best he could; he was defending himself. When Mici was at last permitted to lead them into the lawyer's office and show them the bloodstained pages of Julia's manuscript, the atmosphere changed considerably.

"The lab will have to analyze this before we can be sure it was Miss Schuyler's blood," LaRock muttered.

"Who else's could it be, sir?" Donald demanded, rising to the occasion. Sensing that he was on top, he went all out. He cited Mici's help and cooperation. She was a personal friend of all those involved, and she had placed herself at the department's disposal. He not only exonerated Mici for leaving the studio and coming over here but hinted she had acted with his full approval. Mici had briefed him on the phone regarding the logic that led to the discovery of the manuscript and the bloodstains, but he couldn't quite bring himself to give her the credit. Thus, he remained modestly silent. LaRock and Schumacher were forced to offer him their congratulations.

Mici bit back a smile. Let Donald make all the Brownie points he wanted; she didn't care. When she was finally released, well after four A.M., she did take him aside to remind him that having kept her part of the bargain she now expected him to keep his. Then she went home to bed.

At nine she awoke long enough to make one phone call to Adam Dowd requesting that the supervisor set up a meeting for the following day with certain specified people. Having made the arrangements, she fell back on the pillow and slept till dinner time. It was still raining. She fixed herself an omelette, ate it, washed up, watched the news on television, and went back to bed. The next morning she felt like a million.

According to the radio, it had gone on raining most of the night. Even now there was a touch of mist in the air, but the forecaster promised it would clear. The temperature had dropped fifteen degrees. The heat wave was broken. Mici called Donald.

His wife answered and told her he'd gone to the precinct. Mici called the precinct. He hadn't come in yet but was expected.

The meeting she'd requested was scheduled for noon. Plenty of time.

She made three more calls to the precinct during the morning, and each message she left was more urgent than the one before. Then, when she couldn't wait any longer, when she had to leave for the office, she convinced herself that Donald had called her there, that there would be a message from him waiting for her. But there wasn't. Fran Jarrett greeted her warmly and informed her that all the people she'd requested to attend had agreed to come, and that the meeting would be held in Mr. Cornelius's office. Mici mumbled her thanks and fled from the curious eyes of Dowd's secretary to her own private office, closed the door, and leaned against it, heart pounding.

What had gone wrong? Why didn't Donald call?

She couldn't sit still. She was up and down and up

again. What should she do? How was she going to proceed without having heard from Donald? At five before the hour, just as she was expecting to be summoned into Mr. Cornelius's office—he was a stickler for punctuality—her phone rang. She snatched it up.

"Donald! Oh, thank God! You've had me climbing the walls."

"Gee, I'm sorry, babe. I just this minute got in. I called as soon as I saw your messages."

"So? So? Did you do it?"

"What?"

"What? Donald, please, this is not the time to kid around. My meeting is in four minutes exactly."

"Today! I'm sorry, doll, I didn't realize it was today."

"Sorry? What do you mean, you're sorry? You mean you didn't take care of it?"

"I haven't had a chance."

"Oh, no!" The bottom of Mici's stomach dropped; the bottom dropped out of everything. "We had a deal. I was counting on you."

"I'm not welshing. I'm going to take care of it; I just haven't had the time. Listen, while you were in the sack all day yesterday pounding your pillow, I was pounding out reports. I've had a homicide and a suicide to write up. I haven't even had a chance to get out for a bite."

"So how about this morning?"

"Well . . . Jeez . . ."

"Never mind, don't tell me. Why didn't you get somebody else to do it for you?"

"I didn't think you wanted anybody else. I thought you wanted me."

"All I wanted was the information. Just the information. I didn't care who got it or how. I suggested you pick him up for questioning, but it was just a suggestion. I told you that. I left it up to you." She groaned. "That was my mistake. I guess I'll never learn."

"Don't get excited. I promised you and I'm going to deliver."

"Fine. What am I going to tell those people waiting in my boss's office, huh? Come back tomorrow? Next

213

week? Next month? What am I going to tell my boss?"

Swell had never known the redhead to become so distraught. It shamed him. "Listen, I'll come over right away. It shouldn't take me more than . . . twenty minutes . . . or so. You stall them. Of course"—he hedged, he couldn't help himself—"of course, there's no time to get a warrant, but never mind, I'll do my number anyway. Okay? Okay, babe?"

"Forget it." Tears of disappointment and frustration welled up in Mici's eyes. "I'll do it myself," she said and slammed down the receiver.

But how? How was she going to do it?

Magisterially ensconced behind the sleek slab of his desk, Mr. J. Hammond Cornelius peered through squareshaped, black-rimmed glasses that gave distinction to his small, myopic brown eyes. His jutting jaw was set at the angle for reviewing the troops, yet the commissioner had adopted a casual air by slanting his chair sideways, crossing his legs widely to reveal a section of hand-knitted, wildly colored argyle socks, and puffing energetically on his ever-present pipe.

He did not rise when Mici entered—she hardly expected it—but he did remove the pipe and used it to wave her forward.

"Ah, Miss Anhalt. Come in, come in. Sit down."

The geniality was somewhat forced but surely that he had made the effort at all was a good sign? Mici told herself that indeed it was and crossed to the chair he'd indicated, looking around as she did so. They were all present, those she'd asked to attend. Disposed about Mr. Cornelius's office were the Marins, seated side by side on the tufted leather sofa, as well as Adam Dowd and Wally Lischner sunk into the depths of down-cushioned easy chairs. It seemed like a haphazard, informal grouping, but Mici knew that Mr. Cornelius did nothing without planning. As she passed him, Dowd turned his face sideways and winked with the eye his boss couldn't see. Wally Lischner leaned a millimeter forward and mumbled something, hardly moving his lips; it could have been, "Good luck." Clay

214

Marin made no acknowledgement of her presence one way or another, but then he was the adversary. His wife Sandra, a cool, reserved blonde, a Vassar girl trained to understatement in looks and manner, turned away. That, too, was to be expected; Sandra would naturally side with her husband. Mici was sorry because she liked Mrs. Marin; they had the same kind of background and, Mici assumed, the same set of values. At least she'd come, Mici thought, and she hadn't been sure that Mrs. Marin would. She had invited the blind man's wife as added insurance. Now, with Donald having failed her, Sandra Marin was the only leverage she had.

Though Mici was the one who had requested the meeting, it was obvious that Mr. Cornelius intended to conduct it. Mici obediently took the place assigned to her and let him get on with it.

"Now, Mr. Marin," J. Cornelius began in his clipped Harvard accent which with the years grew more clipped and more related to London than to Boston, "I am bound to inform you that the investigation into your allegations against Miss Anhalt has turned up no confirmation whatsoever." Turning to Mici, he intoned with the same pontifical neutrality, "As you are undoubtedly aware, Miss Anhalt, that does not constitute a verdict of not guilty. However, under the circumstances, it would not be fair to penalize you by continuing your suspension. Therefore you are herewith reinstated with all privileges."

He beamed on her. Adam beamed on her. Wally grinned.

"Thank you, sir," Mici replied. "But I don't want my job back."

Consternation. Dismay. And from one person in that room the edge of triumph barely showing.

"Not under these circumstances, Mr. Cornelius," Mici continued. "I won't come back unless I'm completely exonerated and restored to your and Mr. Dowd's trust and respect and to that of my colleagues."

"You never lost my trust and respect, Miss Anhalt," Dowd announced with a pomposity equal to his chief's.

The looks flashed at him in response from Cornelius and Mici were quite different.

"Thank you, Mr. Dowd," Mici matched the formality. Then she turned again to the commissioner. "I asked for this meeting with the intention of clearing myself. But first I would like to ask Mr. Marin to withdraw his charges."

Everyone looked at the blind man. Clay Marin was well shaved this morning, with accessories matched to his best gray suit, gold cuff links gleaming at his wrists, shoes freshly polished, and yet he managed to look seedy.

"Why should he do that?"

Wally Lischner spoke for Marin. He, too, had dressed for the occasion wearing a straight business suit with proper shirt and discreet tie. His beard was meticulously trimmed. His manner matched his dress: subdued, honestly puzzled.

"Because Mr. Marin has been misrepresenting his situation to us for some time. To all of us," Mici replied. "He has been misleading us on two counts: his medical condition and the situation at home. First, his medical condition. Mr. Marin has become very skilled in the use of his laser cane. I checked that out with his Lighthouse instructor. But Mr. Marin has led us to believe that he was getting around so much better lately not because of his expertise, but due to improved vision. I'm sorry to say that is not the case. According to Dr. Harden's report, of which I have a copy, Mr. Marin's vision has been steadily deteriorating since the original injury." Mici laid the document in front of Cornelius, pausing just long enough for him to glance over it. When he signaled that he had done so, she continued.

"As to his home situation . . ." Mici sighed and turned to Sandra Marin. "I'm afraid that Clay has been saying some very unpleasant things."

"What things?" Sandra Marin asked.

"Miss Anhalt . . ." Dowd shook his head at Mici.

"What things?" Sandra Marin demanded.

"That you're never home,"

216

"That's true enough but . . . ."

"I've called several times myself to discuss Clay's treatment with you but have never been able to reach you."

"Yes, all right, but didn't Clay explain . . ."

"He tried to cover for you, naturally. But there came the time when he couldn't. It wasn't easy for your husband to admit that you had turned your back on him, that the house was dirty, the children neglected, that he was the one who had to get them off to school in the morning and fix the evening meal for them when they came home."

Sandra Marin gasped; she tried to speak, but Mici wouldn't let her—not yet.

"It wasn't easy for him to admit that you were having an affair with another man."

Now Mici paused and now that she had her chance, now that everyone waited to hear her side, Sandra Marin appeared incapable of uttering a word. She looked helplessly at her husband, then back to Mici. "I don't believe it," she said at last.

"It's true. We've all heard the story. He has complained to every one of us here in this room, except perhaps Mr. Cornelius."

The blonde shook her head in puzzlement. "Clay . . ." she appealed to the man who sat silent beside her.

Mici came to her aid. "The fact is that you lied, isn't that so, Mr. Marin? Your wife wasn't home because she was working. She has a job. You do get the children off to school and you do fix their meal when they get home because she's at the office earning the money that keeps you all going."

Marin dropped his head.

"Why? Why, Clay?" Sandra Marin asked sadly. "Why did you say a thing like that?"

"I was afraid that if they found out you were working and earning a good salary they'd cut me off."

"Your loss of salary compensation runs a specified period, Mr. Marin. It can be terminated only when you yourself get employment. Weren't you informed?" Cornelius asked sternly.

Marin nodded. "I was afraid . . ."

"You were afraid that if your vision deterioratcd to the point where improvement seemed hopeless, we'd cut off your medical assistance, that we'd give up on you," Mici put in. "We never give up on anyone, Mr. Marin."

"He said you would." The blind man turned his head toward Lischner.

"I did not. I never did." Lischner bristled. "You misunderstood."

"You made it very clear," Marin insisted. "On the day Miss Anhalt missed my appointment, you told me that she had missed it because she was no longer interested in me, because my case was about to be closed out."

"I never said that. Never. It's a lie." Lischner was on his feet and glaring at his accuser. "It's a lie."

"We were in Miss Anhalt's office and you got the records out of her drawer and told me what Dr. Harden had reported. It was the first I knew of it."

"The man's a liar and a cheat." Lischner's cheeks flamed; the neatly trimmed beard served as a catch basin for the sweat pouring off his face. "He's admitted lying about his wife in an attempt to defraud this office. If he can do that, he can certainly . . ."

"You promised me you'd see to it that I got the operation and that all benefits would be extended." Marin's voice topped the investigator's. "You said you'd get rid of Dr. Harden's report, but that I'd have to bring charges against Miss Anhalt."

Lischner's outrage finally drowned him out. "Why should I do such a terrible thing? Against a colleague? Miss Anhalt and I are friends. We've even dated. Isn't that right, Mici? Tell them."

He had given her the opening. "I'm glad you mentioned that, Wally. Yes, it's true. We did go out together. Once. Just once."

"That was your choice. I asked you out again. I asked you over and over and you turned me down. Well, that's another story."

"No, it isn't."

But Lischner ignored her and appealed to Cornelius. "It's Mr. Marin's word against mine, sir. He has a reason for lying. I don't."

"You made a heavy play for me." Mici ignored Lischner's appeal to the commissioner. "A very heavy play and I wasn't interested."

He flushed slightly but shrugged it off. "That was your privilege. This isn't the time or the place . . ."

"This is exactly the time and the place."

His color deepened, turned into an ugly, unhealthy purple. Ignoring Marin, he crossed in front of the blind man to confront Mici. "You're cleared. The man has admitted his charges were false. What more do you want?"

"I want you to admit that you put him up to it."

"I didn't," he hissed, his face so close to hers that his spittle sprayed her.

Cornelius cleared his throat. "I think this matter should be discussed . . ."

Neither Mici nor Lischner paid attention; they were bonded to each other in a struggle of wills.

"Okay," Mici said. "Let's talk about our date. You made a heavy pass and you wouldn't take no for an answer. You were very hard to turn off. Did I laugh too much? I'm sorry. I didn't mean to ridicule you. The truth is, I was embarrassed by the display."

He turned livid. He choked and for a moment Mici thought he was going to have some kind of apoplectic attack. He managed to avoid it and appeal again to Cornelius. "Either you order Miss Anhalt to retract . . ."

"One week ago a man broke into my apartment and tried to rape me."

That silenced Lischner. She had everyone's attention completely, and he knew that he could no longer hope to stop her.

"I defended myself by plunging a pair of small scissors into his back, just between the shoulder blades. I told Mr. Dowd about it, and of course I reported it to the police. It was dark in my room and the assailant wore a ski mask so I couldn't give much of a descrip-

219

tion, but the wound should be sufficient identification. Would you mind removing your jacket and shirt, Wally?"

Wally pulled back as though he feared he would be stripped by force, though no one came near him. He looked to Adam and saw no hope. "I refuse to dignify such a monstrous allegation." He looked to Cornelius and saw distaste. "I was there at her invitation, *her* invitation!" he yelled, his eyes sweeping the room, but each person to whom he appealed looked away till there was only Mici herself.

"You'll never prove otherwise. I could sue you for sticking those scissors into me. I will. I'll charge you with grievous bodily injury . . ."

"Enough!" Roaring, J. Hammond Cornelius got to his feet. "Enough!"

"Nowadays all a woman has to do is scream rape and everybody's on her side," Lischner whined.

"Attempted rape," Mici corrected. "You didn't make it. That's the trouble, isn't it, Wally?"

Her eyes, faded to a platinum sheen, transfixed him.

"That's why you tried to discredit me and get me fired, isn't it? Because you failed and you couldn't bear to have me around as a constant reminder that you'd failed—a second time."

Lischner squirmed but her look held him. He couldn't tear loose; he couldn't speak. A slow flush appeared at the rim of his tight collar and rose till humiliation flamed in his whole face.

And suddenly Mici pitied him. His craven silence was all the admission necessary, she thought, and turned away. No use piling it on.

About the Author

Author Lillian O'Donnell is very familiar with the theatrical setting of FALLING STAR: she was the first woman stage manager in the history of New York theater.

Ms. O'Donnell, who writes the Norah Mulcahaney mystery series as well as Mici Anhalt thrillers, lives in New York City.